CRIME
AND
CATNIP

T. C. LoTempio

BERKLEY PRIME CRIME
New York

BERKLEY PRIME CRIME
Published by Berkley
An imprint of Penguin Random House LLC
375 Hudson Street, New York, New York 10014

Copyright © 2016 by T. C. LoTempio
Penguin Random House supports copyright. Copyright fuels creativity, encourages
diverse voices, promotes free speech, and creates a vibrant culture. Thank you for buying
an authorized edition of this book and for complying with copyright laws by not
reproducing, scanning, or distributing any part of it in any form without permission.
You are supporting writers and allowing Penguin Random House to continue to
publish books for every reader.

BERKLEY is a registered trademark and BERKLEY PRIME CRIME and the B colophon
are trademarks of Penguin Random House LLC.

ISBN: 9780425270226

First Edition: December 2016

Printed in the United States of America
1 3 5 7 9 10 8 6 4 2

Cover art by Mary Ann Lasher
Book design by Kristin del Rosario

This is a work of fiction. Names, characters, places, and incidents either are the product
of the author's imagination or are used fictitiously, and any resemblance to actual persons,
living or dead, business establishments, events, or locales is entirely coincidental.

The recipes contained in this book have been created for the ingredients and techniques
indicated. The Publisher is not responsible for your specific health or allergy needs that
may require supervision. Nor is the Publisher responsible for any adverse reactions you may
have to the recipes contained in the book, whether you follow them as written or modify
them to suit your personal dietary needs or tastes.

For "Meg and Jenny Ferguson"
Wherever you are!

ACKNOWLEDGMENTS

Once again I would like to thank my fabulous agent, Josh Getzler, and his assistant, Danielle Burby, for their encouragement, hand-holding, and prompt answering of all my questions and concerns even when they're trivial! I would also like to thank my editor, Kristine Swartz, and the entire editorial staff at Berkley Prime Crime for the fabulous job they do. A special thanks to the fabulous copyediting team, who managed to keep this manuscript on track, and a big shout out to Mary Ann Lasher for another fabulous cover. Best one yet!

A special shout out to my buddy Carole Nelson Douglas, who's always there with a word of encouragement. (And Midnight Louie, too!) To all of the authors who've appeared on ROCCO's blog—I love all of you so much! A huge thank-you to Emily Hall, Denise LeSeur-Waechter, Robin Coxon, Barb Bristol Weisemann, Laura Roth, and all the BETAS who graciously pre-read CATNIP for me! Your comments were much appreciated.

I would also like to thank my dentist Edward Levey, my pal Frank Saul and his wife Pat and my work buddy Hilary

ACKNOWLEDGMENTS

Anderson for allowing me to make them characters in my series. You guys are the best!

Finally, an author owes a lot to their readers, and I would like to thank each and every person who buys and reads the Nick and Nora mysteries. Your support means the world to me, and I look forward to sharing many more of their adventures with you in the future.

PROLOGUE

The moon hung, a pale silver orb silhouetted against an expanse of black satin sky sprinkled with a generous glitter of stars. Its rays sluiced through the blinds of a darkened room, basking on one particular object: a glass case in the middle of the floor, and the book that lay on the pedestal within.

The curtains at the far end of the room rustled, and a slim, dark shape emerged. Clad entirely in black, the only clues to its feminine gender were its gently rounded curves, highlighted by skintight jeans and a turtleneck sweater. She moved purposefully toward the far corner, checked the nickel-plated cylinder set above the door molding, then removed a tiny key from the jeans pocket, fit it into the hole, and twisted.

Alarm silenced. Check.

Next she moved to the glass case, sliding her hand into the inner pocket of her vest as she did so. Whipping out a tiny torch, she cut a hole into the side of the case, then reached in a gloved hand to grasp her prize. She held it up, smiling in satisfaction as the moon's rays shone off the stones set into the cover, reflecting tiny beams of light. She plucked the largest stone, a brilliant red, from the cover and slipped it into her pocket. As she reached for the next she paused—the hairs on the back of her neck started to tingle.

I'm not alone here.

One thrust and the book was back inside the case. She pivoted at the exact moment another figure, also garbed in black, emerged from the darkness. At precisely the same instant, the sound of running footsteps in the adjacent corridor reached her ears. The other figure heard it, too, for he paused. She tore her gaze away for a split second to glance at the door and when she looked again, she was alone.

How did he do that? Where did he go?

The sound of a door slamming back made her jump. Turning her head a fraction of an inch, she caught the silhouette of a man out of the corner of her eye. He stood in the doorway for a moment before dropping into a crouch. "Halt or I'll shoot," he barked.

She hesitated, uncertain, then suddenly spun around and charged to the left.

A shot rang out and a bullet whizzed past her cheek, too close for comfort. Heart pounding, she forced her legs to go faster. There was another door at the far end of the exhibit room that led to the back stairwell. *If I can make it there, I'll make it anywhere,* her dizzied brain sang out. She was steps from her destination when another figure rose out of the shadows, blocking the door. Without breaking stride, she spun around and headed back in the other direction. Out of the corner of her eye she saw the guard approach, arm cocked, ready to take another shot.

Her gaze settled on the window, and she ran straight toward it just as another shot rang out. This time she felt a searing pain in her left side. She reached down, and her fingers came away covered in a sticky, dark red substance.

Blood.

It took a few seconds for her brain to process the fact that she'd been shot.

Her breaths came in short, labored gasps now. Two more steps and she was at the window. Even though her vision was slightly blurred, she could make out a VW bug, lights out, parked off to the side. Gritting her teeth, she swung her legs over the sill and just hung there for a moment, suspended in time and space. Beneath her, nothing moved. Everything was as still as a tomb.

Do I really want to do this?

Another shot rang out, shattering the pane of glass right above her hand. She heard a loud grunt not far behind her and then the pounding began inside her own head and the ache in her side reached a crescendo.

Her fingers lost their tenuous grip, and her whole body went limp. In the next instant she was sailing through the air, plummeting toward the unyielding concrete walk below . . .

ONE

"I declare, Nora, with food like this, the museum's annual gala can't help but be a success."

I smiled politely at the speaker as I rose to refill my mother's good bone-china bowl with tortilla chips. Nandalea Webb, the Cruz Museum's curator, was a no-nonsense type of gal and as feisty as the Australian meaning of her given name, fire, implied. She waved a red-lacquered hand in the air, leaned forward in her chair, and reached for one of the deviled eggs on the tray in the middle of the table. She took a bite and batted lashes heavy with several coats of mascara.

"Heaven," she murmured, dabbing at her salmon-pink-tinted lips with the edge of a napkin. "I can't tell you how much the committee appreciates your stepping in to cater this year's fund-raiser on such short notice."

"My pleasure," I assured her, reaching for a chip myself. "Not only would my mother have encouraged me, I consider it an honor. Anyway, I've catered events on less notice. Take Mac Davies's retirement from the Cruz detective squad, for example. I had about twelve hours' notice for that."

"True, dear, but that wasn't of the magnitude this is." Nan's teeth flashed in her version of a smile. "This will be a real challenge for you."

"Well, we Charles women always love a challenge. Plus, I can definitely use the extra income." I set the newly refilled bowl of chips in front of her. She took one, plunked it in my spinach dip (actually I can't claim credit; the recipe is my Aunt Prudence's), and popped it into her mouth. "My mother was always a staunch supporter of the museum. I know she would be proud."

"Indeed she would be."

I turned my attention to the other speaker. Violet Crenshaw was a lifelong resident of our little town of Cruz, California, with all the old money that usually implied. A senior member of the museum's board of directors—probably the most senior, at age seventy-one—she was extremely well preserved. Slight of frame, her clothes fit her like a runway model. Today she had on a dress of lightweight, fire-engine red wool that screamed "expensive designer." It was definitely a dress I'd have killed for, if the color didn't clash with my hair. Violet's own lavender-tinted hair was done in a becoming upsweep that set off her high cheekbones and delicate bone structure to great advantage. I could see why the women made such an effective team. Where Nan was outgoing and effusive, Violet was the more laid-back of the two, but just like the old saying went, still waters ran deep. Violet might tread softly but she carried a big stick, just like her idol, Teddy Roosevelt.

On this late autumn afternoon we were seated in the back area of the spacious kitchen that doubled as my office for Hot Bread, the sandwich shop I'd inherited from my mother a few months ago, to discuss me catering their annual fund-raiser. The Cruz Museum fund-raisers were always a big deal; expertly planned to raise a great deal of money, they paid very well. The catering firm they usually used had shut their doors abruptly a week ago. One of the owners had been diagnosed with a heart murmur, prompting the momentous decision to retire in Palm Springs and reap the fruits of their years of successful labor. I'd been approached for the job, not only because no other caterer in a twelve mile radius wanted the responsibility or pressure of catering a gala for two hundred people on such short notice, but also because my late mother, in addition to being a museum patron, had also been a friend to both Nandalea and Violet.

Violet helped herself to one of the finger sandwiches I'd prepared and eyed me with a steely gaze over the rims of her Ben Franklin–style glasses. "Your mother was an excellent cook, Nora. She put her all into Hot Bread. I always felt bad we had that long-standing contract with Phineas Rodgers. She would have enjoyed catering our affairs."

Nan's dark brown pageboy bobbed up and down in

agreement. "Yes, she always supported our cause with generous donations. She loved Cruz and its history, and she loved the museum."

"It's very gratifying to see you taking over where she left off, following the family tradition." Violet coughed lightly then added, "Family is so important. Sometimes one doesn't realize how much."

I caught the wistful note in the older woman's voice and smiled. "I couldn't agree more."

"Er-owl!"

The two women jumped. The large (although portly might be a better word) black and white tuxedo cat sprawled across Hot Bread's kitchen floor pushed himself upright to regard us with wide golden eyes. His ears flattened against his skull as his mouth opened, revealing a row of sharp, pointed teeth. He waved one forepaw in the air in an imperious manner.

"Ah." Nan laughed. "I see your cat agrees family is important. What's his name again?"

"Nick."

"Nick Charles?" The two women burst out laughing. "That figures," Nan said at last, her gaze sweeping the cat up and down. "He looks well cared for. What shelter did you get him from?"

"No shelter, although I do think that's a marvelous way to adopt a pet. He just appeared on my doorstep one night, waltzed inside, and that was that. Honestly, I blame Chantal. She talked me into keeping him. Although I've never regretted it," I added quickly. "It's hard to tell sometimes who owns who."

"Oh, I *so* agree. I've had a few kitties in my lifetime. One never owns a cat, dear. They own you," Nan said with a wise nod.

Nick sat up on his haunches and pawed at Nan's skirt, then flopped over on his back and wiggled all four paws in the air.

Violet peered at the cat over the rims of her glasses. "He's quite the little ham, isn't he?"

I suppressed a chuckle. "You don't know the half of it. Ask Chantal. Nick is her unofficial model for her line of pet collars, and I swear, he just loves the camera and vice versa."

Nick sat up, wrapped his tail around his forelegs, and cocked his head to one side as if studying the women. Then he got up, trotted over to the fleece bed in the corner, swiped his paw underneath the cushion, and reappeared a moment later with a catnip mouse. He trotted back to the group and paused, head cocked as if studying them; then he walked over and dropped the mouse at the foot of Nan's chair and looked up expectantly.

"Well, will you look at that," Violet said with a chuckle, as Nan picked up the mouse and flung it into a far corner. Nick scampered off after it immediately, his rotund rear wiggling. "He certainly knew which one to pick, didn't he?"

Nick returned, the mouse clamped firmly between his jaws. As he started toward Nan again, I put out my hand and lightly touched his back. "That's enough, Nick. We're having a business discussion right now."

He glanced up at me and blinked, then hunkered down

beside my chair and proceeded to attack the mouse with his teeth and claws.

"Goodness," Nan gasped. "It's almost as if he understood you."

Nick's head lifted. *"Merow."* He flopped over on his side with the mouse clenched firmly between his paws, and wiggled his hind legs.

Violet leaned forward in her chair for a closer look. "Intelligent little fellow," she murmured. "I've always been a dog person, myself, but you know what? I think your cat could change my mind."

Nick swung his head around, lips peeled back in what I termed his "shit-eating kitty grin."

"Yes, he is very smart," I said. "Maybe a little too smart, sometimes. His former human taught him well. I don't know what I'd do if Nick Atkins showed up and wanted him back."

Violet's head jerked up and she fixed me with a stare. "Nick Atkins? The PI? This was his cat?"

I nodded, a bit taken aback. The last person I'd have expected to know the hard-boiled PI was the stately Violet. "Yes. I didn't realize you knew him."

Violet opened her mouth to speak, and then paused as her gaze darted from the cat to me and back to the cat again. It seemed as if she were unsure how to answer the question. The next minute the unlikely strains of "California Gurls" chirped from the depths of her purse. Violet a Katy Perry fan? Man, this day was full of surprises.

"Excuse me." She fished the phone out, glanced at the number, and then snapped it open with a brisk, "Yes,

Daisy. What's the matter?" She listened intently for a few minutes then sighed audibly. "Tell him we'll be back shortly, and to wait until we get there. Surely twenty minutes won't make a monumental difference in their schedule." She snapped the phone shut, slid it back into her bag, and turned to me with an apologetic smile. "So sorry for the interruption. Where were we?"

Nan smiled over the rim of her coffee cup. "Well, before Nick distracted us, I believe we were about to discuss the pros and cons of a sit-down dinner versus a buffet."

"Right. Well, I don't think much discussion is necessary," Violet said. "After all, it's a costume ball. Formal dinners are lovely, but who wants to bother with all that at a masquerade?"

"True," said Nan slowly. "But are we absolutely certain we should make it a costume affair? Most people do prefer a sit-down dinner."

Violet peered at Nan over the rims of her glasses. "Nonsense. It's the week before Halloween, so what could be more appropriate than a masquerade?" Her head swiveled in my direction. "What do you think, Nora?"

Uh-oh. The last thing I wanted or needed was to play referee. Fortunately I was spared getting in the middle as Nan held up both hands in a gesture of surrender. "You're right, Violet. The fact it's before Halloween totally slipped my mind. So, a costume ball with a buffet it is."

Violet's lips curved in a satisfied smirk. "Of course I'm right. Pleasant atmosphere, good food and drink, that's the key. We want our patrons feeling good so they'll whip out their checkbooks and give generously. After all, the happier the patron, the bigger the contribution, am I right?"

"Oh, listen to her. She's so wise," Nan whispered.

"Hmpf. Wise has nothing to do with it. It's common sense," Violet said with a snort. "Just like a big part of keeping 'em happy is getting 'em plastered."

"Violet!" Nan's jaw dropped and she shot me a quick look out of the corner of her eye. "You can be blunt as a knife sometimes."

"Well, it's true." The older woman chuckled. "The more they drink the happier and looser they get, and then out come the checkbooks and better yet, the zeros on the checks!" She rubbed her hands together and closed one eye in a broad wink. "We spring for complimentary wine and soda, but the real proceeds flow from the cash bar. Which reminds me—Nora, do you know where we can find a good bartender? The position pays quite well." She named a figure that made my eyes pop, and I immediately thought of Lance Reynolds. He ran the only tavern in Cruz, the Poker Face. I'd known him for years, dated him in high school. I was positive he'd agree. Not only could he use the money, but it would be great publicity for his own bar. I mentioned his name and Violet nodded solemnly.

"I'm ashamed I didn't think of him right off," she said, reaching into her purse. She pulled out a notebook and made a swift notation. "You wouldn't happen to know a good photographer, too?"

"Actually, Remy Gillard is an amateur photographer, and he's quite good."

"The florist? We've already hired him for the centerpieces, so he might not be able to do both, but . . ." She made another notation in her little book. "It never hurts to ask. I'll have Daisy get right on this."

I arched a brow at the second mention of the unfamiliar name. "Daisy? I thought Maude always handled these details?"

"She did—before she decided to retire," Violet said crisply. "She went to live in North Carolina with her daughter, without giving us any notice! Imagine!"

"Now, now, don't be like that Violet. She did give us a week," interjected Nan.

Violet gave her head a brisk shake. "You call that notice? Hmpf."

Nan turned back to me with an apologetic smile. "We were very fortunate Daisy happened along just when she did. It was really a case of being in the right place at the right time. She happened to be in the museum and overheard us talking about finding a replacement. It's a great opportunity for her. She just moved back to the States from London, and she was about to start job-hunting anyway. What do you call it again, when events intersect just so?"

"Fate," I answered, sliding a glance Violet's way. "I guess I always assumed that when Maude finally retired, Nellie would take her place." Nellie Blanchard was a part-time docent who'd worked at the museum forever. It was no secret the woman aspired to an office position.

"So did Nellie." Violet sighed. "Don't get me wrong, she's done a fine job as a docent, but office work is different. She wouldn't have the freedom she does now. Plus,

I'm not all that sure she'd be able to adapt to a nine-to-five routine. Believe it or not, she's got a bit of a temper, and when things don't go her way . . ." Violet fluttered her hand in the air. "Sometimes she can get quite . . . unpleasant, shall we say?"

I nodded. I couldn't dispute any of what Violet had said. Nellie had never made any bones about the fact she enjoyed being able to set her own hours, and I'd once seen her hurl a paperweight at a deliveryman who'd refused to place a box where she wanted it. Still, she'd always hinted that when Maude went, she should be the next in line, and no one could really dispute her claim. She had the background and the experience, if not the formal education.

As if she'd read my thoughts, Violet said quickly, "It wasn't an easy decision but I think it was the right one. Daisy's rather young but her references were excellent. You'll like her, I'm sure. So then"—Violet clasped her hands together—"are we in agreement on the menu? Buffet style?"

I nodded. "I have quite a few ideas on what can be done. I'll outline a menu and get it to you."

Violet's eyes lit up. "You are such a dear to do this for us on such short notice. Now, don't forget we'll need to have some of your dishes named in line with our theme."

I looked at the two of them blankly. "Theme?"

"Yes. We want the flavor of the ball to reflect the exhibit that debuts the following week." She flicked an irritated glance toward Nan. "You *did* mention that when you brought over the contract, didn't you?"

Nan hung her head. "I'm afraid I didn't. I take full

responsibility. It simply slipped my mind, what with all we had going on."

Violet's jaw shot forward, and before the older woman could make a disparaging remark I said, "It shouldn't be a problem. What's the theme?"

They both answered at the same time, talking over each other. "It's a medieval exhibit." "It concentrates on the Arthurian legends."

"Arthurian legends? You mean King Arthur? As in Knights of the Round Table King Arthur? He's a fictional character, right?"

"Well, that's debatable." Nan pushed back a bit in her chair. "The historical basis for the King Arthur legend has long been a point of controversy among scholars. One school of thought sees him as a genuine historical figure, a leader who fought against the invading Anglo-Saxons sometime in the late fifth to early sixth century. Then others . . ."

"Argue Arthur was originally a fictional hero of folklore, perhaps even a half-forgotten Celtic deity, whom they credited with real deeds in the distant past," finished Violet. "There is no concrete evidence proving or disproving either theory, but Sir Rodney Meecham feels otherwise."

I frowned. "Sir Rodney Meecham? The same Sir Rodney who founded the Meecham Foundation?" I'd heard of the man when a reporter friend had done a piece on him several years ago. Not only was he an avid collector of all things medieval, he was richer than King Midas and Bill Gates put together.

"The very same," Violet said, her head bobbing up and down. "It's his collection that will be on display." She leaned in a bit closer to me, her voice now a hushed whisper. "Recently he was able to acquire a very, very rare artifact. It will be shown for the very first time in the United States at our exhibit the night of the gala. That's why it's imperative everything be just perfect."

"I see," I said slowly. "And just what is this artifact, might I ask?"

Once again they answered in unison. "The grimoire of Morgan le Fay!"

As the two of them beamed at me, I frantically tried to remember everything I'd ever read or seen in the movies and on television about King Arthur and his legendary Knights of the Round Table, but the old gray cells were drawing a blank. "Sorry," I said. "I do remember Lancelot and Guinevere. I can't quite place Morgan le Fay, though."

"She's a powerful sorceress in the Arthurian legend. Even though early works describe her character as more of a magician, she became much more prominent in later prose works as an antagonist to Arthur and Guinevere. She is said to be the daughter of Arthur's mother, the Lady Igraine, and her first husband, the Duke of Cornwall. Arthur is her half brother. Oh, she was quite the troublemaker." Nan rolled her eyes skyward.

"And the grimoire?" I asked. "I'm not familiar with that term."

"A grimoire is an ancient book of spells—a witch's textbook, if you will," Violet answered. "Morgan le Fay's is supposed to contain the blackest spells in the entire world. The jewels that encrust its cover are supposed to act as conduits to her power. Legend or truth? It's one of those mysteries that make the study of the Arthurian era so interesting. Was Morgan le Fay real or not, and if so, was she truly a sorceress of that magnitude?"

"She's an important piece of the legend of Arthur, to be sure, and the grimoire, whether real or not, is of interest to many historians," Nan added. "We're counting on it to attract fresh blood to the museum."

I couldn't help but express my own concerns. "A piece so valuable—I just hope it doesn't attract the wrong type of person, if you get my meaning."

Violet leaned forward and brushed her hand against mine. "I do, dear. There have been a few incidents in the past . . ."

"She means attempts at theft," Nan cut in.

Violet threw Nan a black look, cleared her throat, and then continued. "A few incidents, so I made it a point to contact the Cruz police force about stepping up the security detail for the length of the exhibit, and for the gala, of course."

"Yes, so you needn't worry about anything, Nora, other than preparing your excellent food," Nan remarked, and then added with a twinkle in her eye, "Unless you think the grimoire and its history might make a good story for that magazine you write for."

"*Noir.* It might. I'll ask Louis." Louis Blondell, the owner and editor of the online true crime magazine I wrote for part time, was always eager for any article that smacked of mystery—plus I owed him two pieces already. I tucked the tip about previous theft attempts away, determined to do a bit of research on my own regardless of whether or not he'd be interested—although knowing Louis, I was sure he would be. "I can name some of the sandwiches and main dishes after the more popular characters in Arthurian mythology. I'll just need to do some research on them—and I know just the person to help me."

"Splendid!" Nan gushed. "And several food critics will be there—they're patrons of the museum—so it will be a wonderful opportunity for your shop, Nora. Why, you might generate more business than you can handle."

"An increase in business is not a bad thing." Violet glanced at her watch and rose. "We'd best get going. The exhibit manager is waiting for us back at the museum. Apparently there are many cases to unload. At this rate we may have to move the exhibit to the Red Room."

Nan shrugged into her fleece jacket. "We'll give you a key to the kitchen, so you can just stop in anytime to look it over or whatever. You can pick it up tomorrow, and do let me know if there's anything you'll need."

Nan bustled out the door, Violet trailing at a slower pace. She paused to lay her hand on my shoulder. "I hear you've become quite the sleuth. I heard what you did for your sister, and I read the account of the Grainger case. Very impressive. Like that sort of work, do you?"

"I do. Then again, I enjoyed tracking down leads when I was a true crime reporter so I guess it's really not that much of a stretch."

She nodded. "Well, then, when you've got a bit of time to spare, stop by my office. There's a matter I'd like to discuss that the sleuth in you should find quite a challenge." She looked at me, and I caught a glimmer of a twinkle in her eye. "It involves a disappearance, and there's even the possibility it might also involve . . . a murder."

TWO

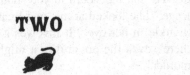

I finally found enough of my voice to squeak out, "A murder? Really?" But Violet had already sashayed out the door and into Nan's waiting car, and I didn't think it appropriate to chase after her. Warm fur caressed my ankles and I glanced downward. "Did you hear that?" I whispered to Nick.

He rubbed his head against my knee. *"Merow."*

She'd spoken so low there was a possibility I might have misunderstood, and Violet did have a dry sense of humor, but somehow I didn't think so. I resolved to quiz her at the first opportunity, certain that a story involving a murder would appeal to Louis more than an ancient grimoire. I stole a quick peek at my watch and looked at Nick. "How would you like to take a ride?"

He detached himself from my body and went immediately to the back door, tail flicking impatiently. I opened the door and Nick padded out and right over to my SUV, and started rubbing against the passenger door. I took that for a yes.

Twenty minutes later Nick and I were driving toward the middle of town and Poppies, the flower shop run by my BFF, Chantal Gillard, and her brother, Remy. Chantal had been away at a psychic convention in Los Angeles until last night, and I needed to fill her in on recent events; besides, I'd missed her company.

Nick chirped his approval when I indicated our destination. He'd always been fond of Chantal, and why not? She was good looking, she was psychic (my friend did possess a certain amount of ESP, which was a good bonding point with Nick, since cats are supposed to possess similar psychic abilities, doncha know?), and she had a delightful French accent (even if it was affected), plus she always made a dreadful fuss over Nick, even to the point of having him model cat collars for her line of homemade jewelry, Lady C Creations. (Okay, maybe that part Nick could do without.)

There was an empty parking spot right in front of the shop, so I pulled the SUV right in. Poppies is divided into three stores. The left side is the flower shop, which is usually brimming with customers and the fragrant smell of whatever buds Remy's decided to have adorn the window for the display he changes on a weekly basis; the right side of the shop is Chantal's, and divided two more ways: One side of the shop is set up like a tearoom slash New Age store. Chantal has a display of crystals, tarot cards, and the like, which she sells, and she also gives psychic readings via whichever method of divination the customer prefers. Another corner of the shop is devoted to her line of homemade jewelry and its newest addition: homemade pet collars. To that end, a large fifteen by thirty photograph of Nick himself wearing Chantal's latest creation, a pale blue stretch collar with the pet name embroidered in colored beads, practically slapped us in the face when we entered the store. Nick let out a yowl of approval upon seeing his handsome puss so prominently displayed on the shop's far wall.

The beaded curtain at the rear of the shop parted and my friend emerged. Today she was dressed in what I called her "gypsy motif." She wore a multicolored maxi skirt with ankle boots and a white off-the-shoulder peasant blouse. A cheerful print scarf was wound through her short, curly black bob. Her wide blue eyes started to sparkle as soon as she spotted us.

"*Chérie!* And Nicky! *Mon Dieu!* Come here and give me some sugar. I have missed the two of you."

I ran forward and let myself be enveloped in a bear hug to end all bear hugs. Chantal might be tiny—five two and ninety-eight pounds soaking wet—but thanks to her gym membership she's pretty much all muscle. She released me and we both looked down at the source of the plaintive "*meow.*"

"Ach, I could not forget about my favorite cat or model! Have you been behaving yourself?" Chantal hefted all twenty-plus pounds of Nick into her arms and snuggled her nose into his soft black fur.

"I think he enjoyed seeing his image on the wall. When did that go up?" I asked.

"Remy put it up while I was away. Do you like it?" Chantal leaned over to coo in the cat's ear. "Nicky is my good luck charm. We sold a dozen collars in the last week!"

I wondered how many sales could be attributed to Nick's poster versus Chantal's sheer determination and salesmanship, but Nick's lips peeled back and he rubbed his head against Chantal's arm. She scratched him in his favorite spot, the white streak behind his ear, before turning to me. "So, how are you, *chérie*? You look—excuse the expression—like the proverbial cat who ate the canary."

"That's because I just landed a fabulous catering job, and, drum roll please, I may have another mystery to solve."

Chantal grinned broadly. "Well, I can guess which of those two is responsible for your Cheshire Cat expression. As far as the catering goes, you know I will help you in any way I can, *chérie*, just as long as I do not have to do any actual cooking."

I laughed at that. My friend is probably one of the only people on the planet who can't boil water.

"No cooking. I just need a crash course in the Arthurian legends. I'm catering the Cruz Museum Gala. They're—"

"Hosting that medieval exhibit," Chantal finished. "I know. There was much discussion of this upcoming exhibit and the grimoire at the fair. Everyone was surprised

23

Sir Meecham agreed to show the grimoire over here after what happened in London."

I eased my hip against a glass case. "Let me guess. Someone tried to steal it."

Chantal's head bobbed up and down, her eyes wide. "Yes. They did not succeed, but a guard was badly injured and several artifacts were damaged. The guard got off a shot that he thought might have injured the thief, and it was touch and go with his own injuries for a while, but he recovered. After that the security was increased tenfold." Her finger shot out, stopping scant inches from my nose. "This could be a very dangerous undertaking."

"Well," I sighed, "at least now I understand why the Cruz police force has been placed on retainer."

"Hm. Nothing against our erstwhile police force, but it might not be a bad idea to call in the big guns, too—like, say, a certain FBI agent?" Chantal remarked innocently.

I shot my friend a sharp grimace. I'd first met FBI Special Agent Daniel Corleone when I was investigating the death of Lola Grainger, and even though we'd gotten off to a rocky start professionally, personally sparks had flown. Getting together wasn't easy, due mostly to Daniel's heavy caseload schedule, but we'd managed to eke out a few dates, albeit they'd been mostly lunch. "I don't think guarding an ancient sorceress's book of spells is high on the FBI priority list. Besides, Daniel's busy with a case right now," I said.

"It is not just any book of spells. It is considered a valuable historical relic. And Daniel apparently is not too busy to skip meals." Her smirk was firmly in place, and I had to resist the urge to slap it right off her. "Don't think I don't know the two of you had dinner together at Le Bistro two nights ago."

I stared at her. "How in the world do you know that? You were out of town."

She tapped her temple. "Psychic, remember? I see all, know all."

I snorted. "Psychic my petunias. Remy told you. I thought I saw him at the counter getting takeout."

Chantal grinned even more smugly, if such a thing were possible. "It doesn't matter how I know. What matters is how it went. After all, it was your first official date, no?"

"Well, it was the first time we didn't get interrupted by an emergency call from the field office, if that's what you mean. We had dinner, and, yes, it was fun."

"Excellent," she squealed, clapping her hands. "And how did dessert go?"

"I had frozen yogurt. Daniel had chocolate cake."

"Not that kind of dessert," Chantal said, bouncing her eyebrows. "I meant *dessert*."

"We kissed." I smiled reminiscently. Daniel was an excellent kisser. "And that's all. We're taking things slow." At her look I added, "It was a mutual agreement. We've both had less than stellar relationships, and we're cautious. There's nothing wrong with that."

"Hmm?" Chantal cocked her brow at me. "So this desire to take it slow has nothing at all to do with your recent reconnection with a certain homicide detective in St. Leo?"

I bit back the *grr* that rumbled deep in my throat. A few weeks ago, while trying to clear my sister of a murder charge, I'd become reacquainted with a blast from my past in the form of insufferable homicide detective Leroy Samms. Samms and I do share a history, and I'd be lying if I said our recent encounter hadn't stirred up old feelings, but I'm totally over it. I've moved on.

At least that's what I keep telling myself.

"I wouldn't jump to conclusions if I were you."

"It's hard not to," my friend replied with a curl of her lip, "since I, whom you claim am your best friend in the whole wide world, know virtually nothing about your relationship with this mystery man."

I wagged my finger at her. "Nice try, but I'm not falling for the guilt trip act. Besides, there's nothing to tell. It was a long time ago."

Chantal's eyes narrowed. "Uh-huh."

"Suffice it to say Samms is a part of my past and leave it at that. Or you could just ask your tarot cards," I said lightly.

"I have done that. They hint at a relationship much deeper than you profess."

I should have known, I thought, giving myself a mental slap. "Okay, fine. Samms and I met when we worked on the college paper during our senior year. I admit I was attracted to him."

"Ah, now we are getting somewhere. Was the feeling mutual?"

"Honest? To this day, I'm not sure. He had a lot, and I do mean a lot, of girls after him. We were like oil and water from the first day. He knew then and still knows now how to push my buttons, particularly with his nick-names for me." I made a face. "Right before graduation, we were working late. We'd finished up a really rough story, and Samms had some wine, said we deserved a celebration." I pushed my hand through my hair. "We celebrated all right—straight through to the next day actually."

Chantal's eyes widened. "Ooh, *chérie*! Do you mean—"

"No," I said quickly. "There was some kissing involved—okay, a lot of kissing—but nothing else happened. Or at least I don't think it did." I grimaced. "We both got pretty toasted."

"And Samms didn't remember, either?"

"I don't know. I left while he was still asleep, and I avoided him like the plague after that, which was pretty easy, considering we were graduating the next day. I got my diploma, got on the train for Chicago, and that was that."

Chantal's brow lifted. "So the first time you saw him in, what, eighteen years was when your sister was arrested?"

I nodded. "That's right. I threw myself into my career, and as far as I know, Samms never made any attempt to find me. Which only goes to prove we're all wrong for each other."

Chantal frowned. "That's not necessarily true. And you don't know for certain he never tried to find you. Did you ask him?"

"I'm certainly not going to ask him something like

that," I huffed. "Not after all these years. Anyway, he never brought the subject up while I was in St. Leo, so it's a moot point."

"You don't know that," my friend protested. "He might have felt just as awkward as you, broaching it."

"I doubt that. One thing Samms is not is awkward. Anyway, I never gave it a second thought in all these years." *Liar*, my brain screamed. I pointed at Nick. "Right now, he's the only serious male in my future. He's handsome, attentive, and doesn't talk back. Who could ask for more?" Before my friend could answer my rhetorical question I went on, "So, back to the present. What do you know about Violet Crenshaw?"

"Violet? She is richer than King Midas, and a crusty old broad I wouldn't want to tangle with. Why do you ask? Is she part of the mystery you hinted at?"

"You could say that. She and Nan were at Hot Bread discussing the gala. On her way out, she said she had something to discuss with me that she thought I might be interested in. A disappearance and a possible murder."

Chantal's eyes almost popped out of her head. "That is certainly strange, *chérie*. Do you think she was serious?"

"With Violet it's hard to tell, but oddly, yes."

"I wonder who she meant?" My friend started to tick off possibilities on her fingers. "A friend? She doesn't have too many. A relative? She's a widow with no immediate family to speak of. Her husband died of natural causes so . . . who could it be?"

"Don't know, but rest assured I'll find out. I'd have grilled her more but she waltzed out while I was reeling from her little bombshell—which, I think, is just what she wanted." I sighed. "Right now, though, I need a crash course in the Arthurian legends."

Chantal crossed over to the counter, reached below, and pulled up a deck of cards, which she held aloft. "The Arthurian Tarot. The quickest way I know of to get a crash course in the Arthurian legends. Stick with me, *mon cher,* and soon you'll know all of 'em like a pro." She shuffled the cards, laid them down, and turned over the top one. "Let's start with Guinevere, shall we?"

An hour later Nick and I said our good-byes and left. My mind was swimming with character names, descriptions, and possible recipes I could put to each one. Of course I only had three days to do all this but hey, not to sound like a broken record, but we Charles women do love a challenge.

"And speaking of challenges, I think we should research those attempted thefts involving that grimoire when we get home, especially the one Chantal told us about. If thieves tried to steal it once, they might try again. We certainly don't need anything like that spoiling our party, do we, boy?"

Nick, curled up in a ball in the passenger seat, opened his mouth, yawned, and then hunkered back down, his chin resting on his forepaws.

"I suppose you're right. I shouldn't worry about it. I should leave it in the hands of the pros. Sorry to bore you." I had to admit, though, I was a bit concerned. A masked ball seemed the perfect backdrop for a theft to take place. I snapped my seat belt into place and jumped as my cell phone chimed. I glanced at the caller ID and then flipped it open.

"Oliver J. Sampson. You must be psychic. I was thinking of giving you a call."

"Psychic, eh? I've been called worse." Oliver J. Sampson—Ollie to his friends, which include me—is a big man of color, about six three at least, and well over two hundred twenty pounds, but when he snickers, he sounds like a little girl. "Got some time for me? I need to see you."

I sucked in a breath. "You heard back from the lab."

Slight hesitation and then, "I'd rather not talk about it over the phone. Tell you what. I'm free after ten a.m. tomorrow. Can you get away from the shop and stop by?"

"Mollie's working a full day tomorrow so I sure can. See you then."

I hung up and twisted the key in the ignition, sliding a glance toward Nick as I did so. Nick shifted his position on the seat, and I frowned as I noticed a pale brown square wedged under his tummy. "What have you got there, fella?" I poked at his tummy and he shifted slightly, affording me a better look at his prize.

It was a Scrabble tile, the letter A.

I shook my head. I'd long given up on trying to figure out how Nick got his paws on things, especially Scrabble tiles—the only thing to surpass catnip mice as his favorite plaything in the whole wide world. I reached out and picked up the tile, turned it over in my hand.

"A," I murmured. "A is Bronson Pichard's middle initial. It's also the first initial of Nick Atkins's girlfriend—Angelique. The one Pichard thought might know something about what happened to him." I'd meant to quiz Ollie about her when I'd first found out, but our schedules had both been pretty out of sync.

"*Er-ewl*," bleated Nick. He scraped his paw against my seat cover.

"Right. I've been dreadfully remiss in my sleuthing. That's why I have you, right, bud? To keep me on track." I slipped the tile into my jacket pocket and eased away from the curb. "So once we hear Ollie's news, we'll grill him about Angelique, and maybe even Violet Crenshaw, too. Maybe we might finally get closer to uncovering the truth about what happened to your former master."

He just stared straight ahead. Either Nick hadn't understood what I'd said, or he simply didn't care.

I'm not ashamed to say that honestly . . . I hoped for the latter.

THREE

Nick and I arrived at Ollie's office promptly at ten the next morning. He opened the door before I could even raise my hand to knock. "Nora." He grinned, displaying a row of teeth that looked like bright, shiny Chiclets. "You're a sight for sore eyes. Come on in." He smiled down at Nick. "You, too, my friend."

Nick led the way, his black tail straight up in the air. I slid into one of the two leather chairs positioned in front of Ollie's desk while he eased his burly frame into the captain's chair behind it. Nick hopped up on the desk and arranged himself comfortably on one end, one black and white paw dangling over the edge.

"Ah, memories." Ollie smiled reminiscently. "He always used to sprawl across the desk like that when Nick was trying to concentrate. It didn't bother him, though. He always called Little Sherlock his muse."

Nick's ears flicked forward at the mention of the name he'd been christened with. He swiped at his face with one furry black-and-white paw. A sound suspiciously like a grunt rumbled deep in his throat.

Ollie laughed. "Sorry, Little Nick. I keep forgetting you like your new name better."

I leaned across the desk. "Okay, don't keep me in suspense any longer. What did the lab say? Was it from Nick Atkins or not?"

A few weeks ago, Ollie received a postcard from New Orleans that he'd fancied might have been sent by Nick. It had definitely rattled him, because up until then he'd been swearing on stacks of Bibles that Atkins was, in all probability, dead and gone and out of his life—and mine and Nick the cat's—for good. For both our peace of minds, I advised sending the postcard to an expert in handwriting analysis, and Ollie had jumped right on my suggestion. Although he tried to act indifferent, I knew he was anxious to get the question of Atkins's status resolved as well, so he could get on with his own life and decide what to do about the PI business they'd built up together. I confess I'm also interested in the fate of Nick Atkins. Not only does his mysterious disappearance gnaw at my reporter's instincts, but I'm a gal who hates to leave things unsettled—such as the question of my tubby tuxedo's ownership.

Ollie opened the middle drawer of his desk, withdrew

a sheet of paper, and slid it across to me. I picked it up and scanned the few typed sentences, then tossed it back on the table, the corners of my lips drooping down. "This says the results are inconclusive. The card was too smudged to make any definitive match. No prints, either. Damn." I pushed the paper back to Ollie. "I take it you haven't received another postcard?"

"Nope." He folded the report and then reached into the drawer again. He withdrew the postcard and set it on the desk in front of us. "Smudged or not, it sure looked like his handwriting to me. If it wasn't Nick's penmanship, it was a damn good imitation." He brushed one hand through his springy mass of gray hair. "I'm no expert on the supernatural, but as far as I know, ghosts can't write postcards. I just don't know what to think anymore. Dammit, he *could* be alive."

I picked up the card and looked at its brief message:

In sunny New Orleans. Must get going. Ollie you'd love it here. Keen swamp tours.

"N"

I turned the card over. The scene depicted was that of a New Orleans showboat, gliding across impossibly blue waters. I glanced at Ollie. "It doesn't say much. His penmanship is horrid. The writing's so cramped you can hardly read it."

"Nick always was a scribbler."

"Yes, I've looked through his journals." I squinted at the card. "These sentences make no sense. And what, might I ask, is 'keen' about a swamp tour?"

"Not much, I reckon. The English language wasn't Nick's forte. He wasn't much for small talk, either. He loved his puzzles, though. I keep looking for the hidden meaning."

My eyebrow quirked upward. "Hidden meaning? How much can one hide in a dozen words?"

Nick thumped his tail down hard on the desk four times, then blinked and hopped off the desk, walked over to the far corner of the room, and lay down, head on paws. I stared after him. "Now what was that for?"

"Isn't it obvious? The cat agrees with me," Ollie boomed. "You'd be surprised what Nick could do, although to be honest, I can't even picture him writing out a postcard. I guess that's why I have my doubts." He took the postcard from me and pulled it in front of him. "That's the funny way he did an 'o,' and the way he crossed his 't's. If he didn't write this, it's a damn good imitation."

"Can you think of anything he was working on that would have led him to New Orleans?"

He leaned back in the chair and laced his beefy fingers behind his neck. "Let's see. What was Nick working on back then? Well, there was the Adrienne Sloane case, of course. Then there was Mickey Parker's divorce. I handled that one. No New Orleans connection there. Oh, and some rich dame hired him to find her missing niece."

My ears perked up at that admission, but I quickly dismissed it. Although Violet Crenshaw would definitely fit the description of a "rich dame," according to Chantal she didn't have any nieces or nephews. "Anyone else?"

He shifted in the massive chair. "Yeah, the girl he was seeing around the same time. She was from New Orleans, I think." He blew out a sigh. "I knew Angelique Martone was trouble from the moment I laid eyes on her. She was one of those femme fatale types straight out of a James Bond movie. Nick had rose-colored glasses on where she was concerned. They dated for a month, I guess, or maybe a bit longer. Things were going hunky-dory and then one day he got a special delivery letter. He read it, and next thing I knew he stormed out of here. He was gone a long time, and when he came back he was three sheets to the wind. He sat down here"—Ollie patted the desktop—"pulled out the Scotch, and polished off the whole bottle. 'Ollie' he said to me—he never slurred his words, not even when he was shit-eyed drunk—'never trust a beautiful woman. They lie, and not about insignificant stuff, either. She's put me in a heck of a spot. So now what do I do?' Then he finished the Scotch and passed out."

My fingers found the Scrabble tile in my pocket and I rubbed at it. "A heck of a spot? What do you think he meant by that?"

Ollie shrugged. "I have no idea. I'm betting the letter explained quite a bit. I hunted for it, but couldn't find it. I did find some pieces of paper mixed in with ash in the fireplace, though. I've got a feeling he burned it. He threw her picture in the trash can, too, but I dug it out, just in case he ever changed his mind." Ollie opened the middle drawer of his desk, pulled out a white envelope, and passed it across to me. I shook the envelope and a photograph of a man and a woman fell out. I recognized Nick Atkins instantly: the lantern jaw, jet-black hair with the familiar white streak behind one ear. But it was the woman's image that really floored me. I stared into wide eyes the color of brilliant green grass, hair as black as a raven's wing, lips as red as ripe apples; in short, perfection. I looked at Ollie. "When I saw Pichard, he said I should ask you about Angelique. That if anyone would know what happened to Nick, it'd be her."

Ollie laced his hands behind his neck. "Not that Pichard is the most reliable source of information, but he might have something there."

I tapped my finger against the photo. "Would you mind if I kept this?"

He hesitated, and then nodded. "Okay, but if you want my advice, you'll leave well enough alone. That woman's got some sort of secret and mark my words, finding her can only lead to disaster."

FOUR

Back in my SUV, I turned on the ignition and then slid a glance at Nick, curled up in a ball in the passenger seat. I crooked a finger in his direction. "Well, what do you think? Would finding this mysterious Angelique lead us to your former human, or just stir up more trouble like Ollie thinks?"

Nick swiveled his head toward me, made a little grunting sound.

"Yep," I said as I eased the SUV into the late-day traffic, "that's what I thought. So let's concentrate on Violet's mystery instead. Louis has been after me for another article for *Noir*, right? Maybe this can fill the bill."

I turned onto Main Street and realized I was only a few short minutes away from the Cruz Museum. I made a quick right and then another left, and ten minutes later I

backed into a parking spot at the far end of the Cruz Museum's parking lot. Things were certainly hopping here: Several black cars were parked near the rear entrance, some of them taking up two prime spots, and a silver truck was backed up against one side of the building. I walked across the lot and up the front steps, pushed through the heavy oaken door and into the high-ceilinged foyer. A cherrywood reception desk was angled off to the left, and I could see Nellie Blanchard's white curly bob bent over the middle drawer. She rifled through it quickly, then slammed it shut, jerked open a bottom drawer, and proceeded to rifle through that one as well. I approached the desk and cleared my throat loudly. Nellie's head jerked up, and her watery blue gaze fastened on me. She slammed the drawer shut with a bang and a barely concealed grunt, and reached up to straighten her wire-rimmed glasses on her beak-shaped nose. "Nora. Hello."

I gave her a bright smile. "Hello, Nellie. I'm surprised to see you here. I thought today was your day off?"

"It was supposed to be, but it seems there's a lot to do lately." She pushed the chair back and stood up, smoothing her magenta-colored skirt. "Between getting the exhibit set up, the volunteers decorating the main hall for the gala, and half the Cruz police force milling around, a body can't even think straight around here." She glanced at her watch, and then peered at me over the rims of her glasses. "Do you need help with something?"

"Nan Webb asked me to drop by and pick up the key to the kitchen entrance."

She rifled through a pile of envelopes on the desk,

opened a few drawers, and then shook her head. "There's no key here, and no one mentioned anything about you stopping by, *as usual.* Nan is with the security detail and I have no idea what *Ms. Martinelli* is up to." She slammed the center desk drawer shut, a bit more forcefully than necessary I thought, and then she added with a tight smile, "If you've got a few minutes, I can get it for you. I know where the spares are kept."

"No problem." I thrust my hands into the pockets of my fleece jacket and eased my hip against one corner of the desk. "Is Ms. Crenshaw around?"

"I haven't seen her, but that doesn't mean she's not here somewhere. They've both been busy as beavers with this exhibit." She glanced at her watch again and cleared her throat. "I'll be right back."

She glided off and I paced in front of the desk, my hands shoved into my pockets. I heard noise and laughter coming from a doorway down the hall and ambled over. I peered in and saw a jumble of tables covered with boxes, and decorations scattered across the polished floor. Several girls were dressing a large mannequin in a regal-looking cape with a sword, laughing and giggling. I chuckled. Seeing the decorating committee at work definitely brought back memories. I'd been in charge of a decorating committee or two in my college days, and they'd been great fun.

A sliver of light far down the darkened hallway beckoned to me, and I ambled in that direction. As I drew closer, I could hear voices and footsteps and a few seconds later, two figures stood framed in the doorway.

"I totally disagree," said a clipped voice with a trace

of an accent I couldn't quite place. "The grimoire is the focal point of the exhibit. It should be in the main room with all the other artifacts, the centerpiece."

"I personally am not against that, but our security team thinks otherwise," said the second speaker, a decidedly feminine voice. "They believe it will be much more secure off by itself in that little alcove room."

The figures took a few more steps forward and I hesitated, thinking they might not appreciate a third party listening in on what was obvioiusly meant to be a private conversation. I glanced around, saw a small niche, and ducked into it just seconds before they passed within three feet of my hiding place. In the pale light of the hallway, I could see their features more clearly. The woman was a petite brunette in a trim suit, her hair caught in a French twist at the nape of her neck. Large gray eyes snapped behind massive tortoiseshell-framed glasses, and her full lips were drawn into a taut line. The man who towered over her reminded me a bit of the actor Caesar Romero in his prime: tall and thin, with a clipped moustache and goatee, his oily black hair slicked back in a style reminiscent of fifties movie idols—or bikers. His suit was Italian and expensive, not a wrinkle to be seen, and his loafers, polished to a black spit shine, looked well made and had a sleek line to them. An image came instantly to my mind: the old comic strip Mandrake the Magician. If Johnny Depp didn't snag the part, maybe this guy could play him in a movie version. And like Mandrake, his gaze seemed oddly . . . hypnotic.

The woman's jaw thrust forward. "Security was tight

in London, too, and yet it was almost stolen. I imagine if the thief is clever enough, no place will be totally secure."

The man cleared his throat. "Well, you ought to know."

The woman stopped dead and stared at him. A little vein bulged in her jaw. "And what does that mean, Henri? Don't tell me you think . . ."

He held up his hand. "Did I accuse you of anything? You know as well as I that the alarm malfunctioned that night. It happens."

"True. And Ms. Webb and Ms. Crenshaw are taking every precaution there is not to have a repeat. If there should be . . ."

The man's face darkened, his features twisting into a scowl. "You almost sound as if you want something to happen to it, Daisy."

Daisy? She had to be Violet's new assistant. I strained to hear more.

Daisy laughed. "I most certainly do not want anything to happen to it. That is why I feel it is best where it is not too visible, or tempting."

"Well, since neither of us are in charge of security, it's moot, isn't it?" Henri's finger jabbed the air. "It probably would be best if you refrain from sticking your nose in where it does not belong. Unless, of course, you are willing to suffer the consequences."

She arched a brow at him. "And what does that mean?"

"I think you can figure it out." He turned on his heel and stalked off in the other direction. Daisy watched him go, then dipped her hand into her jacket pocket and withdrew her cell phone. She flipped it open and started speaking softly. She took a few steps nearer to my hiding place and I crouched down, flattening myself against the wall, and hoped the sound of my heart hammering in my chest wasn't half as loud as I thought it was.

"Hey," Daisy whispered into the phone. "I told you not to call me here." A pause, and then, "No, it's in the room by itself. It's perfect."

She turned her face away and spoke too softly for me to hear any more. After a few minutes she closed the phone and slipped it back into her pocket, then walked so close to where I was hiding I had to hold my breath. I stayed down low until I heard her footsteps disappear down the corridor, then slowly got up, flexing my left foot, which had fallen asleep from my cramped position. I managed to hobble back into the main hall just as Nellie exited a door at the far end. She extended her hand, and I saw a shiny brass key in her palm. "Here you go," she said, dropping it into my outstretched hand. "One key to the kitchen entrance. Do you know where it is? Out back, just before the loading dock."

My fingers closed around the key. "Thanks. I'll just take a quick look to check out the freezer space, and then I'll probably drop a few entree trays off later tonight." I paused and then leaned in a bit closer to Nellie. "Who is the tall distinguished man I saw walk through here a few minutes ago? Black hair, fancy suit, dark eyes . . . Is he with the security detail?"

Nellie's brow furrowed in thought, and then her expression cleared. "You must mean Henri Reynaud. He's the exhibit director, so they tell me, but if you ask me he's more of a pain in the . . ."

"Nora? Is that you?"

I whirled around and saw Violet standing right behind me. "Violet, hi. I was in the area, so I thought I'd drop by and pick up the kitchen key. Nellie was kind enough to get it for me."

Violet threw the other woman a pointed glance. "How fortunate you were still here, Nellie. Don't forget to mark the extra time on your card."

The older woman gave us both a sharp look, and then muttered something under her breath. She elbowed past us and out the front door without a backward glance.

Violet shook her head. "She's still a little ticked at me about the job, but she'll get over it. Nora, do you have a few minutes? I'd like to discuss something with you."

Encouraged by the melancholy look in her eyes, I decided to take a chance. "Your missing niece? Is she who you think might have been . . . murdered?"

The gaze behind her wire rims sharpened, and Violet's thin lips tugged upward. She gestured toward the stairwell. "Let's talk, shall we? First office on the right."

FIVE

Violet's office was large and comfortable and (not surprisingly) about three times the size of my den at home. A beautiful, polished cherrywood desk sat right in front of a large picture window, which afforded an excellent view of the town square. The two high-backed chairs that flanked the front of the desk were pale blue and lavender, and made of leather so buttery soft you felt like you were sitting on a cloud. I eased myself into the pale blue one, leaned back, and waited expectantly. After all, this was Violet's show. The woman herself perched on the edge of the desk, right in front of me, crossed her arms over her chest, and regarded me with a stare of blue-edged steel.

"So you found out about my niece, eh? I must say, I'm impressed."

"I found out from Nick Atkins's partner that one of the cases Nick was working on at the time he disappeared was a society da—ah, woman's missing niece. I just thought, from the remark I heard you make about Nick, that it might be you." I was thankful I'd caught myself. I was pretty certain Violet would not appreciate hearing herself referred to as a *dame*.

"I knew you were a clever girl, Nora. Not many people could put two and two together and come up with six." She regarded me for a few moments, then walked around the desk and eased herself into the captain's leather chair. "I expect you're curious to learn why I'd engage someone like him in the first place. Well, it's like this.

"I've been a loner for most of my life. I had no use for my family. Most of them were shifty, lazy, no-goodniks anyway. I'm from New Orleans originally. Did you know that? My parents moved out here when I was twelve. It was just the four of us; them, my brother, Durwood, and me. I lost all trace of a Southern accent and my father did very well in real estate, so good in fact that we were able to trade in our modest Cape Cod dwelling for the castle-like mansion I live in today." She let out a humongous sigh. "If Durwood had only seen reason, he and his daughter and I—well, I'm getting ahead of myself.

"Whereas I studied and got good grades and was accepted into one of the best colleges the state had to offer, Durwood was lazy. Typical of young boys, I know, but Durwood was really lazy. He took after our mother's side of the family, I'm sorry to say. He started out shoplifting, then buying exam answers. By the time he was twenty-five my brother had a criminal record.

"In the meantime, I married Roger Crenshaw and began carving out a life for myself as a socialite wife. Unfortunately I could not bear children. It bothered me in the beginning, but Roger was so good about it. 'I don't need progeny, my little petunia flower,' he'd say to me. 'We have each other.'

"Well, my parents died and so did Roger's. Roger was an only child and for all intents and purposes so am I. After my brother's arrest for robbing a jewelry store in Van Nuys, I disowned him, literally and figuratively. Many years passed, and I was very contented with my life. And then, three years ago, my husband passed. I became much more active in charity work, took this position on the museum board, but I still felt my life lacked something. There's a great deal to be said for family, Nora, even bad ones.

"I hired an investigator, Paul Mitchell, to find my brother. I found out that Durwood spent his declining years in prison, once again arrested on robbery charges, but I also found out that he'd had a child out of wedlock, a little girl. He never married the woman, but apparently he kept in touch, and all because of the child. When the mother passed from cancer, Durwood, who was in between prison terms at the time, took the girl to raise and brought her back to Louisiana. She was thirteen, an impressionable age. He tried to stay on the straight and narrow, but being uneducated and unskilled, it wasn't long before he resumed the only career he knew: a premier thief."

Violet paused for a breath, and I leaned forward. "Violet, that's so sad. I understand why you never speak of your family."

"Yes." She put a hand to her eyes, brushed away what looked to me like a tear. "To be honest, I never gave Durwood much thought until Roger died, and I was rattling around in that big old house all alone. By the time I decided to contact him, it was too late. He'd died in prison. I learned his daughter was by his side. Shortly after that Alexa just seemed to vanish into thin air."

"Her name is Alexa?"

"Yes. Alexa Martin is my only niece, my only living relative and someday, please God, my only heir to all I've created. *If* she's still alive, that is."

"What makes you think she might have been murdered? Did Nick Atkins tell you that?"

Violet exhaled a deep breath. "When Mitchell retired and moved to Florida, he suggested Atkins take over. He didn't wait for my approval, which ticked me off; he just turned all his files over to him. Atkins contacted me at that point, an introduction you might say, and then a few weeks later left a message on my machine that he'd gotten a lead on Alexa and was going to track it down. He called me on the phone a few days later, said there had been what he termed an 'interesting development' that needed to be investigated. He was acting rather strange—I guess I should say stranger than usual—so I got a bit aggressive with him, and he finally blurted out there was a possibility my niece might have been murdered. Well, you can imagine my reaction! I pleaded and then I threatened, but I couldn't get any more out of him. He said he shouldn't have told me as much as he had, and to give him two days, and he'd call me back with more details. Well, that call was the last I heard from him. I tried calling his cell and got no response. I called the office several times, and was told he was away. Then the next time I called his cell I was told the number was no longer in service." Violet shrugged. "I hired two other PIs who turned up nothing. Then, today, when you said he'd been missing for several months, well . . . that put a whole different light on things." She was silent for a few minutes then bit out, "Think he'll ever show up again?"

"His partner has his doubts on that score," I admitted. "Do you think his disappearing could have anything to do with your case?"

"I don't know. But I see in the past few months you've become quite the detective." She pinned me with her gaze. "That's why I need you, Nora. You're the only one I can think of capable of picking up where Atkins left off. I need you to find out once and for all if my niece is alive . . . or dead."

SIX

For a minute I was so startled I couldn't speak, and then I found my voice. "Violet, I'm flattered you would put such trust in me, but if you truly suspect foul play, it really is more of a matter for the police."

She pinned me with that hawklike gaze. "And I'd agree with you one hundred percent, if I had an iota of proof she was dead, and if the cause of death were foul play. At the moment, all I have is a cryptic statement from a missing detective. Make no mistake; if Alexa was murdered I won't rest until her killer is brought to justice." She laid her hand on my arm. "How about this? Suppose you just make some casual inquiries, as a personal favor to me? No pressure. And don't soft pedal whatever you might find out for me. If you do find some evidence that what Atkins said was on the level, then I'll take it to a higher authority."

I had no doubt she could, even though right now she looked as if she'd lost everything in the world that meant something to her—and maybe she had. My heart went out to her and I reached out, let the tips of my fingers brush the back of her hand. "Sure, I can do that. After this huge catering contract you've awarded me, it's the least I can do."

"Excellent." She crossed over to a large bookcase, plucked an album from it, and returned to her desk. She extracted a picture from the back of the album and passed it across to me. "That was the only picture we could find, so far. Apparently Alexa wasn't fond of having her picture taken."

I looked at the slightly out of focus photo that depicted a tall, gangly girl, slim, high cheekbones, long light hair that curled at the ends, big round eyes, a wide generous mouth. "She was about sixteen there," Violet said. "She's most likely changed a bit, but the basics would probably still be the same." She shook her head as I started to hand back the photo. "It's a copy, keep it. I've got the original. And I'm sure I don't need to impress upon you the need for discretion where this matter is concerned. There are some people who know I had a brother but as for the rest . . ."

"I get it." Violet, being an upstanding pillar of the community, certainly wouldn't want it getting out that her brother had had a criminal record. Gossip traveled quickly in a small town, and Cruz was no exception.

"I've spent a lifetime disavowing my family and shirking my responsibilities," she said. "Maybe if I'd intervened sooner, Durwood wouldn't have returned to his life of crime and his daughter could have gotten a proper education, taken a place in society. I just pray it's not too late."

I rose and smoothed out my skirt. "By the way, Violet, were you aware that there was an attempted theft of the grimoire in London not long ago?"

She nodded. "Yes. Sir Meecham told me when we were making the arrangements. It was a rather clumsy attempt, too, from what I understand. But don't you worry, Nora, Sergeant Broncelli is on it. He understands the importance of an efficient security detail."

I frowned. Curtis Broncelli was new to the Cruz police force. I'd only met the guy once, at the retirement party for his predecessor. From what I'd heard he'd spent quite a few years in Louisiana building a stellar reputation before his transfer to California. He impressed me as someone good at playing politics, at doing whatever was necessary to climb up the promotional ladder. Lance was buddies with a few of the guys on the force, and the scuttlebutt was none of them were particularly impressed with their new boss, although it wasn't an unusual reaction when a beloved supervisor was replaced.

Violet walked with me to the door, where she squeezed my arm. "I knew confiding in you was the right thing to do. I've got a feeling you'll succeed where Atkins failed."

I was partway out the door when I thought of something and turned back. "By the way, Violet, I thought I heard someone mention Daisy worked at a museum in London before she came here."

"Oh, yes, dear." Violet smiled. "That's quite true,

except it wasn't a museum, per se, but the Meecham Foundation. She was hired right after that attempt was made to steal the grimoire. Isn't that a coincidence?"

I retraced my steps downstairs and asked a girl wearing a tag that read *Museum Volunteer* the way to the kitchen. She told me to go straight down the main corridor, but midway down it branched out in two directions, so I was faced with a decision, "The Lady, or the Tiger" style, left or right? I closed my eyes, went eeny meeny miny moe, and turned right. A few minutes later I found myself in a large room filled with tables and cases covered with white tarp.

Definitely not the kitchen. This had to be the main medieval exhibition room.

I confess there are times when my curiosity rivals that of my cat. I was dying to see this famed grimoire that required the attention of half the Cruz police force. I sidled up to the first table and peeked under the tarp. A collection of swords was laid out underneath the Plexiglas, some with ornate jeweled handles. There were placards in front of each one, but I really wasn't too interested in them. I lowered the tarp, glanced around, and saw a small, low-lit room off to my left. The door was open a crack, so I walked over and pressed my eye to it. The room appeared empty, save for a single tarp-sheeted case. I pushed on the door and it creaked inward on hinges desperately in need of an oiling. I slipped in, soundless in my kitten-heeled mules, and inched over to the display. Very slowly, I raised the cloth.

The book that lay on the black-walnut pedestal hardly looked impressive. What it looked was . . . old. It had a well-worn purple leather cover, embossed in a silver scroll design. There were several stones embedded in the cover, a large red stone flanked by a smaller green one and a blue one. In this dim light they hardly looked like the conduits to power Nan had implied they were; rather they more closely resembled cheap crystal knockoffs. Shouldn't a book rumored to be so enchanted be more . . . well, more exciting? This looked like a prop from a cheap B movie. I started to turn away when a dark shadow suddenly fell across the room and an all-too-familiar voice said, "Nora Charles. Who let you in here?"

I swallowed over the king-sized lump in my throat and slowly turned on one heel to look into the slightly amused glance of none other than . . . Detective Leroy Samms, St. Leo Homicide.

For a minute, neither one of us spoke. Leroy Samms is even better looking now than he was in our college days, and he was pretty darn perfect then. He's six foot three, well-built, broad shouldered, hair the color of ink and eyes to match. He also has a smile that could light up a room, when he chooses to use it, that is. Right now his lips were clamped tightly together, his steely gaze locked with mine. The two of us stared at each other for what seemed an eternity, and at last I gave in and cleared my throat.

"What am *I* doing here? I've got a perfect right to be here. A better question would be what are *you* doing here? This is Cruz, not St. Leo. Oh, wait, don't tell me. You're lost?"

He snorted, his fingers brushing at the lock of inky hair falling casually across his forehead. "Sorry, I'm not lost. I'm here at the request of Sergeant Broncelli to help out with the security detail for this exhibit."

My jaw dropped. "You're kidding. How on earth will St. Leo Homicide ever get along without you?"

"Oh, trust me, they'll manage."

I frowned at the note of bitterness evident in his tone. Samms seemed unaware of it, however, as he reached up to flick an errant curl off his forehead in a careless gesture. He jerked his thumb in the grimoire's direction. "I'll grant you that book doesn't look like a valuable treasure and yet I understand it's quite in demand."

My eyebrow rose. "Then you're aware an attempt was made to steal it in London?"

He nodded. "Yep. Whoever the thief was, they knew a lot about the Meecham Foundation's alarm system. The wires were expertly cut. It seemed like the work of a pro."

"I understand both Violet's assistant and the exhibit manager were employed at the Meecham Foundation at the time of the attempted theft. What are the odds they'd be together again here?"

Samms scratched at his chin. "Probably about as good as the odds of you and me running into each other again after all this time."

I resisted the urge to smack him. "You have to admit though, doing guard duty is a bit out of your bailiwick. You are Homicide, after all, not security."

"Lee's doing this as a favor to me."

I turned to see a tall, wiry man with a shining bald

head and neatly trimmed goatee step through the doorway and stride toward us. Samms nodded at the newcomer and turned to me. "I don't believe you two have met. Nora Charles, this is Sergeant Curtis Broncelli."

"A pleasure, Ms. Charles." Broncelli gave a curt nod in my direction.

Samms smiled politely at the newcomer. "I'm surprised to see you down here, Curt."

Broncelli tossed me a frosty smile. "I like to keep a low profile and I trust my men to handle things. However, my approval was needed for that comprehensive alarm system, so . . . here I am." He spread his hands. "As far as Lee's being here—well, we go way back to my days working in Monroe Homicide. I wouldn't want anyone else on this detail."

Samms's lips twitched upward. "And I can't think of anyone more qualified to head this. We were lucky to get him, fresh from a stint overseas."

I decided it was time to end this mutual admiration society before I puked, and pushed my hand through my hair. "Just what does a comprehensive alarm system entail?"

"It's a combination of policies procedures, personnel, and hardware, used by many museums. We've just made a few slight improvements."

"Such as?"

"What are you, writing a book?" Samms growled.

"No," I responded sweetly. "Just a monthly column for *Noir* crime magazine. I'm thinking this might be a good topic."

Those ink-blue eyes narrowed. "Ever the reporter, aren't you?" he murmured very softly, but I heard him and flushed.

Broncelli turned to me. "In layman's terms, a comprehensive system is one that adds more and tighter security precautions as you get physically closer to a high value object, like the rings on a bull's-eye. For example"—he pointed upward—"we've got concealed cameras recording everything in this room and the main one as well. We've also got an infrared alarm on the case that will kick in if someone tries to break in. Try it."

I glanced at Samms, who merely sighed and stepped aside. I walked up to the case, balled my hand into a fist, and pounded on its side.

Nothing.

I turned and looked questioningly at Broncelli, who smiled. "No loud alarms go off—it's silent. But we're notified and our men come immediately!" He pointed to two uniforms who'd suddenly appeared in the doorway, guns drawn. "Sorry, guys. Demonstration."

The two officers looked a bit annoyed, but they holstered their guns and backed out of the room. Samms crossed his arms over his chest and glared at me. "Satisfied?"

"You two are the experts. If you're satisfied then it's good enough for me."

Broncelli turned to me. "Well, I have a few other matters to attend to. It was nice meeting you, Nora. I hear you're catering this soiree."

"Yes, I am."

"That's good to know. At least the food will be top notch." He made a little bow. "I'll have to drop into your shop one day. I've heard nothing but raves from all the men about it."

"Good to hear, thanks."

Broncelli glanced briefly at Samms, then turned on his heel and left. Samms turned to me but before he could say anything, his cell chirped. He pulled it from his pocket, and I was standing close enough to get a good look at the name lit up on the screen. Startled, I angled for a second glance, but Samms had already clicked it into voice mail. As he slid the phone back into his pocket he met my curious stare. "Something the matter?"

Lots, but I wasn't going to give him the satisfaction. I hefted my tote bag back onto my shoulder and gave him a brisk wave. "Nothing at all. I can see everything's under control here. See you at the gala."

He started to say something, and then stopped. He gave me a halfhearted wave. "Yeah. See ya."

Back in the corridor I leaned against the wall, my thoughts in a whirl. I closed my eyes and the name from Samms's caller ID popped up, crystal clear.

None other than my current boyfriend, FBI agent Daniel Corleone.

What was up with that?

SEVEN

I checked out the kitchen and its two freezers and king-sized fridge, which, thank the stars above, had more than enough space for all my entree trays, and then drove back home. I pulled in the driveway just as Mollie was locking up and I beeped my horn. She waved and hurried over to the car as I got out. "No problems. Chantal came over and helped with the lunch crowd, but she had to get back to Poppies by two."

"Great. Did Nick behave himself?"

"Oh, you know," Mollie said with a grin. "He was Nick. I'll say this, he's mastered the art of scarfing up any tidbit that hits the floor."

"Yep. That's Nick, all right."

I said goodbye to Mollie and let myself in the back

door, and Nick lurched up from his post by the refrigerator door to amble over and rub against my legs. I reached down to pick him up, but paused midway as my cell phone chirped. I glanced at the caller ID and snapped it open. "Hey, Sis. I was just thinking about you."

"You were? Me, too. Guess this is what Chantal would call a psychic connection," my sister said with a laugh. While I had to admit we'd never been particularly close, the events of the last few months had forced both of us, and Lacey in particular, to reassess our relationship. Narrowly avoiding a life sentence in prison will do that to a person. We'd been getting along better the last few months than we had all our lives. "I just thought I'd call to let you know I got accepted into the accelerated program. If I get a B plus or better, I can graduate early."

"Hey, that's wonderful. So, have you given any thought to a job? What about the one Peter recommended you for?" Peter Dobbs, an attorney friend of Daniel's, had represented my sister. I had a sneaking suspicion he figured in her decision to stay on in Carmel with Aunt Prudence while she finished art school.

"Hm, it didn't pan out. Lee got me a part-time job down at the station, though. Their resident sketch artist retired, so I help out when I don't have class and on weekends. It's pretty cool."

Lee? My left eye started to twitch and my stomach did a flip-flop. "Lee?"

She let out a snort. "You know, Leroy Samms. My former arresting officer."

My eye started to twitch harder. "Well, the two of you certainly have gotten chummy."

Lacey laughed. "He's not so bad, once you get to know him. And I think he was trying to make up for, you know, what happened." She let out a giant sigh. "Too bad he's not on the force anymore. Irene heard he went into free-lance consulting."

Irene, my aunt Prudence's best friend, was, for want of a better word, a real yenta. She knew what was going on in the neighborhood before the people involved did. I took a deep breath, exhaled slowly, and said, "I know. He's here."

Silence, and then, "He's there? In Cruz?"

"Yep. I don't know about the consulting part, but he's helping out with guard duty for a valuable exhibit at the museum."

"Well now that the two of you are in the same town, I guess he'll be giving Daniel a run for his money, eh?"

Ah, my darling sister, tactful as always. "My relationship with Samms isn't like the one I have with Daniel."

"Of course it isn't. For one thing, you don't get the same goofy look on your face around Daniel like you do with Lee."

"Excuse me," I snapped, "I do not get a goofy look on my face around Samms. I hadn't seen the guy in nearly twenty years until you got arrested. And how would you know how I act around Daniel, anyway? You saw us together at the hospital for what? Twenty seconds?"

"Sometimes that's all it takes," she responded. "Tell

the truth, Nors. You'd like to get to know Lee again, wouldn't you?"

I knew just where this was headed, and I intended to nip it in the bud right now. "Not particularly. You do know I'm dating Daniel."

"Mr. Hunky FBI? Yeah, I know, but you've had, what, like two dates?"

"More than that." I frowned into the receiver. Both Daniel and I had been burned badly by past relationships; as a result, we'd mutually agreed to take ours slowly and see what developed. However, I saw no reason for filling my sister in on that detail. "And just where are you getting this information?"

A long pause, and then, "Oh, around."

I frowned deeper. That, no doubt, meant Chantal.

"Listen," my sister continued, "loyalty's great, but there's no ring on your finger, is there? That means you should play the field."

"Yeah, well, I've never been very good at that. What I am good at, though, is leaving the past in the past where it belongs, and concentrating on the here and now."

Fortunately, my sister, who usually manages to be obtuse, took the hint and allowed me to steer the conversation away from my love life. We chatted for a few more minutes about her school, and Aunt Prudence's effort to cure her precious African Gray parrot, Jumanji, of a constant cough, using a method gleaned on the Internet. With promises to see each other soon, I hung up, and my phone chirped again. I looked at the caller ID and flicked it on. "Hank! Hey, thanks for calling back."

My longtime buddy and Confidential Informant, Hank Prince, is a private investigator whose endless string of contacts had proven invaluable to me during my time in Chicago. "Nora! Don't tell me you've stumbled on another mystery?"

"Two," I said, and immediately launched into the details of my conversation with Ollie, ending with the arrival of the mysterious postcard. "Bottom line: Ollie and I both think there's a good chance Nick Atkins might still be alive, and that he might be somewhere in New Orleans."

"I've got a few contacts down in New Orleans. Remember Petey Peppercorn? He's living down there now, plus one of my frat brothers works in the Department of Records there, so hopefully I'll have something for you in a few days, maybe sooner if we get lucky."

I chuckled. "You belonged to a fraternity? Why does that not surprise me?"

"Pi Kappa Alpha, I'll have you know. We stick together like glue, like you sorority gals. You said there were two mysteries?"

I gave him a brief rundown on Violet's brother and missing niece. "Her name is Alexa Martin. Apparently after her father died she vanished into thin air. Nick Atkins was trying to track her down around the time he disappeared. Right before that, he called Violet and told her there was a possibility the girl might have died under mysterious circumstances."

"Wow." Hank whistled. "What sort of circumstances?"

"Your guess is as good as mine. It could be her

disappearance and possible death plays a part in his vanishing act as well. Violet wants to find out if the girl's still alive, and if so, where she is."

"You think Atkins tracked her to New Orleans?"

"It's possible." I hesitated and then said, "Could you do me one more favor? Check out a girl named Daisy Martinelli."

"You think she figures into these other two disappearances?"

"No. It's more to satisfy my curiosity. She's the new admin here at the Cruz Museum. And also a guy named Henri Reynaud. He's the director for an Arthurian exhibit here." I twirled a red curl around one finger. "Let's call this Unofficial Mystery Number Three. They both worked at the Meecham Foundation at the time an attempt was made to steal a valuable artifact. I'm just wondering how much of a coincidence it is that they're both here together again, at its first US showing."

"Well, you know how I feel about coincidences."

I sure did. Hank felt the same way I did, that there was no such thing. We chatted for a few more minutes and then I hung up and dug out my trusty laptop. I keyed in "Meecham Foundation—Morgan le Fay Grimoire—theft" and hit enter. To my surprise, I only got two hits. Both were from London newspapers, and both were very small, sketchy articles. All they said was that an attempt had been made to steal Sir Rodney Meecham's latest acquisition, but the theft had been thwarted. The second article, by a Doris Gleason, carried the additional information that a guard had been wounded and was in critical condition. Neither article carried any mention of the thief being hurt or wounded, as Chantal had implied.

I printed out the articles, shut off the laptop, and went back downstairs into my shop, Nick trailing at my heels. First I checked out the trays I'd gotten up early this morning to prepare: eight each of lasagna, chicken, and beef stroganoff. Then I sat down at the counter and pulled out the cream place cards I reserved for special catering occasions. I carefully lettered four of each—*Lancelot's Lasagna*, *Merlin's Magical Chicken*, *Mordred's Beef Stroganoff*. I leaned back to survey my handiwork. My fancy script was a bit rusty, but they still looked nice. I had the appetizers all in place, but I still needed to prepare something really special after Morgan le Fay. I was poring through my mother's old recipe cards when I heard a tap-tap at my back door. I peered through the curtain and opened the door with a squeal to admit the six feet, two inches of dirty blond, masculine, total hunk that is Daniel Corleone.

"Daniel! When did you get back?"

"I just got in. My bag's still in the car. I have to check in at the office but I wanted to see you first."

He stood very close to me, and I sucked in a deep breath. He smelled faintly of sage and sweat, definitely manly. His hands slid up my arms to rest on my shoulders and we just stood there for a moment or two, gazing deeply into each other's eyes. It was what my sister Lacey would have called a "heart-stopping moment," the point in the romance novel or the movie right before the hero and heroine lock lips in a passionate kiss to end all kisses, one that usually ends up in the bedroom.

We didn't do that, probably because at the moment when Daniel's lips started to veer in my direction, I got a mental image of his caller ID popping up on Samms's cell phone, which produced a sudden fit of coughing on my part.

Daniel's hands came off my shoulders. We both took two steps back.

"What's all this? Looks like you've got a big catering job." His sharp gaze took in the disheveled appearance of my kitchen, from the empty pans scattered across the floor to the recipe cards strewn all over my counter.

"I do." I plucked the gala flyer from its place on the wall and pushed it under his nose. "I was a last-minute substitute, but it's a big job. It pays really well, too."

He plucked the flyer from my hand and studied it. "You're catering this?"

"Yep, but mainly because I was the only caterer willing to accept the job on such short notice. But if it's a success, there's no telling how much new business it'll generate. Why, Nick might be able to have steak three times a week, instead of when I have a special once a month."

At the word *steak*, Nick lifted his head and warbled out a loud "*Merow.*"

Daniel laughed. "Seems the way to your cat's heart is through his stomach. And it would appear a big catering contract is the way to yours."

I chuckled. "So, does the FBI have any galas coming up that need catering? Better book me now."

"None on the immediate horizon." He set the flyer

back on the counter and eased his long frame onto one of the stools.

"How did your trip go? Or can't you talk about it?" Daniel never could talk about open FBI cases. He shrugged.

"Not as well as expected. It's just a temporary setback, I hope." He inclined his head toward the flyer. "On a more pleasant note, I have Saturday afternoon and Sunday off." He reached out and touched the tip of my nose with his finger. "How would you like an escort to that gala?"

I raised my eyebrow. "Really? You'd want to go to this? It's a work event for me, remember."

"But not for the whole evening," he said with a boyish grin. "I'm sure if we put our heads together we could manage to have some quality time for the two of us."

I leaned both elbows on the counter and stared him straight in the eye. "This offer, along with this unscheduled time off, wouldn't have anything to do with your earlier call to Leroy Samms, or the fact he's pulled guard duty on that grimoire, would it?"

He didn't even bat an eyelash. "I guess you ran into Lee at the museum, huh?"

"Sure did. He informed me he'd been drafted for guard duty right around the time your name popped up on his caller ID."

Daniel shrugged. "I'd originally been going to turn down his request to help out, but now that I know you're catering the affair, I'm glad I said yes."

I looked him straight in the eye. "Are they expecting another attempt to steal the grimoire? After all, a masked ball's a pretty good venue for a thief. I can think of half a dozen movies where it worked out perfectly."

"I believe it's just a precautionary measure. The owner, Sir Rodney Meecham, is a fanatic about his collection."

"So I've heard. That grimoire must be pretty valuable, to rate an FBI guard."

"An off-duty FBI guard," Daniel amended. He pulled a stick of mint gum from his pocket and held it out to me. I shook my head, and he unwrapped a piece, popped it in his mouth, and then leaned over the counter. "So, what do you say?"

I threw up both hands. "Okay, you've convinced me. It's a date."

He flashed me a full wattage smile, dimples and all. "Okay, then, I guess the next step is to decide on a costume. I thought about . . ."

"No, no, no!" I held up my hand, traffic-cop style. "Please don't tell me you want to go as an FBI agent!"

"I was thinking of a profiler." He chuckled. "Or a spy, like James Bond. Tell you what, though. I'll let you pick my costume."

I looked at him. "Really? You mean it?" At his nod, I waved the flyer under his nose. "Sucker."

"Meow."

We looked down. Nick squatted his entire furry length across Daniel's feet. I laughed. "See, even Nick agrees." I peered closer, and could see the edge of something white peeping out from underneath his rotund belly. "Looks like he's brought you a present."

Daniel gave him a poke and Nick rolled to one side. I gasped as I saw what Nick's body had covered. The photograph of Nick Atkins and Angelique. I could have sworn I'd put it in the zipper compartment of my tote but, as I full well knew, mere zippers never seemed to stop Nick from acquiring things he perceived as his property.

Daniel stared at the photo. He turned it over in his hands. "Where did you get this?"

I reached for it but Daniel held it out of my grasp. "Ollie gave it to me. That's Nick Atkins and his last girl-friend, Angelique Martone."

Daniel's brows drew together as he stared at the photo. "Angelique Martone?"

I nodded. "Yep. Apparently she and Nick Atkins had quite a serious relationship, but they had a big fight and she took off." Daniel didn't reply, just kept staring at the photo. For a brief second I thought I caught a flicker of annoyance in his blue eyes, and then his expression cleared. He set the photograph back on the counter and abruptly stood up. "Sorry to cut this visit short, but I've got to get going. I've got a few reports to file at the office. I'll give you a call about the details."

"Still trust me to pick out your costume?"

He hesitated only slightly. "Absolutely." He bent over, gave me a quick peck on the cheek. "Later, alligator," he whispered, his breath hot on my cheek.

He walked out the door with a wave. I leaned against my counter, tapping the photo of Angelique against my palm. At my feet, Nick bleated out a plaintive meow. I set the photo on the table, reached down, and hefted him into my arms, cradling him against my chest. I buried my face in his soft fur.

"Daniel's not telling the truth, Nick," I whispered. "He knows Angelique somehow."

Nick burrowed deeper into my arms. *"Merow."*

"Right. What if she's involved in some way in this new case of his? What if the FBI's after her for some reason? What if . . ." I stopped speaking and gave a little shudder. There were starting to be entirely too many "what ifs" for my taste. As much as I hated to admit it, maybe Ollie was right.

Finding Angelique might only lead to more trouble, indeed.

EIGHT

I locked the door after Daniel, finished arranging my trays, and then, because my curiosity would not be stifled, trotted back upstairs, Nick at my heels, to fire up the laptop once again. Forty minutes later I leaned back in my chair, frustrated. I'd tried everything I could think of but had found nada on Angelique Martone, other than one brief mention on the Whitepages website. I said a silent prayer that Hank's sources would have better luck, then went back to load the trays of food into my SUV. Nick cantered at my side, and when I'd finished he hopped into the passenger seat and looked expectantly at me.

"Merow."

I grasped him firmly around the middle and took him back inside. "Sorry, bud. There's no detecting to do at the museum, just the boring unloading of food trays. Maybe next time."

He cocked his head, blinked twice, then held out a paw. *"Merow?"*

I shook my head. "No, I mean it. You can't come with me."

He abruptly turned his back on me, tail high in the air, and marched directly to the far table. He wiggled underneath without a backward glance. I sighed.

"Cattitude I don't need, Nick. Tell you what, you be a good boy and I'll give you an extra-big bowl of cat food when I get back."

Silence greeted me. Well, what did I expect from a cat who was used to getting his way ninety-nine percent of the time? I made certain, though, to check the SUV thoroughly before I started off. It wouldn't have been the first time Nick tagged along for the ride, and I was positive it wouldn't be the last, either.

It was quarter past eight when I pulled into the parking lot. I noted all the other cars and trucks were gone save for one lone black sedan parked a few spaces away under a spreading elm tree. It no doubt belonged to one of the security detail personnel. Apparently guard duty was a 24/7 job. I wondered idly if it were Samms who'd drawn the late shift. Resolutely I squared my shoulders, putting all thoughts of Samms, Daniel, grimoires, missing nieces, and missing PIs from my mind and just concentrated on unloading my food.

I'd just slipped the last tray into the freezer when I thought I heard a slight sound in the corridor outside. I tiptoed over to the door and opened it just a sliver, enough to peek out.

The corridor was deserted.

I paused. What I should have done right then was haul ass out of there and go home. So, naturally, instead I slipped out into the main corridor and took a quick look around. Far down I caught a glimmer of light, so I proceeded to follow it. A few minutes later I found myself in the main exhibition hall again, with the familiar white-sheeted cases. I glanced in the direction of the room where the grimoire was kept and noticed that the door was closed. Impulsively, I walked over and twisted the knob.

Locked.

I moved into the rear corridor, which was also dark, but I could see a circle of light all the way at the end. Hopeful of finally running into someone who might be able to help, I inched my way along the corridor. As I approached the source of the light, I heard voices raised in anger. I paused and flattened myself against the wall, inching along until I came to the opening. I peeped cautiously around the corner and saw Daisy, her face flushed, facing another woman wearing a long black skirt and blouse, whose back was to me.

"I refuse to continue this discussion with you, Magda." Daisy's voice rose slightly, enough so that I could hear every word. "As usual, your babbling makes no sense."

The other woman thrust out her arm and grabbed Daisy's wrist. "You seem to forget, I was there in London, too. I know you would like to discredit me with Henri." Her long finger jabbed into the younger girl's chest. "I am warning you, mind your own business."

"You're nuts. If anyone should mind their own business it should be you." Daisy shook her arm free and took a step backward. The other woman turned and I caught a glimpse of a beaked nose, sagging skin, and glittering eyes. This woman could have easily played any one of the three witches in the opening scene of *Macbeth* without benefit of makeup.

"Hah!" She shook her mane of greasy hair. "You think I don't know about you and your agenda?"

"What agenda? I have no idea what you're talking about." Daisy jabbed her finger in the air right under the older woman's nose. "Stop being dramatic. You and I both know . . ."

Her voice dropped to a whisper, and I couldn't make out another word. I inched a bit farther along the wall, so intent on doing that, I didn't see the loose floorboard until it was too late. My foot caught and down I went. A few seconds later both women were framed in the doorway, staring at me.

"Ms. Charles," Daisy stammered. "What are you doing here?"

"What do you think she's doing?" Magda snorted, folding her arms across her chest. "She is spying."

"I most certainly am not," I lied, struggling to my feet. I noticed neither woman offered to help me. "I was just finishing unloading the entrees."

Magda's eyebrows rose. "And what? You thought you'd take a walk and snoop through the museum." She glared at Daisy. "How do we know she's not a thief? That she's not after the grimoire?"

I brushed off my pants. "I'm most certainly not a thief, but I confess I was a bit curious to see the exhibit. Is that a crime?"

Magda shot a black look in my direction, one that clearly said she wasn't buying my innocent act. She turned to Daisy. "I'll be in the prop room. We're not finished with our . . . discussion." With another dark look in my direction the old woman stalked off.

Daisy brushed her hand across her forehead. "I'm so sorry, Ms. Charles. Magda is one of Reynaud's exhibit assistants. She's worked for Meecham, golly, it seems like forever. She can be a bit . . . testy, and a mite overprotective of her brother."

My eyebrow lifted. "Brother?"

"Yes. Henri."

Wow, there was a shocker. That was like saying Rosie O'Donnell and Brad Pitt had been separated at birth. Aloud I said, "No need to apologize. I get the sibling thing, and she was right. I shouldn't have been snooping around after hours, but I confess I am curious about this exhibit. Until I drew this job, what I know about King Arthur and his Round Table would fit on the head of a pin."

Daisy's eyes twinkled. "If you're that interested, I can give you a preview."

I nodded. "I'd like that."

She started to move away. "Give me five minutes, and then come on in."

I did as she requested. The first thing I noticed was all the tarps and covers had been removed. The glass cases gleamed in the pale overhead lights with their bounty. I stood in the doorway for a moment, taking it all in.

"Overwhelming, isn't it?" she said. "We tried to make it look just as it does at the Meecham Foundation in London." She gestured toward a large case filled with swords. "This case contains swords used by the Knights of the Round Table."

I peered at the assembled collection, each with a beautifully scrolled placard in front of it. "I don't see Excalibur. Isn't that the fabled sword in the stone?"

"Because it is not here. However, Excalibur is by no means the only weapon associated with Arthur, nor the only sword. For example," she pointed to a dagger with a jeweled hilt, "this is Carnwennan, the dagger Arthur used to slice the Very Black Witch in half. And this," she pointed to a long spear, "is Rhongomyniad, a spear also used by him. And this," she pointed to another long sword with a handle of green and red stones, "is Seure, which belonged to Arthur but was used by Lancelot. The placards in front of each tell a bit about their history."

"Fascinating." I glanced around the crowded room. "You've certainly assembled a very impressive exhibit, not only of Arthurian artifacts, but all things medieval."

"Sir Meecham has," Daisy said. "It's an honor to work with him."

"It seems as if you enjoy your work," I said. "Although I imagine you didn't enjoy that theft attempt."

Her jaw tightened just a bit. "It's to be expected when one possesses an object many people find desirable."

"The grimoire is desirable?"

Both her eyebrows rose. "Don't sound so surprised, Ms. Charles. Of course it is, to historians and to those who believe in the occult. There are many who would like to possess it, to see if it does indeed have the power it is purported to have."

"And you? Do you believe it has power?"

She shrugged. "It's not my place to believe or disbelieve. What I can tell you is that if this exhibition goes well, Sir Meecham is open to leasing the exhibit to other museums here."

"And by going well I assume you mean no attempts at robbery?"

Her lips twisted into a wry grin. "Something like that."

"Do you have any regrets? About leaving your job with Meecham, and not being able to travel the world with the exhibit?"

She shot me a startled glance. "How did you know—oh, yes." She let out a short laugh. "Investigative reporter, I almost forgot. You're pretty good, Ms. Charles. I see why Violet asked you to help find her niece. I overheard Violet telling Nan about it." She paused and then added, "I hope she isn't making a mistake."

I frowned. "Why would you say that?"

"Oh, I don't know. I've learned people don't always

turn out exactly the way you hope. Sometimes it's best to leave the past where it belongs—in the past." She glanced quickly at her watch. "Goodness, I didn't realize it was so late. I have to go. I'll see you at the gala, Ms. Charles."

She turned on her heel and walked away swiftly. I stared after her. My gut was telling me there was more to Daisy's comment than she let on, but just what it might be, I had no clue.

I arrived back at Hot Bread and let myself in the side entrance. Nick came over and brushed against my ankles, meowing softly. I looked down at him. "Does this mean I'm forgiven?" I asked.

He rubbed his head against my shin. *"Merow."*

I hefted him into my arms and buried my face in his ruff. "Okay, you're right. I did promise you food, didn't I? Okay, one late dinner is coming right up."

I'd just finished filling his bowl with his favorite Fancy Feast when a tap-tap-tap at the shop's rear door caught my attention. I peeped through the curtain and then flung the door wide to admit Ollie. His cheeks were flushed and his eyes bright, and I knew immediately something was up.

"I know it's late," he said. "But I had a busy day and only started going through the mail an hour ago." He whipped an object out of his breast pocket and laid it on the counter in front of me. It was another postcard, a scenic view of New Orleans—a shot of the outside of a jazz club on Frenchman Street—and I turned it over to read the message written in the cramped handwriting I'd come to associate with Nick Atkins:

Here on Frenchman Street. At St. John's Bar. Damn, the music is great! Too good to pass up. Ollie, you would love it here. Good beignets. Ollie, keep the faith.

"N"

I set the card back down. "It's a bit wordier than the first message, and makes about as much sense. Which is none," I said.

Nick hopped up on the table. He bent over, sniffed at the card, licked the edge, and then smacked his tail down on it, once, twice . . . all in all a total of seven times before he stood up, stretched, and leapt back onto the floor.

"Well, what was that all about?" I picked up the card, which looked none the worse for wear from its beating.

"Maybe Little Nick can't decide if it's from Big Nick or not, either. Myself, I'm starting to think these are forgeries," Ollie said. At my look he continued. "The message is out of character. Nick would never say the music was great at St. John's Bar, trust me."

I pored over the card again. "It does look similar to the handwriting in his journals. If it's a forgery, it's a damn good one. At least this card isn't smudged. The lab should be able to tell whether Atkins wrote it or not."

"Maybe," Ollie agreed. "I'm taking it there first thing in the morning." He swiped at his broad forehead with the back of his hand. "I'm not sure anymore what to believe."

As he started out the door, I called him back. "Why would you say he would never think the music was great at St. John's bar?" I asked.

He tossed me a rueful grin. "Simple. Nick's always hated jazz. He wouldn't be caught dead at a jazz bar. No pun intended."

NINE

By three forty-five Saturday afternoon I'd finished preparing the dish I'd named after Morgan le Fay. The Pepper Steak Stir-fry from my mother's recipe cards was not only quick, it served a large number of people, two big pluses in my book. Chantal and Mollie had volunteered to run Hot Bread's Saturday breakfast and lunch crowd so I could finish the preparations. Nick watched me from his perch atop the rear counter, occasionally dropping to the floor to scarf up a stray piece of meat. Chantal stuck her head in just as I was putting Saran Wrap over the last tray.

"Lunch crowd all gone and the place is pretty well cleaned up," she reported. "Mollie had a big homework assignment so I let her go around two." She eyed the trays, stacked neatly on my counter, and sniffed the air. "Um . . . that smells wonderful."

"Morgan le Fay's Pepper Steak Surprise." I grinned. "I saved the best for last, I hope."

Chantal eased herself onto a nearby stool. "Something is bothering you, *chérie*, I can tell. Want to talk about it?"

I told Chantal about what had happened with Daniel and Daisy, and my belief that both of them had lied to me. Then I told her about the second postcard from Nick. When I finished she closed her eyes and was quiet for several minutes, then she said, "I get a sense that they are from Nick, *chérie*. As for what he's written . . ." Her shoulders lifted. "Ollie is right. I believe there is a message from Nick hidden somewhere in them."

I crooked an eyebrow. "I don't suppose your sixth sense can enlighten me as to how I can decipher it, or better yet what this message is?"

She opened her eyes and shook her head. "I can only sense so much. The rest is up to you. You're the detective, after all. But I have every confidence you will figure it out."

"Thanks. That makes one of us."

A sharp "*Meow*" warbled out from underneath the table, and a sleek black paw swiped at the edge of the tablecloth.

"Sorry. Two of us," I amended.

Nick hopped up on the counter. He lifted his paw, tapped it once against the counter, paused, tapped once more, and then thumped his tail down hard for a final time before turning around and then sitting—*plop!*—

right on the furry appendage. He looked at me with his steady, unblinking gaze.

"I think he is trying to tell you something, *chérie.*" She laughed. "See how serious he looks."

I had to admit he did indeed, or at least as serious as a cat could. He flipped his paw in the air, waved it. *"Merow,"* he croaked.

I groaned. "Oh, Nick. I'm not fluent in cat speak. It would all be so simple if you could speak English."

Chantal laughed. "Oh, and by the way, Remy wanted me to thank you for referring him to Violet and Nan for his photography skills."

"Not a problem. Is he going to do it?"

Chantal shook her head. "He has two other floral jobs that same night so regretfully, no." She tapped the face of her watch. "I've got to get back. I have some ladies coming over. They ordered custom jewelry to wear with their medieval costumes. This gala might improve my business, too. I'll check in with you later." As she shrugged into her coat and departed, Nick's paw darted out and touched my wrist. He inclined his head toward his food bowl.

I shook my finger at him. "How can you possibly be hungry after all the samples I slipped you, you little scavenger? You've eaten better today than I have all week."

"Merow," Nick said. He jumped down from the counter, landed right at my feet, and waddled over to his bowl. He placed his paw on it and blinked twice. *"Merow."*

"An endless stomach, that's what you have, Nick," I muttered. I reached beneath the counter and pulled out a can of Fancy Feast Yellowfin Tuna. I emptied the contents of the can into Nick's bowl. He looked at me, tapped his paw twice on the floor, and then hunkered down in front of the bowl. A few moments later the sound of contented slurping reached my ears. My stomach rumbled, apparently not satisfied with the half English muffin I'd had for breakfast or the small portion of samples I'd scarfed down for lunch. I pulled two slices of honey whole wheat bread out of the breadbox and was headed toward my display case when I heard my cell phone chime. Seeing Hank Prince's number on the display, I wiped my hands on the first available rag and eagerly scooped up the phone.

"Hey. I didn't expect to hear back from you so fast."

He chuckled. "I got lucky. Got a minute?"

I pulled out a stool and eased myself onto it. "Sure. Shoot."

"Well, this Angelique Martone seems to be quite a woman of mystery. I managed to dig up her last address in Cruz and called her landlady. Unfortunately, the woman had zero information on her. Apparently Angelique kept pretty much to herself. She did, however, describe Angelique's gentleman caller. Tall, lantern jawed, dark hair with a white streak behind one ear."

"Nick Atkins," I murmured.

"He fits the description," Hank agreed. "Seems they had a humdinger of an argument the night before she moved out. And, a few days before that, the landlady saw Angelique having an altercation with another girl. The girl stood in the shadows, so she couldn't see her face; the only description she could give was she was about the same height and weight as Angelique."

"How about New Orleans? Anything turn up on that end?"

"Not so far. Petey's out of town on another case, and my other guy isn't having much luck. It's like this Angelique doesn't exist."

"I'm sure she does," I said, and then slapped my forehead with my palm. "Wait, I've got a photo of her. Ollie gave it to me. I can scan it and send it to you."

"That would be a big help," he agreed. "Now, you also asked about Henri Reynaud. The guy graduated summa cum laude from Oxford with a degree in Art History, and has been working for the Meecham Foundation for a number of years. Apparently he's regarded as a valued and trusted employee. Local authorities did investigate him when the near-theft of the grimoire occurred, but apparently he had a good enough alibi that they dropped him from the suspect list."

"What about his sister—Magda? I understand she worked at the gallery at that time as well."

"Didn't hear anything about a sister, but I'll check." Hank paused. "Now here's the part you'll really be interested in.

"Alexa Martin—daughter of Durwood Martin. Graduated from Edna Karr High School, attended Our Lady of the Lake College in Baton Rouge. Dropped out in her second year—that was when her dad took ill."

I frowned. "Isn't that a nursing college?"

"Primarily, but they do have other programs. Alexa was enrolled in the Arts program, and her major was Art History. I managed to pick up her trail right after her dad's funeral. She withdrew all the money in her account, a little over two thousand dollars, and boarded a plane for London, England. Guess where she got a job about a week later."

"Not the Meecham Foundation?"

"Bingo! Even though she didn't finish college, her grades were excellent. Plus she got a good recommendation from one Mr. Henri Reynaud."

"Reynaud!" My jaw dropped. "You have got to be kidding! How on earth did she manage that?"

"Well, here's the thing. She might not have. I read through Paul Mitchell's notes. He investigated that angle before he retired to Florida. When he interviewed Reynaud, the guy denied ever writing the letter, and he said he didn't know anyone named Alexa Martin."

"So the letter's a forgery?"

"It could be. There's no confirmation either way. Apparently the Foundation is a big place. Alexa's job permitted her to work from her home a good deal of the time."

"Work from home." I sighed. "That's a sweet setup."

"Sure is. As a matter of fact, her neighbor across the hall had a similar one. Seems she worked for the same place, too."

"Oh, don't tell me. Her neighbor was Daisy Martinelli?"

"No. This girl's name was Doris Gleason. She took a job at the Foundation so she could put herself through journalism school. She continued it after she got her degree and a job; no one's quite sure why. Maybe she planned on furthering her education at some point and wanted to sock some extra money away."

I let out a low whistle. "Now that's interesting. So Doris and Alexa knew each other?"

"You'd think so, wouldn't you, but I can't find anything that would substantiate a relationship between the two. Although here's something you'll find interesting. A week after the attempted theft, Doris Gleason abruptly quit both jobs, moved out of her flat, and, as far as anyone knows, the country. Daisy Martinelli moved into the flat and got hired in her place immediately afterward. Now here's something real odd: The day after the theft, Alexa Martin phones in, quits, and seemingly vanished into thin air."

"Both of them?"

"Yep. No one's heard from either Doris or Alexa since. I checked hospitals, morgues, newspapers—no record of an obituary for either girl. No Jane Does unidentified in the morgues, so maybe Atkins's info on Alexa being dead didn't pan out." He paused. "There's something else you should know about Alexa Martin. Apparently when she was sixteen, she got into a pretty big scrape, bad enough to be hauled down to jail. From what I understand, charges were dropped, but since she was a minor, the records were sealed."

I tapped my chin with the edge of my nail. It was possible Alexa had started to take after her father early on. "What about the injured thief? Anything turn up on that angle?"

"Zip. Listen, I've got to dash, but send me that photo."

I hung up and then just sat for a minute, cupping my chin in one hand, staring off into space, mulling over everything Hank had told me. More and more it seemed as if Alexa Martin might have followed in dear old dad's footsteps with her career choice. But what had happened to her? I was almost afraid to find out.

I decided to concentrate for the moment on my second woman of mystery—Angelique. Maybe her photo would produce a breakthrough with the Nick Atkins angle. I'd been certain I'd slipped it into the front compartment of my tote, but a quick look revealed it wasn't there. I turned the whole bag inside out and when nothing turned up, I rummaged through all the drawers in the kitchen and storeroom before heading upstairs to do the same to my kitchen, den, and bedroom.

No photo.

I stood in my bedroom, scratching my head, and saw something out of the corner of my eye, peeping out of the corner of Nick's fleece cat bed. I walked over and lifted its edge.

The photo of Angelique lay there, on top of a square bit of paper. I lifted both up and saw that the latter was Daisy's business card. The corners of both had been chewed clean through, tiny teeth marks discernible in the edgings of both.

"Nick, for goodness' sakes."

As if on cue, he appeared in the doorway. He saw what I had in my hand, threw his head back, and let out a loud yowl. Then he stamped his paw twice on the carpet, turned around, and wiggled his rotund bottom underneath my bed.

I leaned down and peered underneath. He was curled up in a ball in the far corner, tail wrapped around his body. Two golden eyes stared balefully at me, and no amount of coaxing could make him come out. At last I gave up and straightened. I looked at the two objects I held in my hand.

It would appear that Nick wasn't particularly fond of either Angelique or Daisy, and I had to share his sentiments, at least where Daisy was concerned. The jury was still out on Angelique, but from past experience even I had to admit Nick's intuition was rarely wrong.

Like his former owner, my cat had a sixth sense about crime.

TEN

"**N**ora, you look so charming! Are you supposed to be Gretel? Or Little Miss Muffet?"

It was a little after four on Sunday afternoon. I glanced down at my short red-and-white gingham-checked dress and frowned. "Isn't it obvious?" I pointed to a scarlet hooded cape draped over the back counter and the little wicker basket that sat next to it. "I'm Little Red Riding Hood." I looked appraisingly at Chantal's costume. The gold gown with its miles of creamy lace edging went well with her fair complexion, and its low neckline showed off her slim shoulders. A wig of flowing blond locks covered her own cap of dark curls, a twinkling tiara nestled in its middle. "You look like the fairy tale princess you're supposed to be," I assured her. "So am I to assume Rick Barnes is Prince Charming?"

"And a handsome one he will be, if he got to the rental shop on time, that is." Her eyes widened and her lips formed a perfect O. "Please do not tell me that Daniel is going as Grandma!"

The thought of Daniel Corleone decked out in a granny nightgown and gray wig made me chuckle. "Hardly. Daniel's going as the Big Bad Wolf, complete with full head mask! Thank goodness it was still there when I called yesterday."

"I bet he is thrilled." Chantal chuckled. "What did he say when you told him?"

"He didn't complain, but I did hear him gulp a lot." I laughed. "Honest, I'll be shocked if he shows up in it. I'm fully expecting him to come up with some excuse to don a suit and tie and say he's either James Bond or Bruce Wayne." I picked up my red cape and slung it around my shoulders, then went over to the basket, where I paused.

Nick lay curled up inside.

"Sorry, fella." I dipped the basket sideways. Nick's portly body tumbled half out, and he opened one golden eye and raised a paw as if to say, "Hey, you're interrupting my beauty sleep. Can't you leave me alone?"

"This ball is no place for a cat, Nick." I tipped the basket again and both his hind legs landed *plop!* on the counter. I lifted him up and set him on the floor. "See here, I've filled your bowl with some leftover lobster and shrimp! A banquet just for you, a feast fit for a kitty king!"

Nick ambled over to his bowl, leaned over, and did a cursory sniff. He glanced over one shoulder at me and then dove into the food. I watched him for a few minutes and then glanced over at Chantal. She was just closing her cell phone.

"Rick just texted me that he and Daniel will be a little late, but they will show up."

I shrugged. "If they do, they do. If not, don't worry, we'll be plenty busy."

My friend arched a brow. "How broad-minded of you. Might I attribute this casual attitude to the fact Leroy Samms will also be on the job tonight?"

I wrinkled my nose. "You may not. I'm looking forward to spending at least a part of the evening with Daniel. What I'm not looking forward to is running into Samms on his security detail. All in all, I'll consider this a successful evening if those food critics are pleased with the menu."

"I did a tarot reading for you before I came here. Basically it was very good."

I lifted a brow. "Basically?"

She shifted her weight. "The gist of it was success is imminent and you are moving in the right direction."

"But?" I prompted as she hesitated.

"The Moon appeared in the reading. It often signifies illusion, and mystery. The card encourages you to trust your intuition for the answers you seek."

"Great," I said. "Well, right now my gut is telling me we've got to get a move on."

Chantal picked up her dainty lace shawl and arranged it around her shoulders. "I do not think that reading referred to the gala at all. I think it was a warning to you to proceed with extreme caution on Violet's mystery."

"I'm always cautious."

Nick looked up from his food bowl. "*Er-Owl*," he said.

Chantal laughed. "I think Nick disagrees with that statement."

I sighed. "He would." I held my wrist up and tapped my nail against my watch face. "Come on, or we'll be late. I told Nan we'd be there no later than five-fifteen to start setting up. We can sort it all out later." I walked over to Nick and looked down at him, my hands on my hips. "And you, sir, stay here and behave yourself. I know you're disappointed you can't come, but don't worry. I'll be sure to save some *Morgan le Fay Pepper Steak* for you."

Nick blinked, then turned and stalked over to the staircase leading to the upstairs apartment. With one final sulky stare at me, he vanished through the doorway.

"Nick," I called after him. "I mean it. You be good and stay here."

No answering meow. All I heard was the thump-thump of his tail on the stairs.

Cats.

B y seven p.m. when the museum doors opened to admit a swelling throng, the food had been artfully arranged on the buffet tables that lined the east end of the museum's massive exhibition hall. Candles twinkled and punch flowed around the sterling silver chafing dishes that held my creations, with cream-colored cards in front of each dish proclaiming its title in elegant script. My *Lancelot's Lasagna* and *Merlin's Magical Chicken* were joined by

Guinevere's Pasta, which was a linguini in a delicate cream sauce, with shrimp and mussels. *Mordred's Meatloaf* was actually a turkey meatloaf, and, for the lighter eater, *Lady of the Lake Sandwiches* which were turkey, roast beef, and ham sandwiches cut in the shape of—that's right—coffins. The pièce de résistance, *Morgan le Fay's Pepper Steak Stir-fry*, sat squarely in the middle of the table, surrounded by beautiful flower arrangements provided by Poppies. The appetizer table looked good, too—the arugula salad and shrimp cocktail were joined with a pumpkin curry soup served in a hollowed-out pumpkin shell, a meatball soup, confetti cornbread, as well as the good old pigs in a blanket, all with names of Arthurian characters and places. Large crystal punch bowls containing my special punch sat at either end of each table, replete with frozen hand peeping over the edge. Everything looked and smelled great, even if I had to say so myself.

"Too bad Remy couldn't stay," I said. "Those floral arrangements are fantastic, especially the ones on the individual tables. Only he would have thought of surrounding those mini-pumpkins with chrysanthemums and black and orange roses."

"Perhaps it's for the best," Chantal said with a laugh. "His head would get swollen with all the praise, and trust me, it does not need to get any bigger." She tossed me a wink. "BTW, the chrysanthemums were *my* idea."

She sailed off, leaving me to absorb the atmosphere and glance over the crowd of gaily dressed patrons. While most had elected to dress in Arthurian garb, there were many other types as well. I noticed two Sir Lancelots with swords, a King Arthur in a purple velvet robe, a roly-poly Harry Potter, two Edgar Allan Poes complete with stuffed ravens perched on their shoulders, a Miss Marple, a Scarlett O'Hara . . . even a woman in a suit carrying a book and bicycle handlebars I took to be Jessica Fletcher. I spotted my part-time boss Louis Blondell wearing an Inverness cape, deerstalker hat, and pipe in the tradition of Sherlock Holmes. I moved off quickly before he could spot me. I had two articles past due that I knew I wouldn't be able to finish in the foreseeable future. So far I'd seen no sign of Daniel, Samms, or Broncelli, just Danny Travis, who'd drawn guard duty. I slid into a quiet corner and looked around, craning my neck for a glimpse of Nan or Violet, and finally spotted Violet. She stood in the midst of what appeared to be a group of knights, wearing a green velvet gown and floral head wreath I'd noticed in some paintings of Guinevere. There was a figure standing next to her, in black robes with wild red curls cascading down her back, and Chantal, who had reappeared, gasped and pointed.

"Look at that! Nan came as Morgan le Fay. Can you imagine that?"

I shook my head, trying to imagine the effervescent Nan as an evil sorceress. "Hardly."

"Neither can I. I do like Little Bo Peep, though, although the girl wearing the costume looks as if she's just swallowed a toad."

I followed Chantal's gaze and saw Little Bo Peep in a full-skirted shepherdess dress complete with white stockings, black Mary Janes, and a little stuffed lamb tucked under her arm. A short black cape graced her shoulders. She stood by the appetizer table, and as she lifted her black half mask to sample a shrimp I gasped. "Omigod that's Daisy! Violet's assistant."

"Ah, no wonder Nellie is giving her dagger looks."

Nellie Blanchard stood right behind Daisy in the line. The older woman wore a black hood with an attached collar and crown that hid her curly white bob, but I had to admit she looked positively regal in the black and violet medieval gown, a gold sash looped around her waist.

"Who's she dressed as?" I asked Chantal.

"If I had to guess I'd say the Evil Queen from *Snow White*. Judging from the look on her face it seems appropriate. Poor Little Bo Peep. If looks could kill she'd be six feet under."

I had to agree. Nellie's thin features were drawn into a dark scowl as she glared at Daisy's back. I wondered if the younger girl could sense it, because Daisy suddenly seemed to give a little shiver, and stepped out of line. I considered following her when a hand dropped on my shoulder, and I spun around to face Morgan le Fay or, rather, Nan Webb.

"Isn't it just thrilling? What a turnout! And people are raving about the food!" Nan's eyes were bright as she looked my costume over. "Gretel, right? What a cute costume!" Her gaze roved over Chantal's outfit. "And you look divine," she cooed. "So . . . princessey." Her hand darted out to give mine a quick squeeze. "This is such a raging success. Violet is *so* pleased."

A man dressed in a colorful court jester costume suddenly appeared at our elbows. His belled hat jingled as he fingered the pricey Nikon D90 hanging from a leather strap around his neck. He aimed the camera, shot off three or four pictures in quick succession, then made a low bow and sashayed over to another small group off to our left.

"Yowsa!" I blinked my eyes rapidly to dispel the lingering effects of the powerful flash. "Who was that?"

"Wally Behrens. He's the cousin of Edward Levey, the dentist. Wally's a professional photographer. He just rented that small studio on Atkins and is trying to promote his business. We asked him to take publicity pictures," Nan said. She was blinking rather rapidly herself.

"Yeah, well I hope he's good." I glanced pointedly across the room where Wally crouched in front of a group of giggling girls dressed as fairies.

Nan shrugged. "He's doing it for free to get exposure. As Violet would say, the price was right." She glanced over my shoulder and let out a little squeal. "Oh, you must excuse me. I see a reporter from the *Carmel Post*!" With an air kiss and a quick wave, she fluttered off. `

I watched her red wig bob and weave through the crowd and glanced around again. If Broncelli and Samms were here, they were well disguised. I turned to Chantal. "There are supposed to be food critics here . . . somewhere. Maybe we should meander over toward the buffet and try to find them—maybe we can get a feel for what they think of my creations."

Chantal didn't answer because at that moment Rick

Barnes, dressed in elegant white tie and tails as Prince Charming, walked up to us and slipped his arm across Chantal's shoulders. Black head bent over blond as he gave Chantal a kiss on the cheek and then he nodded at me.

"Wow, Nora, it all looks fantastic." He sniffed the air ravenously. "Smells even more so."

"Thanks, Rick. It's always nice when hard work pays off." I glanced around. "Where's Daniel?"

"Oh, he's coming," he answered, a bit evasively, I thought. "There were a few loose ends that came out of that meeting he has to tie up, and then he had to run home and get that costume." He chuckled. "But don't worry, he'll be here."

Chantal took Rick's arm and the two of them meandered over to one of the banquet tables. Left solo, I decided this might be a good time to seek out Daisy to finish our conversation from the night before. As I passed one set of partially open double French doors I caught a glimpse of my quarry in the hallway. Her face was flushed and her body language definitely indicated she wasn't alone. I flattened myself against the wall and pushed the door open a crack so I could peer out without being seen.

Daisy was indeed not alone. Another woman stood opposite her, dressed in a colorful skirt and blouse. I would have recognized her from the unkempt fall of curly dark hair before she turned, affording me a glimpse of a sharp nose and glittering eyes.

Daisy's companion was Magda.

The older woman's hand snaked out and grabbed

Daisy's wrist. She leaned over, whispered something to the girl. Daisy jerked her arm free and for a minute I thought she might slap Magda, but she just turned on her heel and walked away, leaving the other woman standing there muttering under her breath. As I debated following Daisy, Magda suddenly turned and strode in my direction. I backed up, prepared to blend in with the crowd, and then stopped as I heard a soft "Ow." I glanced over my shoulder and saw Louis Blondell rubbing his shoulder.

"Hey, Nora. Great to run into you, literally speaking." He held up a coffin sandwich. "Absolutely delicious."

"Thanks." I glanced casually over my shoulder. Magda stood on the threshold, her chest heaving. She glanced around the room, then flounced off in the opposite direction from the bar and was swallowed up in the crowd of gaily dressed revelers.

Louis peered down at me from under the brim of his cap. "Is something wrong? You look upset."

"Upset? Me? I guess I'm just a bit anxious, that's all. I've got a lot riding on tonight."

I started to move away but he caught my arm. "Well, if those food critics don't rave about these dishes, they don't deserve their jobs," he said, licking his fingers as he popped the last of his sandwich into his mouth. "Oh, and speaking of jobs, you"—he waved his finger in the air—"owe me two articles. Any idea when I can expect to see them?"

"Louis? Louis Blondell, you rascal, that is you. Where have you been hiding? You were supposed to call me!"

I breathed a silent sigh of relief as a girl dressed as a

Victorian lady, hair up in a French twist, sidled up to
Louis and laid her hand possessively on his arm. I noted
the haggard expression on Louis's face and figured she
wasn't exactly someone he'd wanted to run into. I wiggled
my fingers and took the opportunity to slip away and
retrace my steps back into the hall. Daisy was nowhere
to be seen. I returned to the main ballroom, being careful
to avoid the corner where Louis and his "friend" were in
deep conversation, and decided to check out the bar. I
hadn't spoken to Lance in a few days, so I had no idea if
Violet had hired him or not. I started toward it, and then
stopped as I saw the lady herself talking to a Sir Lancelot
and a Lady of the Lake, no doubt wealthy patrons. I
swiftly changed course, sidling up to her just as Lancelot
and the Lady moved off. Violet's eyes lit up when she
saw me.

"Nora, how cute you look. Red Riding Hood?"

"Yes, as a matter of fact." I smiled at her. "It's a great
ball, Violet."

"Due largely to the excellent food." Her hand reached
out, squeezed mine. "Any progress on our other matter?"

"A little. It's slow going. I hope to have some sort of
news for you soon."

"Favorable, I hope," she said and there was no mistak-
ing the anxious note in her voice.

"I hope so."

Two more costumed patrons came up demanding Violet's attention, so I slipped away and continued my trek
toward the bar. The large, black-lettered sign above the
wood-paneled bar read CAPTAIN JACK DANIEL'S WATERING

HOLE, and the man behind it was dressed in full pirate regalia. The line wasn't too long, so I slipped into place behind a girl dressed as Peter Pan, and when my turn came I ordered a Bloody Mary.

"So, are you Captain Jack Daniel?" I asked the bartender. I scrutinized him closely. He had what looked to be a year's growth of beard hanging from his chin, an eye patch over one eye, and a scarf wound through long dark hair that I assumed had to be a wig. As he passed me my drink he grinned and then spoke in a rough voice.

"Captain Lance is the moniker I prefer, but the powers that be insisted I go under the name of Jack Daniel. Arr-arr-arrgh."

He raised his eye patch and pulled his beard down low, and I laughed. "Lance! I wondered if Violet contacted you. That's some getup. You had me fooled!"

He wiggled both eyebrows. "I meant to stop by and thank you. She said you recommended me highly. As for my 'getup;' well, that's the idea of a masquerade, isn't it, me pretty? To revel in disguise?" He dropped his "pirate" voice and whispered, "You wouldn't believe what they're paying me. Phil still wanted to keep the Poker Face open tonight, though, so he's manning the bar." He glanced around the crowded room. "All I can say is I'm working my booty off to earn these big bucks. This is some crowd."

I held up my glass. "This drink is good. You're not skimping on the liquor here, like you do at the Poker Face."

He stuck his tongue out. "This place isn't my livelihood. Besides, there's enough liquor here to blitz a third world country."

"Well, my food's going pretty quickly. I just hope I made enough." I glanced around. "You're flying solo?"

"Heck no." Lance grinned. "I brought Jose."

I wrinkled my nose. Jose was a cousin of Lance's former barkeep, Pedro. Pedro had been an excellent bartender and an acceptable short order cook. Jose, not so much. But, according to Lance, the guy had promise and he was learning. I leaned over and peered underneath the bar. "I don't see him. Is he hiding?"

"He went on break about twenty minutes ago, and he seems to have gotten lost in the crowd." Lance craned his neck and glanced around the room. "He's dressed as Smee, the pirate from *Peter Pan*. I think I saw him chasing Carmen Miranda a while ago."

I chuckled and glanced at my watch. "I have to put the desserts out at nine, and the exhibit opens at ten. You haven't seen Daniel around have you?"

"Sweetie, in this crowd I wouldn't recognize my own mother. What costume is he wearing?"

I pointed to my gingham dress and dropped a little curtsy. "Why the Big Bad Wolf of course."

Lance slapped his palm down on the bar. "Oh no! You got him to rent that wolf costume from Girard's? What did you threaten him with?"

I batted my eyelashes and assumed an innocent expression. "I beg your pardon. He was quite agreeable about wearing it."

"I'll bet." Lance laughed. "Well, for an FBI guy it's probably the perfect disguise. Listen, I'd love to chat more, but duty calls. If you see my buddy Smee, tell him to get his behind back here. He would be the guy in black and white stripes, a stuffed parrot on one shoulder, chasing all the pretty girls."

I laughed and moved off, noticing as I did so the line behind me had grown. I left Lance to wait on Princess Leia and Luke Skywalker and took up a position near the rear of the room. I sipped my Bloody Mary, and glanced around the milling throng at all the colorful costumes: fairies, clowns, pirates, ghosts, witches. I caught sight of Wally, over by the buffet, snapping away, and I hoped for Violet's sake the "free" pictures wouldn't end up being a big waste. As I turned toward the large bay window, one costume in particular caught my eye. A tall woman, dressed head to toe in scarlet—scarlet gown cinched with a scarlet sash, ankle-length cloak, shoes, stockings . . . even her sleek pageboy bob, which I guessed was a wig, was a muted shade of red. Her features were partially obscured by a red-and-white half mask that covered the upper portion of her face, so only her full, scarlet-glossed lips and chin were visible. I thought she personified the "Red Death" from the Edgar Allen Poe mystery, and idly wondered if that was the image she was trying to project. She stood for a moment, glancing around, and then turned and made her way toward an alcove at the far corner of the room. I saw her vanish into it. A few seconds later she emerged, and Bo Peep was with her. The two of them were whispering, and at one point the Red Death wagged her finger under Daisy's nose. Then she pulled an object from underneath her cloak, but before I could get a good look at whatever it was, Daisy took the other woman's arm and pulled her into the hallway. As she did so, a figure in a bright orange skirt disengaged itself from the crowd and slipped into the hall after them.

I frowned. I'd been too far away to see faces clearly, but it certainly looked like the outfit Magda had on. Why was she following them? Impulsively I started in that direction, but I hadn't taken two steps before a heavy hand dropped on my shoulder. "Hold it right there," a raspy voice hissed in my ear.

I froze.

ELEVEN

"**W**ell, well, Nora Charles. Nice costume."

The familiar voice grated in my ears. Oh no, it couldn't be? Could it?

The hand dropped away from my shoulder and I turned around slowly, not quite sure what to expect. It certainly wasn't the tall figure in tight black jeans, a black silk shirt, and black boots that towered over me. A black silk mask covered the upper portion of his face, leaving only the lips and chin visible, and those lips were curved upward in a maddening grin.

"Th-thanks," I stammered. "Who are you supposed to be? Zorro?"

"Hardly. Zorro's weapon was a sword."

Samms pulled back his cape, revealing a holster with

a shiny .45 clipped to his side. I shook my head. "I thought you were on guard detail?"

"I am." He grinned. "But even the most stalwart guards need a break. Just between you and me, I've been trying to avoid that clown in the jester suit. You know, the roving photographer." He rolled his eyes upward. "He's a bit overzealous."

I laughed. "He's just starting up a photography business."

Samms winced. "That would explain it." His gaze roved over me, taking in every detail of my costume. "Very nice," he said. "Gretel?"

"She's Little Red Riding Hood, of course," said a muffled voice behind us. I let out a loud squeal as the tall figure in blue jacket, red bow tie, and large wolf mask swept me into his arms and against his chest. "Hey there, Little Red. Been behaving yourself?"

"Why certainly. I wouldn't want the Big Bad Wolf to get angry at me."

"Good." Daniel pushed the mask up to reveal his face and glanced at Samms. "Everything okay here?"

"No sign of trouble," Samms said. He touched two fingers to his forehead. "I'm headed back to relieve Bristol at the grimoire room. Stop by when you get a chance."

Daniel nodded. As Samms was swallowed up in the throng, he turned to me. "Hey, sorry I'm late. I got a bit held up after the meeting."

I brushed a strand of auburn hair out of my eyes. "It's okay. I had every confidence you'd show up sooner or later."

A figure appeared in the archway—Sergeant Broncelli. I noted the lawman had opted to wear a dark suit and tie and not a costume. He motioned to Daniel, who squeezed my arm. "I'm just going to check in. I'll be right back."

I watched him disappear into the hallway with Broncelli and I let out a small sigh. I had the definite impression this "working date" was going to turn out to be more work for Daniel than for me. Bo Peep stepped up to the podium just then and commandeered the microphone. "Good evening, everyone. We hope you are all enjoying the delicious food, catered by Ms. Nora Charles of Cruz's premier specialty sandwich shop, Hot Bread!" There was a smattering of applause and a few catcalls and whistles I attributed to Chantal, Rick, and Lance. Once everything died down, Daisy continued. "Please continue to enjoy our appetizers and entrees. Dessert will be served shortly, and then we will have the unveiling of our medieval exhibit, featuring the prized grimoire of Morgan le Fay! In the meantime, please eat, drink, and be merry."

"Hmpf. I could have done just as good a job."

I turned and saw Nellie Blanchard, arms crossed over her chest, standing just behind me. "Hello, Nellie," I said. "Enjoying the party?"

"It's okay," she grumbled. "The food's good."

"I like your costume."

Nellie glanced down, and then brushed at a speck of lint on one sleeve. "Yeah, it's okay. This material's a pain, though. It picks up everything."

Nan pushed her way through the throng and caught Nellie's arm. "Ah, Nellie, there you are. We need to get more napkins out of the storeroom. Could you possibly lend a hand?"

Nellie cast a dark glance toward one of the buffet tables where Daisy stood, chatting with a girl dressed as a fairy. "Sure. I guess the princess can't handle it," she muttered under her breath. Her fists clenched and unclenched at her sides, and she expelled a sharp breath. Then with a slight nod to me, she followed Nan out into the hallway.

"Looks like disgruntled employees are all over," said a figure to my left. "I've noticed that woman can have a short fuse, too."

I turned my head and met Reynaud's hypnotic gaze. He was dressed in a black suit, black tie, with a black cape looped around his shoulders. He held a white mask in one hand, a glass of punch in the other. "It is a fabulous soiree, with equally fabulous food. Kudos."

"Thanks."

I moved over to the table to get a glass of punch, and out of the corner of my eye saw Daisy coming in this direction. As she approached the table, Reynaud reached out and grabbed her arm.

"We need to talk," he hissed.

Daisy backed up a step and removed her mask. She looked quickly around. "Not here," she murmured.

"Where, then?"

"I don't know." She took another step away from the man. "Tonight is not a good time."

"There never seems to be one lately," he hissed back. "But you and I will settle things one way or another. Tonight."

Reynaud turned on his heel and moved toward the bar. Daisy looked after him a moment, then slipped her mask back on and hurried through the double doors into the hallway. I set my glass of punch on the table and followed, curious as to what "things" they might need to settle. When I entered the hallway I saw her standing in a far corner, her back to me, shoulders hunched. From her stance it appeared she was talking on her cell and as I drew closer I could see my assumption was correct. She finished her conversation, slid the phone into the pocket of her skirt, turned, and bumped right into me. "N-Nora," she stammered. "You startled me."

"I've been looking for you," I said. "I was hoping you and I might have a talk about Alexa Martin."

Her brows knit together; her lips slashed into a taut line. "I already told you, I do not know anything about Violet's niece. If you will excuse me . . ."

She started to move past me but I planted myself firmly between her and the exit into the adjoining hall and whispered boldly, "Who are you afraid of, Daisy? Reynaud? Magda? Someone else? Maybe that woman in red I saw you with earlier."

Her face paled and she sucked in her breath. I noticed her gaze seemed fixed at a point just beyond my left shoulder. I turned my head quickly, but there was no one there, although I had a fleeting impression of a door at the end of the hall closing. I swung my gaze back to Daisy. In the dim hall light, her skin looked almost transparent. She had the most startled expression on her face, like she'd just seen a ghost. Impulsively, I touched her arm. "Are you all right?"

Her head snapped up and she fixed me with a stare. "I'm sorry," she murmured. "I like Violet a lot, and I wish I could help you, but trust me, there is nothing I can tell you that would put Violet's mind at ease about her niece. Now if you'll excuse me."

She started to push past me but I stepped forward to block her way. "Something has upset you, I can tell. Maybe I can help."

Down the hall a door opened and more costumed revelers emerged, laughing and giggling. Daisy's fingers plucked at the string that tied the black cape around her shoulders.

"I'm sorry. I must go."

A girl dressed as Pocahontas popped her head out of a far doorway and started waving her hand. "Ms. Charles," she called. "The food critic from the *Monterey Herald* would like to speak with you. He's been sampling your food like mad!"

"See?" Daisy hissed. "An excellent opportunity for you. Forget about me, Ms. Charles. You should concentrate on taking care of your own business."

With that, she pushed past me and marched swiftly down the corridor. I sighed, squared my shoulders, and followed Pocahontas back into the ballroom.

Fifteen minutes later I'd completed my interview with Nate Blasdell, head food critic for the *Monterey Herald*, one of the largest papers in the Northern Cal area, which I personally thought had gone rather well. He'd been exceptionally pleased with my dishes, the *Morgan le Fay's Pepper Steak Stir-fry* in particular, and I extended an invitation to him to come down to Hot Bread the following week to sample more of my specialty sandwiches. I was checking my watch when a hand brushed against my waist. I jumped, and then relaxed as I spun around to gaze into a leering wolf's head.

"Everything okay?" Daniel asked, his voice muffled.

"It's great. I have to check on the desserts, so you'd better grab yourself a plate of real food. We'll be starting to put it away soon."

He patted his stomach. "I'm not worried. I know the chef."

I chuckled. "Did you happen to see Chantal or Rick anywhere around?"

"No, sorry."

"Well, if you do see Chantal tell her I'm heading on down to the kitchen. I've got to start getting the desserts ready."

Samms appeared in the doorway. He nodded curtly at me, then crooked his finger at Daniel and stalked off. Daniel leaned over, pecked my cheek, and then hurried off down the hall after Samms. I saw the two of them pause for a moment, and it looked as if Samms were showing Daniel something, but I was too far away to be sure. The two of them moved off toward the grimoire room, and I turned to go the opposite way toward the kitchen. My hand was on the knob when I paused. The sound of angry voices was coming from behind the kitchen door. They were too low-pitched for me to distinguish anything, so I slid the door open just a crack, enough to peer inside. I saw Daisy, her face flushed, talking earnestly to a figure all in red who stood in front of her—the Red Death. As I watched, the figure in red shook her head emphatically and started gesturing with her arms. Daisy shook her head, leaned over, and whispered something in the other's ear. Whatever she said must have really rubbed the Red Death the wrong way, because she gave Daisy a push backward. Daisy regained her footing, and then, eyes blazing, jabbed a finger under the other woman's nose.

"I mean it," I heard Daisy say loudly. "You've got to get out of here now, before you're seen. If anyone's in danger here, it's you."

The other woman's arm shot out. "Don't be a fool. If you're right, you're in as much, if not more, danger than I."

"Let's just agree we are both at risk." Daisy dragged her hand through her hair. "I've got to be positive before we move forward, though, so just put a lid on it. Don't do anything until I tell you to."

"You mean you don't want me to break—"

"NO!" Daisy's response was vehement. "Not until I say so. Let me handle it."

"You are so stubborn. It will be the death of you," spat out the woman in red. With that remark she pulled the red cloak from around her shoulders and flung it at the other girl.

I hesitated. What had Daisy's companion been going to break? My first thought was *break into the grimoire room*. I was just about to push the door open and confront them when loud laughter sounded from farther down the hall. Cursing bad timing, I quickly backed away from the door and leaned against the wall as three girls dressed as a fairy, a witch, and a clown sailed past me, giggling and laughing. They stopped a few feet away from me, huddled in a circle, and it was a good ten minutes before they meandered on their way again. The minute they vanished, I hurried back and pushed the door wide open.

The room was empty.

I walked all the way inside. "Daisy?" I called softly. "Are you all right?"

No answer.

At the far end of the room was a door. I hurried over and jerked it open. Beyond was a storeroom, with canned goods and paper products cramming every shelf. Off to the left was another door. I crossed over, opened it, and peered out. There was a long corridor outside, and far down the darkened hallway I could hear laughter and music. Apparently this was a back entrance into the main ballroom— and it explained how they'd disappeared so fast. As I started to turn away, the toe of my shoe crunched down on an object by the doorjamb. I leaned down to pick it up.

It was a small purple stone.

I slipped it into my skirt pocket, and then retraced my steps back to the kitchen. I was anxious to track Daisy down, but right now my energies had to be focused on dessert. I crossed to the double-door refrigerator and opened it. For a huge crowd like this, sheet cakes were the best bet. I'd made eight of them, all covered in yummy orange and black frosting. Cupcakes and cookies worked, too, and I'd made huge batches of pumpkin-shaped cupcakes and cookies in the shape of cats, bats, and spiders, all covered in frosting and sprinkles. I pulled the cupcake trays out of the refrigerators, and then went into the little side room where we'd stored the cookies. I counted the trays, frowned, and then counted them again.

I was one tray short. Dammit. Somehow it must have gotten left in the SUV. Well, no matter. It was parked right outside the service entrance. I had my car keys. I could just run out, get it, and no one would be the wiser. Then I could search for Daisy with a clear conscience.

I stepped outside and immediately wished I'd put on my jacket—the night air was cold! I hurried over to my SUV and, as I hit the button to open the rear door, suddenly paused. The hairs on the back of my neck were all standing at attention, and I had an idea it wasn't from the cold. I was just about to open the door when I heard a raspy voice at my ear.

"Watch your step, Red. You shouldn't take what doesn't belong to you."

I gasped and started to turn. My hood slid back, and I heard a sharp intake of breath. Then something strong and hard slammed into my back, sending me pitching forward. I caught a flash of something black out of the corner of my eye before my head hit the side of the SUV. I saw flashing lights dance before my eyes and then . . . nothing.

TWELVE

"Nora! Nora! Can you hear me?"

My head pounded like a little guy was inside it, shaking a pair of maracas, but I could hear Daniel's voice over the din, though it sounded weak and far away. My eyes were heavy, as if two giant weights rested on them, and there was a queasy feeling in the pit of my stomach.

Another voice, not the comforting rumble of Daniel's but harsh and raspy, reverberated through my brain.

Watch your step, Red. You shouldn't take what doesn't belong to you.

My eyes flew open and I sat up, startling Daniel. He'd shed the wolf mask but still wore the blue jacket and red bow tie. I gulped in breath after breath. "I—someone pushed me into the car—from behind—" I finally managed to gasp out.

"Yes, you have quite a lump on the back of your head. Just lie still."

Daniel eased me back to the ground, but a few seconds later I was straining to sit up again. "The desserts," I mumbled. "They have to be served."

"The earnest businesswoman right to the end, aren't you?" Daniel chuckled. "Don't worry, Chantal and Rick have it under control. I can call an EMT. Just relax, now."

"EMT!" I strained to sit back up. "I don't need an EMT."

"Oh, yes you do." He put both his hands on my shoulders and eased me back onto the ground. "Just lie still. You might have a concussion."

"Honestly, Daniel. We Charles's are known for our hard heads. I'm fine. Help me up, please." As he hesitated I added, "If you don't, I swear I'll do it on my own."

He rolled his eyes, then stood and offered me his hand. I'm not quite sure exactly how I managed it, because my legs did feel like jelly, but somehow I got to my feet. I took two steps and leaned against the side of my SUV. "See. Perfectly fine."

"Uh-huh. I know better than to argue with you." Daniel shook his head. "What were you doing out here anyway?"

"I noticed I was short one cookie tray, so I came out to see if it had been left in the car." I touched my sore spot gingerly. "I heard a noise, like something rustling, and then someone whispered in my ear."

Daniel's brows drew together. "Do you remember what was said?"

I found it hurt a bit to nod. "Yeah. It didn't make much

sense. Something about watching my step, and taking what doesn't belong to me."

I touched the back of my head gingerly. "Black."

"Pardon?"

"Right before I conked out, I saw a flash of black. It could have been a cape, or a coat. Or—oh my God, that's it."

A picture rose in my mind's eye of the scarlet woman flinging her red cloak in Daisy's face. I whipped my gaze to Daniel's. "I had my hood up, covering my head. So when my attacker called me Red, obviously he or she wasn't referring to my hair color."

Daniel frowned. "Meaning?"

"Meaning there are lots of other people here with red capes that have hoods." I crossed my arms over my chest to ward off the sudden chill that snaked down my spine. "I don't think my attacker was targeting me, specifically. I think I was mistaken for someone else wearing a red cape."

Daniel tapped his chin with his forefinger. "You think it was another person dressed as Red Riding Hood?"

My mind flew immediately to the Red Death. Even though she wore a longer cloak, it was the same shade of tomato red and had a similar hood. To someone who wasn't particularly fashion conscious, the two items looked pretty similar. I hesitated. I really didn't want to reveal anything about the argument between Daisy and the woman in red until I found out a bit more about just what was going down, which would entail me tracking down Daisy. I shrugged. "I don't know. It could be. There

117

are tons of red costumes here, though. It could be any one of them."

He didn't say anything for a few minutes, and then he nodded. "Okay, I'll check it out." He draped his arm across my shoulders. "In the meantime, let's get you back inside."

I still felt a bit woozy, so I was glad of Daniel's strong arms helping to support me. We walked back inside the museum and into the front room. The gala was still in full swing—apparently news of my attack had not gone any further, which I had to admit was a good thing. As people milled around, sampling the desserts, I stood on the fringe of the room with Daniel, looking around. I saw two more Red Riding Hoods (although their costumes weren't as cute as mine), a couple of red devils, even a fallen angel with red-tinged wings. However, the one I'd christened the Red Death was nowhere to be seen. I thrust my hands into my skirt pockets, then frowned. I'd been certain I'd put the purple stone I'd picked up in the kitchen there, but now both pockets were empty.

As I debated whether or not to tell Daniel about the stone and the conversation I'd overheard, Samms glided up to us. He stared at me, his arms folded across his burly chest, and if I didn't know better, I could almost swear that was a look of genuine concern on his face. "Everything okay here?"

"Yes," I responded, tapping at my temple. "As I told Daniel, I've got a pretty hard head."

Samms looked as if he wanted to say something, but then Daniel pulled him to one side. Chantal appeared at my elbow, bearing a mug of hot tea. "Cinnamon ginger. It will relax you." She pressed it into my hand. "What a shame, *chérie*. Things were going so well. I hope Daniel and Samms can catch whoever's responsible." She held her wrist up in front of my eyes and pointed to her watch. "Shouldn't the exhibit unveiling be starting soon?"

I nodded. "Daisy should be here to make the formal announcement," I murmured.

"Now that you mention it, *chérie*, I have not seen Little Bo Peep in quite a while."

I set the mug down on the edge of one of the long tables, the vision of Daisy and the woman in red arguing sharp in my mind's eye. "She might have gotten sidetracked with something. Maybe we should look for her."

I started forward, but Chantal grabbed my arm. "Not so fast. Your attacker is still walking around out there. We need some protection."

My lips twitched. "What, like a gun?"

My friend laughed. "No, like a big strong man. I see Rick over there." She inclined her head toward the other end of the room. "Wait here and I'll get him. Don't move."

She glided off and melted into the crowd before I could protest. I tried to keep my eyes fixed on her, but it was impossible in the sea of brightly colored bodies flitting from table to table, to the bar and back again. A lightheaded feeling stole over me and I leaned against the doorjamb for some extra support. Suddenly I felt something furry and warm wind itself around my ankles. I looked down at the black pool of fur curled around my feet and let out a little cry.

"How the devil did you get here?"

Nick raised his paw, clawed the air.

I bent down to rub his head. "You always turn up at the most unexpected times," I murmured. "Almost as if you're my personal guardian angel."

Nick opened his mouth, wide and long, flashing white fangs and crimson tongue. "You must have snuck into the van when we were loading the trays," I murmured. "My bad," I told the cat. "I'll take the heat for being careless, although with you I should know better."

Nick's claws shot out and embedded themselves in the hem of my skirt. "*Yer-owl*," he said, giving the fabric a little tug.

"Hey, hey," I cried, disengaging his shivs from the gingham. "Take it easy, will ya? These are rented goods, Nick. I can't bring them back damaged."

He thumped his tail twice and then raised his paw and began to lick it.

I sighed. "Look, we've got to get you out of here, buddy, before your presence is noticed. Pets weren't invited to this soiree. Plus, I've got to track down Daisy and ask her a few questions."

He regarded me with his catly stare, then got up and made for the doorway. Could it really be this easy? I jumped up and followed him as he trotted down the hall. He cantered past the closed exhibition hall doors and made a left.

"Nick," I hissed. "You're going the wrong way. The car is that way." I pointed in the opposite direction. Nick glanced over one shoulder at me and then trotted on, making another left, leaving me no choice but to follow. As I passed, I could see Samms, Daniel, and Broncelli in front of the grimoire room, surrounded by half a dozen policemen.

"Merow!" Nick squatted at the end of the hallway, his tail thumping impatiently against the carpet. *"Merow!"*

"Okay, okay, I'm coming." I put my finger to my lips. "Not so loud."

I started down the hall. Nick picked himself up and trotted off, and I hurried to keep up with him. We went down another long corridor, made two more turns, and then we were in a deserted display room, where he plopped himself in front of a large oak door on the far wall. He meowed softly and began to rub his body against it. Then he raised himself up on his hind legs and scratched at the wood with his shivs.

"Meower." He glanced over his shoulder at me and when his actions elicited no response, he started to scratch harder. *"Meower,"* he said, more insistently this time.

I frowned. Usually when Nick got into this mode nothing good resulted from it; in fact, it usually led to finding someone dead. I looked again at Nick, who had stopped scratching and was now running around in a circle in front of the door.

"Fine. But there had better not be a you-know-what inside here."

I twisted the knob and the door swung inward, almost hitting another furry shape crouched behind it. The cat that charged at me out of the darkness had a white body and an orange and white face. Its fluffy white tail waved like a flag signaling surrender. It landed on all four paws and stood, back arched, bright blue eyes glittering.

"Yowl!"

I looked at Nick, who'd sat back on his haunches and was calmly regarding the newcomer. "Is this what you wanted me to find, Nick? You wanted me to let this cat out of here?" I made an impatient gesture. "I told you I had things to do."

I could swear that Nick shook his head. *"Meeoow,"* he yowled.

The other cat turned around twice, echoed Nick's cry, and then shot like a guided missile back through the door. I peered cautiously inside. The room beyond was black as midnight, and I had no flashlight—nor did I have the cat's extraordinary range of night vision. I felt along the wall and found a switch, which I flipped. Illumination revealed a flight of steps leading downward into what was most likely a basement or a storage area. Nick and the other cat were halfway down the stairs. Both paused, turned and looked at me, and meowed plaintively.

"I do not have a good feeling about this," I muttered. I cautiously crept down the stairway, emerging into what appeared to be the museum storeroom, filled to overflowing capacity with boxes, cabinets, and trunks of varying sizes. I walked over to one and read the white-and-red printed label:

PROPERTY OF MEECHAM EXHIBIT

"Oh great," I muttered. This was obviously the place where the packing materials were stored for the exhibit articles. The cats were dashing madly around the room—

off to a large trunk on the left side, then back to me, around in a circle, and then back to the trunk. The orange and white cat began to mew pitifully as Nick chased a few red threads on the floor. Fighting the tingling feeling inching up my spine, I moved forward and saw a black Mary Jane dangling over the trunk's side, partially obscured by a swath of red satin.

With a sinking feeling, I walked all the way around, stopped, and bit back a scream.

Daisy Martinelli sat sprawled in the trunk's center, her neck cocked at an awkward angle, the red scarf tied around it pooled like a puddle of blood in her lap. One finger was caught in the scarf's frayed edge, almost as if she were pointing. Her sightless eyes stared straight ahead, and a little bit of drool trickled out of the side of her mouth. Her arms were tangled in the folds of a scarlet cape looped carelessly around her shoulders.

I didn't need to feel her pulse to see that she was quite, quite dead.

Rats.

THIRTEEN

"**S**o you found another body."

The words rolled off Samms's tongue almost as if he were pronouncing a curse. He hooked his thumbs in the loops of his belt and stared at me, brows drawn together. "You've really got to stop doing this," he continued. "Being a magnet for death isn't a real attractive quality for a woman."

"I am not a magnet for death," I huffed back.

"Okay, fine. Your cat is, then. Have you considered maybe giving him up and adopting a Yorkie? Or a King Charles Cavalier spaniel?"

"Never happening, pal." I didn't add that if I were to adopt a canine, I'd probably choose a Rottweiler. Or a Doberman. Something with a lot of bite. "I'm a cat person."

"I figured. Oh, well, it was worth a shot."

I bit my lip, swung my legs off the divan I'd been lying

on, and stood up. I felt a bit shaky but otherwise okay, so I began to pace back and forth across the small room I'd been confined to with Samms. "How much longer do I have to stay here?"

"Till your boyfriend arrives," Samms said with a grunt. He slid a glance over toward the doorway and added, "Here he is now."

Daniel crossed the room in two long strides and enfolded me in his arms. "Are you okay?"

"Yes," I mumbled against his shirt. His arms felt good, and I leaned into him. "It's been quite a night, though." I lifted my head to look into his eyes. "How did Violet and Nan take the news?"

"Better than expected," Daniel admitted. "Nan was her usual dramatic self, moaning about what a nice, efficient person Daisy was and who would want to murder her, while Violet was more concerned how it would affect the fund-raising portion of the evening."

"That sounds like Violet, but in spite of the brave front she puts up, I'm sure she's just as upset. She seemed genuinely fond of Daisy." I pushed the heel of my hand through my hair and peered up at Daniel. "Is everything all right with the exhibit?"

The smile faded from Daniel's face, replaced by an expression I could only describe as stonier than any president's on Mount Rushmore. Before he could answer me Samms walked over and clapped a hand on his arm. "If Nora's up to it, we really should get her statement now," he said quietly. "We should get the facts while they're still fresh in her mind."

Daniel flashed Samms an odd look. "True, but I'm not certain she feels up to that right now."

"I'm fine," I said quickly. "I can give a statement now. The sooner, the better. I'd really like to get it over with." I sat back down on the divan and folded my hands in my lap. "Chantal and I noticed that it was almost time for the exhibit to start and Daisy wasn't anywhere around. We thought we'd go look for her, and Chantal went to find Rick so he could act as our bodyguard. I felt something warm and furry by my ankles and I saw that somehow Nick had gotten into the gala. I knew I had to get Nick out of there, but all of a sudden he took off down the hall. He led me right to the storage room door. I opened it, and a cat jumped out—"

"Wait . . . another cat?" both Daniel and Samms chorused in unison. I half expected one of them to call out "jinx" any second.

I nodded. "Yes, an orange and white one. Anyway, Nick and this other cat kept meowing and running around in circles, and then they raced down the cellar stairs, so I followed them, and there she was, sprawled dead in that trunk." I squeezed my eyes shut. "She was strangled, right?"

"I can't say officially till the coroner delivers his report, but it appears so, yes," Daniel said.

A mental picture of Daisy's body rose before me, and I visualized the ribbon of red looped around her neck. I pursed my lips, trying to remember if the woman in the Red Death costume had been wearing a red scarf. I glanced up and saw both Samms and Daniel looking at me somewhat expectantly.

Samms placed a hand on each hip. "Perhaps you noticed something strange, or something struck you as out of the ordinary tonight? You've got good instincts, after all."

I eyed him. An actual compliment? Would wonders never cease? "I did see Daisy arguing with some people here tonight."

Daniel reached in his jacket pocket and pulled out a small black notebook and pen. "Did you recognize any of them?"

"Yes. One is an exhibit worker. Her name is Magda. She's not a very pleasant person. I heard them arguing at the beginning of the evening. She got pretty rough with Daisy."

"In what way?"

I scrunched my lips up as I tried to remember her exact wording. "She said she knew what game Daisy was playing and it wouldn't work. Daisy told her to mind her own business. Then Magda implied that Reynaud might not trust Daisy, and it would be wise not to cross her."

Samms cocked a brow. "She threatened her?"

I nodded. "It certainly sounded that way."

Daniel scribbled something in his notebook. "Who else?"

"Daisy had a brief exchange with Reynaud. He mentioned a matter they'd been discussing, and he told her it would be settled tonight, one way or another. She didn't exactly look thrilled by this."

"Interesting. Any idea what this 'matter' was?"

I shook my head. Daniel mumbled "Hm" again and

scribbled more in his notebook. "Any more confrontations with anyone else?"

I hesitated. Part of me felt I should let Daniel and Samms know about Daisy's argument with the mysterious Red Death, but my gut was telling me that despite what I'd witnessed, the woman in red was no more responsible for Daisy's death than I was. Right now, my money was on either Magda or Reynaud, with Magda in the driver's seat.

I shook my head. "Nope. That's all."

Samms's steely gaze bored into me. "Are you sure?"

"Well . . . there is one more thing." I cleared my throat. "When I was attacked earlier, I remember seeing a flash of black before I conked out. It could have been someone wearing a black cloak, or costume . . . or with long, black hair." I paused. "That woman Magda has very long, greasy hair, the color of midnight."

Daniel frowned. "You think this Magda attacked you? Why would she?"

I chuckled. "Well, I've had a run-in with her myself, but I still think I was mistaken for someone else tonight. And Daisy had a red cape on when I found her."

Samms looked at Daniel. "That's right, she did. But earlier in the evening she had on a black one."

"Hm, good point. Why did she switch capes? Or did she? We'll have to check on that." Daniel snapped his notebook shut and held out his hand to me. "Okay, Nora. You've been a big help. Come on. I'll get someone to take you home. You need to get some rest after the night you've had."

I ignored the proffered hand. "Oh no, you're not getting rid of me that easily. I'm not leaving. I've been around a crime scene or two in my day, you know. I could be helpful."

"Or you could still be in danger," he said.

"I agree with Dan," said Samms. "This isn't the time for you to switch back into investigative reporter mode."

I planted my feet apart and glared at both of them. "Nick is still missing. I'm not leaving here without him."

"For all we know, your cat might be back at your house," Daniel suggested. "Animals can be remarkably resilient when it comes to returning to the place that houses their food bowl."

It wouldn't be the first time Nick had found his own way home, but I wasn't about to be put off so easily. "Maybe, but I want to make sure he's not hiding anyplace around here before I desert him."

"Stubborn as usual," Samms muttered to Daniel. He turned to me. "I know from past experience arguing with you does no good. You always somehow manage to find a way to do just exactly what you want."

I tossed him a smug grin. "Yes, and it took years of practice to perfect that technique."

Daniel looked at me, then at Samms, then back to me and shrugged. "Fine. You can stay until we find your cat. Then you go home. Understood?"

I bobbed my head up and down. "Certainly."

"And you stay out of the way of the investigating team. Okay?"

"Of course."

I smiled sweetly, hoping neither of them noticed my fingers crossed behind my back.

I'm no stranger to murder scenes. It doesn't mean I like them, by any stretch of the imagination; it just means I know my way around 'em. The storage area where I'd found Daisy's body was now cordoned off with familiar yellow-and-black tape. I saw a black gurney just off to the left, a sure sign the coroner and his team were downstairs, no doubt also accompanied by a forensic photographer. I walked swiftly past, not caring to see Daisy's body transported up in a black body bag.

The sense of revelry that had dominated the evening had long dissipated. Now costumed revelers sat huddled in groups, waiting their turn to be questioned by the CSI team before being ushered off the premises. Cruz Homicide boasted a team of six detectives, counting Sergeant Broncelli, and I had no doubt they were all here tonight. Daniel stopped to give instructions to two uniformed policemen, and I couldn't help thinking that he appeared to be the one in charge, even though it was supposed to be Broncelli's show. Speaking of which, where was the erstwhile sergeant? I hadn't seen him around, save for those few moments outside the grimoire room. It crossed my mind I hadn't seen him all night. Chantal's tarot reading came back to me: Proceed with extreme caution. Follow your gut.

Too bad those two didn't necessarily go hand in hand.

I was so lost in my thoughts I didn't hear Daniel come up next to me. I jumped as he touched my arm.

"This is the reason I wanted you to go home," he said in an accusing tone. "You're dead on your feet. No pun intended."

I stretched my arms wide. "I still have to find Nick. He's around here somewhere."

"Did you check your car? For all you know he might have gone right back there." He held out his hand. "Give me your keys. I'll check it out and be back in a few. Stay here till I get back."

I handed over the keys and Daniel hurried off toward the kitchen. I ambled over in the direction of the bar. A quick glance showed it was closed. A uniformed policeman was over there, talking to Lance. I noted that he'd finally tracked down Jose, who stood right beside him, looking decidedly uncomfortable. I could sympathize. Crime scene interviews aren't exactly a barrel of fun.

I knew that all crime scene investigations begin with the interview. The interview process is an exacting one. It's used to determine the type of crime (in this case, murder), what happened during the criminal act, and how it was committed. Back in Chicago, the CSI team would interview the first officer who arrived on the scene, and then branch out to any actual victims or witnesses of the crime. In a case like this, with no eyewitnesses, the team would question people to determine who, if anyone, might have seen or noticed anything of value. With a crowd like this, that would be a gigantic undertaking. Most of the information collected during these types of interviews was not always factual; much depended on first impressions, witness testimonials, and memories. In a case where multiple witnesses and interviews are involved, the information will not correlate with the evidence collected at the scene nine times out of ten.

Nonetheless, it was this information that would become the foundation of the investigation. The officer in charge, most likely Broncelli in this instance, would have the unenviable job of disseminating and dissecting the information collected, determining what was useful and what was not.

And ultimately using said information to track down a killer.

I was feeling more than one pang of guilt. I was, in police vernacular, "withholding pertinent information." Well maybe not so much withholding it as just not sharing it. But I couldn't help it.

I had a gut feeling, or what Chantal would call a vibe, that Daisy's death might somehow be linked to the prior attempt to steal the grimoire, and also to Violet's niece, Alexa Martin. Just what that connection might be, however, I hadn't the faintest idea. Somehow that woman in red was part of it, but I hesitated to say anything without some proof. I'd done that once, early on in my career, and a criminal had nearly gone free because what I'd said had pointed the police in the wrong direction. I was loath to do that again, especially if Violet's niece was involved. No, I needed something more tangible to go on before I said anything to either Daniel or Samms.

And I had an idea, albeit a risky one, of how I might go about getting just that.

FOURTEEN

"**Y**ou look like you could use a drink."

I looked up and into the somber face of Lance. His lips crooked up at the corners and he placed his hand gently on my elbow, guiding me back toward the bar. He helped me up on one of the stools then slid around to the back and started rummaging beneath the counter.

"Heard you were the one who discovered the body," he said, his voice muffled. I could hear the clink of glass as he shuffled bottles around.

"All in a night's work," I said, leaning both elbows on the wood counter and cupping my chin in my hands. "Actually, it was Nick and another little furred friend of his who led me downstairs."

"Yeah? Well ain't that somethin'. Bet it wasn't a pretty sight. That gal had something on her mind all right. She came over here, ordered a Horny Toad—don't give me that look, it's a nice sweet drink." He threw his hands up as I raised both eyebrows. "The ladies love it. Anyhow, she didn't drink much of it. First that guy who looks like Mandrake came over and tried to talk to her and she cut him right off. Then some lady dressed as a gypsy hag started to approach her, and she took off thataway." Lance pointed to a set of French doors. "And then some chick all in red followed her out. Yep, she was one busy lady. Think one of them did her in?"

Since he'd named all three of my prime suspects, I couldn't help but nod. He dipped his head below the counter and a minute later he straightened, a bottle of Ketel One clutched in both hands. "I think this calls for a Thin Man special, and I'm not talking tuna melt."

"A Thin Man special, eh? And what would that be?"

"Think about it. What was Nick Charles's drink of choice in those movies?"

I chuckled. "A very dry martini. But I don't like martinis."

He closed one eye in a broad wink. "You'll like this one."

He poured a generous amount of vodka into a nearby blender, added some pink liquid and sugar, blended it for about twenty seconds, then poured it into a tall glass and pushed it in front of me. I eyed it, took a tentative sip.

"Oh, that is good."

"You can use any juice but I like pink grapefruit. Add in a generous helping of sugar and vodka and—voilà! It'll calm your nerves."

I'd been watching the preparation, and judging from the amount of vodka he'd put in, I hoped that was all it would calm. "My nerves are fine."

He leaned across the bar. "You think they're fine, but finding a corpse isn't exactly something one does every day."

"Yeah, well, Nick and I have found more than our share lately, or at least Samms seems to think so."

Lance's gaze traveled to the other side of the room, where Samms stood in conversation with another policeman. "You know, when I first heard he was in town I thought maybe he'd come to pay you a visit."

I picked up the glass, took a sip, and made a face as the liquid burned a trail of fire down my throat. I set the glass back on the bar, swallowed, and said hoarsely, "Why on earth would you think that?"

Lance poured himself a generous helping of the juicertini and downed it in one swallow. He wiped his lips with the back of his hand and looked me straight in the eye. "Chantal mentioned the two of you have a past."

Oy, how many people had my friend told about Samms? "College. Long time ago. Over it."

Lance waggled his eyebrow. "Yeah? You never really forget your first love, you know."

"Who said Samms was my first love?" I said quickly. I tossed him a devilish grin. "And here I thought you were."

"Aw, thanks, but we both know that's not true." He poured some more juicer-tini into his glass. "I, for one, will not forget the shabby way he treated Lacey, even if deep down he did believe in her."

"Lacey's forgiven him. Apparently they've struck up a sort of friendship. He even got her a part-time job as a sketch artist. She was pretty upset when he left St. Leo."

Lance tossed back more of the drink and then set the glass down on the bar. "Well, there's one bright spot anyway. If he's doing guard duty for that exhibit, he'll only be here for another week or so. That's a relief, right?"

"Why do you say that? Oh, wait!" I held up my hand. "Please don't start that again. Samms means nothing to me, and I'm sure I mean even less to him."

He topped off my glass with the remainder of the juicer-tini and pushed it toward me. "Maybe you don't think so, but I'm a man, sweetums. I can tell when a guy's got a thing for a girl, and it's very evident Samms has . . . well, let's put it this way. He feels *something* for you."

Almost as if he knew we were talking about him, Samms turned his head and looked straight across the room at us, or rather, at me specifically. He scowled darkly, then turned back to the other patrolman.

"Yeah," I said, picking up the glass. "He feels something all right. Can you say disgust?"

"That's not disgust, sweetums. That's lust."

"Riiight."

He took both my hands in his. "Listen, you're not the first person to be torn between two suitors. History is full of love triangles. For example, there's Superman, Lois Lane, and Lana Lang. Rick, Ilsa, and Victor. Scarlett, Rhett, and Ashley . . ."

"You do realize those are all fictional characters."

"Hey, life imitates art."

"Enough." I jerked my hands free. "I hate to burst your bubble, but there's nothing for me to feel guilty over. No love triangle here."

"Uh-huh, if you say so. Just remember, there's a fine line between love and hate."

I was spared more soul-searching advice from Lance by the appearance of Bill Kelly, a detective who often came into Hot Bread. He walked over to us and nodded at Lance. "Mr. Reynolds, we have just a few more questions, if you don't mind," he said, throwing me an apologetic look. I said good-bye to Lance and wandered over to the bay window. I pulled over a nearby chair and proceeded to mull over the evening's events. I replayed Daisy's altercations with Reynaud, Magda, and the woman in red over in my mind. Out of all of them, the one with the woman in red had been the most dramatic.

"It sounded as if they were working together on some matter that put the two of them in danger. Yet, at the end, Daisy seemed unsure about something. What?" I muttered to myself.

I wished Nick were here. Even though the cat couldn't answer me, I always felt better going over my theories aloud with him. And he somehow found a way to either agree or disagree, to point me in the right direction, something I sorely needed right now. I brushed my bangs out of my eyes and thought about the information Hank had supplied.

Doris Gleason had worked at the Meecham Foundation, ostensibly putting herself through journalism school. She'd obviously worked part-time on a London paper, because she'd written one of the two articles I'd found about the attempted theft of the grimoire. Then Doris vanishes. Enter Daisy Martinelli, who takes over not only Doris Gleason's flat but her job at the foundation. But what if Doris hadn't disappeared? What if she'd merely dropped out of sight, maybe to work on a story undercover? If the story concerned the grimoire and the Meecham Foundation, she might have needed another pair of eyes and ears to remain there, to keep her informed on current events.

Those eyes and ears could have belonged to Daisy.

I tugged at a stray curl. There were a lot of holes in my theory. For one, I had no proof that Doris Gleason and Daisy Martinelli had ever known each other. For another, what sort of story would Doris have dropped out of sight to follow? And did it have anything to do with Alexa Martin, or was that just wishful thinking on my part?

The scenario that made more sense was that Alexa and Doris knew each other, had plotted the grimoire theft together, and had barely escaped. Or had they? A thief supposedly had been shot, and neither girl had been heard from since. That could have been the basis for Nick Atkins cautioning Violet her niece might be dead. As far as Daisy's murder went . . . who had a motive? If Doris were the woman in disguise as the Red Death, and she and Daisy had indeed been working together toward a common goal, it was doubtful Doris would have murdered her; she would have had no reason to. But possibly Magda or Reynaud did. It would certainly help to know just what beef each of them had with Daisy, and if it were strong enough to kill over. Furthermore, if Daisy and

Doris were that close, it was also a good possibility that Doris might have a good idea who the murderer was, and that would have put her in danger.

Watch your step, Red. You shouldn't take what doesn't belong to you.

Thinking about my attack made me shiver. My thoughts went to the missing purple stone, and the fact that it had mysteriously disappeared out of my pocket right afterward. Had that been what my attacker had referred to, or could it be something else? And if retrieving the stone had been the reason for my attack, what significance could it possibly have?

Nothing made sense.

I set my lips. Back in the day, I used to assemble clues on cases I was working and keep them locked in my desk. Perhaps Daisy might have done the same. Better yet, I knew the museum personnel had lockers near the offices. Lockers were always a good place to secret stuff you wanted to keep hidden. Hey, it had worked in high school.

I started to make my way over to the main staircase when a heavy hand clamped down on my shoulder.

"And just where do you think you're going?"

I met Samms's stony stare with one of my own. "What are you, writing a book? Leave that chapter out."

"Very funny." The grip on my shoulder tightened. "I thought you promised Daniel you'd stay out of the crime scene."

I bit down hard on my lower lip to keep from screaming my answer. "The crime scene is downstairs, in the basement. I was just about to go *up* the stairs."

"So you were." He quirked an inky brow. "And what's the attraction up there, may I ask?"

I thought fast. "I wanted to get my purse and things, you know, so I'd be ready to go home when Daniel got back."

"Bzzt! Wrong answer." His eyes flashed sparks. "I happen to know that you and Chantal locked your purses in your van."

I bit down hard on my bottom lip, trying to cover up my consternation. "And just how do you know that?"

"I'm an ace detective, after all." He smirked. "Plus, Chantal told Rick that before they left. She called her brother so he'd leave the door open for her. Oh, and I almost forgot. She asked me to tell you she'd pick up her things in the morning."

Rats! "Oh, all right, if you must know . . . I wanted to see if Nick was up there. With all the commotion down here, he might have opted for a quieter place." As Samms remained stonily silent, I added, "You know, the faster I find my cat, the faster I can get out of here . . . and your hair."

His gaze raked over me, and then he sighed. "Fine. But I'm coming with you."

I felt my stomach lurch. "That's really not necessary. I'm sure you have a lot to do here."

He held up his hand. "No buts. After all, in case you should stumble across *yet another* dead body, as you are wont to do, at least this time you'll have a police officer right on the scene."

I had no answer to that, at least none I could say out loud. We climbed the rest of the stairs in silence.

The second floor of the museum was where its administrative offices were located. We stood for a minute at the edge of the long hall, getting our bearings.

"The offices are off to the right, if I remember correctly," I said. "There are a few empty rooms they keep for file storage down the left end, so how about if we split up? You take the right, I'll take the left. It'll go faster that way."

"We'd much rather be thorough than fast, right? Two pairs of eyes are better than one, particularly when you're looking for cats. They're devils when it comes to picking out hiding places, am I right?"

I set my lips. Shaking Samms wasn't going to be easy, but I had to think of something if I was going to hunt for Daisy's locker. I squeezed my eyes shut and said a quick prayer.

"I see a door ajar. Let's start at this end," Samms suggested. We'd only taken two steps when his beeper went off. He swore softly and looked at it, then turned to me. "I've got to get back downstairs."

I noted the granite expression on his face. "Is something wrong? What's happened?"

"Nothing you need concern yourself with." He slipped the beeper back in his pocket and let his arm sweep wide. "Go ahead, start looking for those cats. I'll be back as soon as I can. Try not to find any more dead bodies, too, okay?"

I made a face at his retreating back, said another silent prayer of thanks, and turned toward the door that stood partially open.

As good a place to start as any.

I knew the minute I entered the room I'd hit pay dirt. Coats were tossed carelessly over desks and chairs, and I could see the edges of purses peeping out from some of them. There were a few lockers positioned against one wall. I moved toward the lockers first, and started to pull them open. The ones without locks were all empty, but there were a few in the bottom row that had bright, shiny combination locks dangling from their handles.

I sighed. I hadn't even thought about a lock. It would be just my luck if Daisy's locker were one of those.

Fortunately, luck was with me. The last locker on the bottom row yielded a snappy brown twill jacket that was very stylish and modern and something I could easily envision Daisy wearing. The bag on the floor was an envelope-style purse, made of buttery soft mocha leather. It had a chain strap and an outside pocket. I was just about to slip my hand into the pocket when I heard the soft creak of a floorboard. I dropped the purse and whirled around.

And saw no one there.

I turned my attention back to the purse, thrusting my hand into the slim outside pocket. My fingers closed over something hard and I drew out a plastic room key from the Cruz Motel with UNIT 13 stamped across its face.

Hm . . . if this was Daisy's purse, then apparently she hadn't gotten around to renting an apartment yet.

I snapped the purse open and peered inside. The contents of this purse were all neat and orderly. There was a Laura Geller lip gloss, a small compact of MAC blush, Mally mascara—all high end, quality products that a young woman might use. There was a small packet of Kleenex, a key ring with two keys on it, a pin in the shape of a pink ribbon, and a small coin purse, which I opened. Empty. I replaced the coin purse inside the larger bag and pushed it back under the jacket, shoving the motel key into the pocket of my costume. After a minute I picked up the pink ribbon pin and slipped that into my pocket, too. I turned toward the door and then paused.

In the hallway beyond I could hear the murmur of voices.

I stepped up to the door and peered through the small crack. A tall, imposing figure dressed all in black was standing just outside the door, its back to me. As it turned slightly, I caught a glimpse of its profile.

Reynaud.

The man was muttering to himself. He leaned against the wall and reached into his pants pocket. He withdrew two stones, held them up to the light.

I gasped. The stones he held in his hand looked almost exactly like the green and blue stones in the grimoire!

My mind flashed to the group huddled outside the exhibit door. Had there indeed been a theft attempt, a successful one? Was I looking at the thief right now? I pressed my eye closer to the crack. Reynaud closed his

143

hand and put the stones back in his pocket. Suddenly he stiffened, and I heard a sharp intake of breath. "What the devil!"

"*Er-owl!*"

My heart stopped. I knew that wail. I angled my face so I could peep downward and sure enough there stood Nick in front of Reynaud, hackles raised, back arched in the classic Halloween black cat pose. His lips peeled back and his sharp white fangs were exposed. He let out a hiss.

"Who let *that* in here?" Reynaud rasped. "Get it out of here. Black cats, any kind, are bad luck, bad luck indeed."

Whoa, black cats must really get to him. He had to be talking to himself—as far as I could tell, he and Nick were the only two out there. I saw Reynaud's hand lash out, and I knew I couldn't stay hidden and let him harm Nick. I closed my fingers over the knob, prepared to jerk it open and reveal my existence, but just at that moment Nick spun around and took off like a rocket down the stairs. I held my breath and pressed my body against the door. My heart was pounding so heavily in my chest I was almost certain Reynaud would hear it. A minute passed, and then two . . . and then I heard footsteps, shuffling away. I edged the door open and peeped cautiously around the side.

I saw a flash of black melding into the shadows at the far end of the hall. I leaned weakly against the doorjamb, remembering the last flash of black I'd seen. Hm. Reynaud was wearing a black cape . . . Was it possible he'd been my attacker? My hand closed over the plastic room key in my pocket.

"Nora!" came a shout from the stairwell. "Nora, are you still up there?"

I quickly exited the room, pulling the door shut behind me. I hurried over to the stairwell and saw Samms at the bottom, his hands on his hips. He smiled up at me. "I've found your cat," he said, pointing downward. Curled around his feet was Nick. I threw another quick glance behind me and then took the stairs two at a time. When I reached the bottom I scooped Nick up in my arms and gave him a big hug.

"You rascal," I whispered.

Nick blinked at me. "*Meow*," he said, and then snuggled contentedly into my arms. His pink tongue darted out, licked at the back of my hand.

Daniel rushed up, the tense expression on his face softening as he caught sight of me and Nick. "Good," he said. "You found him."

"Samms did." I looked at Daniel. "No trace of that other cat, huh?"

He shook his head. "No, sorry. I did tell Nan Webb about it, and she promised to put her staff on alert."

"Thanks." I shifted Nick in my arms. "I think we're ready to go home now." I let out a loud yawn. "Believe it or not, I'm tired. The events of this evening are catching up with me. After all, I was conked on the head you know. It wears down a person."

Daniel stepped in between us and slipped his arm around my shoulders. "Of course, it's been a very trying evening for you, Nora. I'll be glad to take you home."

I shook my head. "Oh no. You're needed here, after

all. I don't feel dizzy now, and besides, it's not far. Nick and I will be fine, won't we, Nick?"

Nick snuggled deeper into my arms and let out a loud, rumbling purr.

Daniel and Samms exchanged a glance, and I got the definite feeling one or the other was going to offer to be my personal police escort slash bodyguard, a complication I so did not need right now. Fortunately, before either of them could utter a polite phrase in my direction, a patrolman hurried up to us. "Detective Samms? Sergeant Broncelli needs you right away." He glanced at Daniel. "You, too, Agent Corleone. He wants to discuss the gri—"

"We're on our way." Daniel cut the policeman off mid-sentence and turned to me. "You'll go straight home? You promise?"

I made an "X" over my heart. "Of course." Daniel leaned over, gave me a quick kiss on the cheek, and then motioned to Samms. Samms gave me a thorough once-over before he fell into step behind the patrolman.

"He knows I'm up to something, damn him," I muttered, my grip on Nick tightening. "So we'd better get a move on, Nick. Anyway I wasn't lying . . . much.

"We are definitely going home, but it's just a pit stop for me to change into something a little less conspicuous. I know it's almost one a.m., but most people would call it the shank of the evening. You and I have a sleuthing date at the Cruz Motel."

FIFTEEN

I made it home in record time, and under Nick's watchful eye peeled off my costume, replacing it with a pair of black jeans and a black turtleneck. I shrugged into a black fleece jacket and put a few little necessities into a black cross-body bag. Then I took my red hair and bundled it up under a black knit cap. One glance in my full-length mirror assured me that I definitely gave new meaning to the phrase *second-story man*, or more appropriately, *cat burglar*. Nick, sprawled across my bed, fixed me with an unblinking stare.

"Don't look at me like that," I chided him. "I know, I know. I should have told Daniel and Samms about finding that purple stone, and about Reynaud with those stones, but let's face it, it's only speculation. Not actual proof of anything."

Nick sat up and blinked.

"Okay, maybe I should have told them about the motel key but, once again, I have no proof that it belongs to Daisy. There was no identification in that purse. It could be anyone's. So we'd best get a move on. If it's not Daisy's key, we don't want to get caught in an innocent person's motel room now, do we?"

Nick studied me with his golden gaze for a few seconds then hopped off the bed and pranced over to the door.

I grinned. "Okay, then. We're off. With a little bit of luck we might even get back in time to get an hour's nap in before Hot Bread opens."

The Cruz Motel was about ten minutes away. I pulled into a spot at the rear of the lot and then walked over to the large single building with its connected rooms as Nick padded along beside me. I found Unit 13 without much difficulty and was just about to pull the purloined key out of my bag when I noticed the door was slightly ajar.

Uh-oh, I thought. *This can't be good.*

I pushed the door and it swung wide open. I took a cautious step inside, feeling along the wall for the light switch. I found it, turned it on—and bit back a cry of dismay.

The room was one freakin' mess.

Drawers were pulled out and clothes and underthings were strewn everywhere. The bedclothes had been pulled off the bed and rolled into a tight ball and flung into one corner. The mattress was askew; a suitcase, devoid of contents, lay overturned on the floor beside the bed. The folding closet door was open. Lying on its end was a soft-sided black suitcase, and propped against the wall off to its left was a hard-sided one in a funky purple leopard print. I picked my way through the maze of clothing and went into the bathroom. Everything was thrown about in there as well. I retraced my steps into the main room and just stood, surveying the wreck, my hands on my hips. Nick raced off to a far corner and bent over, his rotund bottom wiggling. I walked over to see what had interested him and saw a pile of brown nuggets on a paper plate. Nick was chomping on some of them. I reached down and picked the plate up, sniffed.

"Cat food?" I frowned, remembering the orange and white cat. Had it been Daisy's? I set the plate back down on the floor, but by this time Nick had lost interest (he's spoiled with my leftovers—mere cat food rarely satisfies) and had moved on to something else. I saw him now half under the bed, his claw fiddling with the underside of the mattress.

"Nick, this place is in bad enough shape. Don't make it worse." I sighed. I stood in the middle of the room, hands on hips. Someone had certainly performed a thorough search—but for what? And had they found whatever it was they'd been looking for?

"Er-OWL!"

I whirled around. Nick was squatted beside the bed, one claw caught on the mattress. I knelt down beside him and gently disengaged his paw. "Hey, I told you not to mess things up, didn't I?"

Nick's paw shot out, tapped the side of the mattress. I

saw a white edge peeping out from underneath it. I grasped the edge and pulled out a photograph. I crossed over to the desk, switched on the lamp, and studied it. It was of a group of girls, all wearing pink vests and white blouses, posing underneath a banner that read: WALK FOR BREAST CANCER. I squinted at the tiny faces. Yes, there was Daisy right in front, between a brunette and a red-head, and just behind her, a tall woman with light-colored hair, a turned-up nose, and a determined chin.

A girl I recognized from another photograph.

Alexa Martin.

I tapped the photo against my wrist. Well, here was surefire proof Daisy and Alexa Martin had indeed met, if not known each other. I squinted at the other girls' faces. It was possible one of them might be Doris Glea-son. I'd have to have Hank work that angle. I slipped the photo into my jeans pocket and shut off the desk lamp.

"Meower."

I peeped around the corner of the desk. My four-footed assistant was clawing madly at a threadbare section of the rug, threatening to put a huge hole in the cheap material. I knelt down and gently pulled him away.

"Nick, I know this place gives new meaning to the phrase *a holy mess*, but let's not destroy it any more than it has to be."

"Meower."

He clamped his paw down on a section of the rug. I leaned over for a closer look. A bit of the rug was curled up, revealing a small cavity underneath. I threw Nick a look, but he was sitting back on his haunches now, head cocked and looking supremely pleased with himself.

I touched the curled portion of the rug and it flapped back, revealing a small hole. Nick's paw darted out, and before I could do anything, he'd snagged an object that had been secreted in the hole and now clenched it tightly between his forepaws.

"What have you got there, buddy?"

Nick rolled over, loosening his grip on his prize. He looked at me almost expectantly as I picked it up.

It was a small, red leather pouch, tied with a drawstring. I took it back to the desk, sat down, and loosened the tie. Then I shook the pouch.

A large red stone tumbled out, making a small *clink* as it hit the desk's scarred surface.

I switched the desk lamp back on and held the stone up to the light. A few years ago I'd done a story on synthetic gemstones. Sophisticated technology today made it possible to manufacture stones that not only looked like the real thing, but were created using the same general process as that of Mother Nature. I turned this stone over in my hand. The two major categories of man-made stones were glass and synthetic, of which glass was easiest to recognize. It usually had little bubbles or scratches, and the cut often had a rounded edge. This stone had none of those, so I ruled out glass.

Determining if a stone was synthetic or real was a bit harder. I knew synthetic gems sometimes had a scissor cut in the shape of an X, and often little grooves. Real gems had what was called inclusions (internal air bubbles or cracks, if I recalled the interview correctly). Not being a jeweler or a certified gemologist, I couldn't make a call about this one. It did shine when I held it up to the light, but there were ways to make synthetics duplicate the luster of a real gem as well.

This was a call I couldn't make. I started to slip the stone back inside the pouch when my fingers touched something crinkly. I reached in and pulled out a small slip of paper. On it was printed:

318 4181516

I frowned. What did this number have to do with the stone? If it were a fake stone, maybe it was some sort of ID number. I slipped both back inside the pouch and tucked that in my purse, along with the photo, and then I stood up and looked over at Nick, sprawled in the corner near the bed.

"Well, Nick," I murmured. "Looks as if you're two for two tonight for valuable clues. Now we just need to figure out what they're clues to."

"*Er-ewl*," mewed Nick. His tail went straight up and his eyes gleamed in pure kitty satisfaction. The cat was good and he knew it, damn him.

"Okay, Sam Spade Junior. Let's get back home."

Nick suddenly tensed, tail straight, back hunched. His head swiveled toward the motel room door, and I heard a loud rumble, almost a *grr* sound, deep in his throat.

Someone was outside that door.

I tiptoed over to the window and moved the curtain a fraction so I could peep out. I could hear a gusty wind blowing, and I saw swirls of leaves flit across the parking lot. There were a few cars, including my own SUV, but not a sign of a human anywhere.

Nick had stopped growling, but he still paced to and fro in front of the door, keeping his eyes fixed firmly on it. I stepped away from the window and moved back to press my ear against the door. I listened for a few minutes, but no other sound reached my ears. I slid the safety chain into place and opened the door a crack, peering first right, then left.

Nothing. The walkway around the motel was deserted.

I opened the door, walked back to the bed, grabbed Nick, and then got out of there and over to my SUV as fast as my legs could move. As I put Nick in the passenger seat, I thought I saw out of the corner of my eye a shadow flit. I whirled around, but the parking lot appeared to be deserted. The only shadows I saw were those of the trees, their branches swaying in the late autumn wind.

Imagination. It's a wonderful thing, and the mainstay of every writer, but right now I had no time for it.

I buckled myself in, started up the car, and swung back out onto the main road. I could save time getting back to Hot Bread if I took a shortcut, a little-traveled road that ran along the coast. In the interest of time, I opted for that route. The road was narrow and quite dark, as there were no lights, and I sped rapidly along the road. I heard a sound beside me, and spared Nick a quick glance. He'd risen in the seat, hackles up, and his head was cocked to one side, listening. Since a cat's hearing is way more sensitive than ours, I didn't doubt for a second he'd heard something.

"Hey, relax, buddy," I said. "This is a shortcut. We'll be home before you can say 'Friskies'—say what?"

The car had come up from out of nowhere. I saw the lights in my rearview mirror and heard its motor gunning a second before the car's front fender connected with my rear one.

"Hey!" I shouted, gripping the wheel tighter. "What are you doing, you lunatic?"

I cast a quick glance out the window. The road wound along the coast, and there were no guardrails on this stretch. If the other car should bump me along the side, and run me off the road . . . well, there would be nowhere to run. It would be a good fifty-foot drop down into the raging waters of the Pacific.

"Hang on, Nick," I said through gritted teeth. "Fasten your seatbelt, buddy, it's gonna be a bumpy ride."

I slid a glance in the cat's direction. He had his head buried in my purse. "Don't worry, boy," I whispered. "I won't let this nut hurt us."

I pulled hard on the wheel and pushed my foot down on the accelerator, turning the car sharply to the left just as the car following me was about to smack my rear fender again. I made a swift one-hundred-eighty-degree turn and started racing down the road back the way I had originally come.

"I guess this shortcut wasn't such a hot idea," I ground

out. A quick glance in my rearview mirror showed the twin headlights boring down on us again. It closed the gap between us in record time. Now its grille was about ten feet away from my rear bumper.

I gritted my teeth and then a soft whirring sound made me look over. Nick had his paw down on the automatic window release and was lowering the passenger window. He had an object clenched between his teeth. The pouch!

"Nick! What in Hell—"

I slowed down just a fraction and Nick took that opportunity to leap out of the car. Headlights reflected in my rearview mirror blinded me for a second, and I gave the steering wheel a sharp twist to the right, sending my SUV up over a grassy knoll just as the other car whizzed past.

"Whew," I murmured, glancing over at the taillights of my pursuer as it vanished. "That was close—DARN!"

The tree loomed large in front of me. I pressed down hard on the brake, but it was too late. I braced myself as the hood of the SUV made contact with the tree, and the last thing I remembered was the airbag deploying and enveloping me as I slipped into unconsciousness . . .

SIXTEEN

"Nora? Hey, Nora!" A male voice cut through the haze of fog that enveloped my brain. "Twice in one night is a little much for this, don't you think?"

I winked one eye open. I saw the black, starless sky above me and cautiously moved one hand. I could feel a thin blanket beneath my body, and as my fingers explored further, felt a few rough blades of grass. I moved my head slightly to the left, caught an arrowed glimpse of Daniel's pale face as he checked my pulse.

I coughed. "Did anyone get the number of the tree that hit me?"

"Very funny." Daniel's voice was tinged with concern. "This could have been a lot worse, you know. You're lucky that Patty and Frank Saul were on their way back from spending an evening with his sister in St. Leo."

I turned my head slightly to the right. Off to the side of the knoll I saw a tan Cadillac, and leaning against it were the Sauls. The elderly couple were good customers of mine at Hot Bread, came in at least twice a week, and sometimes Frank made an extra stop if he was out that way walking his two dogs, Lois and Lola. I'd have to remember to give the Sauls lunch on the house the next time they stopped in. "Nice to see there are Good Samaritans left in the world."

"They saw you run off the road and called it right in. The minute I heard the description of the vehicle, I knew just who it was." He peered down at me. "You're a careful driver, that I know. Care to tell me what happened?"

I hesitated. This was the perfect opportunity to come clean with Daniel, to tell him everything, particularly about my motel break-in but . . . it all came back to the burden of proof. There was nothing concrete that indicated the stone I'd found had anything to do with Daisy's murder. For that matter, there was nothing to indicate that whoever had run me off the road was after the stone. It could just have been a careless or drunk driver, although deep down I didn't really believe that. No, best to wait a bit until I had everything sorted out. "I was minding my own business, just out for a little drive and I guess . . . I lost control of the car."

Daniel's lips were slashed in a straight line. "So a dark-colored sedan had nothing to do with this, eh?"

"A dark sedan?" I tried to sit up, discovered my head hurt like the dickens, and flopped back down on the grass again. "Where'd you get that from?"

"Both Frank and Patty say they saw one try to ram your rear fender before you took off up the hill." He put his thumb under my chin and raised my face to his. "It's two-thirty in the morning. You do remember promising me you were going to go straight home?"

"I promised to go straight home, and I did." I moved one arm down the length of my body, indicating my change of clothing. "I never said I'd stay there. I couldn't sleep. I thought a drive would help."

The pounding in my head stilled a bit, so I sat up again, this time successfully. I moved my hand, felt my rib cage gingerly. "Nothing seems to be broken but it sure hurts like hell. Bruised, most likely."

"Apparently you weren't going fast enough to cause too much damage to either yourself or your car," Daniel said dryly. "You're a bit banged and bruised but it's mostly from the airbag deployment. We'll get you checked out at the hospital, though, just to be on the safe side."

"No." I shook my head. "No hospitals. I hate them."

"Who likes 'em? I'm afraid, though, this isn't your call," he said firmly. "You're going."

I saw lights flash out of the corner of my eye. I turned my head and saw an ambulance making its way up the grassy knoll. I also saw a tow truck from Fagin's Garage preparing to hook my SUV to its back end.

"Your car doesn't appear to be too badly damaged," Daniel said in response to my unspoken question. "Really, Nora, you were very lucky."

"I've got nine lives, just like my cat." Which reminded me—where was Nick? I craned my neck, but didn't see him anywhere around. The last thing I remembered was his leaping out of the passenger side window . . . with the pouch. The photograph of Daisy and Alexa Martin, though, should still be in my purse. I started to rise, felt woozy, and dropped back down to the blanket. "I need to look in my purse," I murmured.

Daniel brushed the back of his hand against my cheek. "Why is it women always want a comb and mirror in a crisis? You look fine," he assured me.

"Not that," I croaked. "I don't care what I look like. I mean, I do, but . . . I just . . . need to see my purse."

Daniel straightened and said something to one of the EMTs. A few minutes later the guy returned with my black purse in tow. He handed it to Daniel, who dangled it in front of my eyes.

"Here it is, safe and sound. Feel better now?"

I reached out a hand. "Can I see it? I just need to make sure everything's still there."

"Do you mean this?" Daniel pulled an oblong object out of his pocket and held it up. My stomach lurched as I recognized Daisy's purloined motel room key.

"It was lying on the grass by the driver's door." Daniel waved it before me. "Am I correct in assuming your little nocturnal activities involved a visit to this room?"

"I can explain." I pressed a hand to my head. The little vein above my right eye was suddenly throbbing like a sonofabitch. "Just not right now."

Daniel slid the key into his jacket pocket. "Why do I have the feeling this key belonged to Daisy Martinelli?"

I swallowed. "I'll have to plead the Fifth right now."

"There is such a thing as interfering with a police investigation, you know. Particularly when it involves murder. Dammit, Nora." Daniel ran his hand through his hair. "Have you forgotten you were attacked tonight, in addition to being run off the road? Someone apparently thinks you're onto something."

"Yeah, well, then they know more than I do."

He ran his hand through his hair again, riffling the sides just a little, giving him that tousled, oh-so-sexy look that had attracted me to him from the get-go. "Don't think this is over. I've got a lot of questions for you, young lady."

"I might have a few for you, myself." I let out a shaky breath. "Did something happen with the grimoire tonight?"

He wagged his finger at me. "Don't try to change the subject."

"I'm not," I protested. "It's just that I can't help feeling the grimoire figures in this somehow. I'm just not sure how big a part it plays. As for why I had Daisy's key, I'll tell you. Violet asked for my help in tracking down her missing niece, and I have reason to believe Daisy knew more about that than she let on. I was hoping to get some more information out of her, but then she was murdered."

Daniel's brows knit together. "Violet has a niece?"

"Yes. And she asked me to keep all this confidential, so I really can't say any more without her permission."

Two EMTs rushed over just then and Daniel moved aside. "This conversation isn't over," he whispered in my ear. He glanced at the two attendants. "Take good care of her."

The bigger of the two bent over me, and I recognized

him—Mickey Dugan, who worked construction with his brother Harvey. He liked my *Thin Man Tuna Melts*, too.

"Mickey," I said. "You're an EMT volunteer?"

"Yep." He grinned at me. "This is my first night on the job, too. You're my first accident, Nora."

"Swell," I murmured. I pressed a hand to my temple. "Say, why is everything spinning?"

And then my world went black for the third time that night.

"Feeling better?"

"Not really." I groaned and threw my hand over my eyes to block the glare of fluorescent lights. I turned my head in the direction of the speaker. Samms was sitting in the chair next to my bed, thumbing idly through a magazine. "What," I croaked, "it's your turn to watch me again?"

"Someone obviously has to."

I swiped at my eyes. "How long have I been out?"

"A couple hours. You needed the rest." He set the magazine down and stood up, walked to the side of the bed. "You are a very lucky woman. Usually a vehicle rolls over upon the impact of hitting a tree. All you got was a crumpled hood and a deployed airbag, which probably kept you from being more severely injured. Instead of head or face injuries, or damage to your chest or pelvic areas, apparently all you got is a few bruised ribs."

"Yeah, well." I touched my side gingerly. "We Charles women come from tough stock."

He didn't answer, just gestured toward the foot of the bed, where a neatly folded pile of clothing rested. "Doc Morris says as soon as you feel well enough to walk, you can go home. You'll feel a bit banged up for a few days, but just stay on the medication"—he indicated a small bottle on a nearby table—"and you should be back to full speed in a few days."

I eyed him warily. "And you're here because?"

"I'm here to make sure you do just that. No more little side trips to motels, or nighttime sleuthing excursions."

"Daniel told you to do this."

"Daniel would have done it himself, only he's a tad preoccupied at the moment." He tilted his head. "I, ah, volunteered."

"You did? Well, wasn't that nice of you?"

"I thought it was the least I could do," he answered, "considering."

"Considering?"

Both corners of his lips turned up. "Our illustrious past, of course."

We were both silent for a long, awkward moment and then I huffed, "I thank you for your concern; however, I've no need of a babysitter."

"You sure about that, Red?"

In answer, I threw back my blankets and swung my feet over the side of the bed. An icy chill raced up and down my spine and across my back. I reached out, curled my fingers in the side of the bed for added support.

A nurse bustled in at that moment and took in the scene before her with a tight-lipped stare and hands fisted on ample hips. "Ms. Charles, you shouldn't be out of bed just yet. You're still sedated."

No shit. I sat down on the edge of the bed and took a few deep breaths. "I'll be fine," I ground out. I tossed Samms a significant look. "Some privacy to get dressed would be nice."

He tossed my look right back at me. "I'll be right outside this door. Don't even think of trying to sneak out of here without me."

Once he'd gone, I ripped off the hospital gown and reached for my clothes. A wave of dizziness swept over me, but I steeled myself and waited for it to pass. I caught a look at my naked body in the mirror on the back of the door and winced. Bruises the color of grapes were all over my sides and back. I had two gigantic elastic bandages wrapped around my rib cage. Other than that, it seemed to be business as usual. I slid my clothes on and banged open the door. Samms lounged against the far wall, arms crossed over his chest, a cocky grin on his face. I took a tentative step forward and felt my knees wobble. His hand shot out to steady me and I caught a flutter of . . . something; a spark as his hand brushed my arm. Instinctively, I pulled back. "I'm fine," I whispered.

He took a step back, almost as if my touch had burned him. "Okay. My car's out front. You're going home, and this time you're going to stay there." He offered me a lopsided grin. "Since your wheels are out of commission, chances of you making another nocturnal run are slim at best. Oh, and don't bother trying to enlist Chantal's aid. We've already read her the riot act of what will happen if she even tries to assist you in one of your cockamamie schemes."

I coughed. They were probably right. I still felt a bit woozy and my ribs hurt like all get out.

I fell slowly into step beside him. "How did Chantal sound? She wasn't too worried, I hope."

"You've got a real loyal friend there. She wanted to come right down and see how you were, and it took all my charm to convince her that wasn't necessary. She said that you shouldn't worry about opening Hot Bread, she'd take care of it, and stay as long as it takes."

I halted and stared at him. "As long as what takes? My recovery?"

"For you to explain to Daniel and me just what you were doing at the Cruz Motel last night—or should I say earlier this morning." He leaned toward me and said in a heavily accented voice, "And believe me, Lucy, you've got a lot of 'splaining to do."

My lips, probably the only spot on my body that didn't throb, twisted into a wry grin. "Your Spanish accent sucks."

He made a rumbling sound deep in his throat and turned his back. I couldn't help it; I gave into my inner fourteen year old and stuck my tongue out. My hand closed over my purse. I'd checked and the photo of Daisy and Alexa was still there, right where I'd put it. Maybe with a little luck I'd have some good answers before Daniel and Samms started their inquisition. I knew I couldn't hide anything from them for too long, nor did I want to.

Dawn was streaking the sky as Samms pulled up in front of my house. He cut the engine, and before you could say "Easter bunny," had hopped out of the car and come around to open the passenger door. I accepted his arm and let him lead me up the walkway to the rear entrance that led straight up to my apartment. I pulled my key out and turned to give him a tight smile.

"Thanks. I'll be fine now."

He shook his head. "Sorry. I'm seeing you upstairs."

"I'm fine, honest." I lifted first one leg and then the other. "See! And I don't feel a bit woozy." Well, that was a lie, but what the heck. It wouldn't be the first one I'd told.

He took the key from my hand. "All part of the job," he said. "Just making sure you don't have any unexpected visitors lying in wait for you. Besides, Daniel left me specific instructions."

"I'll bet," I murmured.

Samms started to fit the key into the lock and suddenly stopped, his heretofore pleasant expression turning into a deep frown. "You locked up before you left?" At my nod, he pointed to the lock. "It's been forced open. Looks like you've had some visitors."

Samms pushed the door open and we went into the small entryway. "Wait here," he whispered and then he was off, moving soundlessly up the stairs. He disappeared into my apartment and I leaned against the stair rail, my heart pounding. Five minutes passed, then ten, and I was just about to follow him upstairs when he poked his head out, wearing as grim an expression as I'd ever seen. He motioned to me with his hand. "Come on up."

I hurried up the stairs as fast as I could. When I reached the top I called out, "Where are you?"

"In your den."

I stopped dead on the den threshold. Every drawer in my desk had been removed and the contents scattered across my shag rug. The recliner lay on its side, and the cushions from my loveseat had been thrown carelessly in one corner. My laptop had been pushed off the desk but fortunately hadn't been smashed. DVDs and books had been pulled off the shelves and lay in assorted piles throughout the room.

"Take a look," Samms said tersely. "Can you tell if anything's missing?"

I swallowed. I had a good idea of what whoever had done this might be looking for, but I also didn't have the faintest idea if Nick was here, or if he'd brought the pouch with him. I moved slowly around the room and finally shook my head. "If anything was taken, I sure can't tell."

He snorted, and then we repeated the same procedure in my bedroom (where Samms got a good eyeful of my entire Victoria's Secret underwear collection thrown madly about) and the kitchen.

"Someone was definitely looking for something," Samms remarked. "Any idea what it might be?"

Once again, the perfect opportunity to come clean, and once again, I passed it up. "I didn't take a complete inventory, of course, but everything appears intact."

He looked at me for a long moment. "That's not what I asked."

"If I knew for certain what this person was after in my home, I'd tell you," I said. I brushed a hand across my eyes. "Do we have to call the police?"

His lips twigged upward. "Well, technically, I am the police so . . . no. I'll file the report. But you're going immediately to bed, right?"

"Right. My body aches too much to do otherwise."

He looked as if he didn't quite believe me, but in the end he left. Once he'd gone, I stripped off my clothes, pulled on my comfy pajamas, and went into my kitchen to make a cup of tea. I reached for the kettle and jumped as something warm and furry twined itself around my ankles.

"Nick," I cried. Even though it hurt to bend over I did it anyway, scooping the portly kitty into my arms and placing a big wet one on his cheek. "Goodness, I was worried about you. And thanks for taking off like that, bud, although I can understand why you did it. No sense in the two of us getting injured on the job. Did you see who did this?"

Nick looked at me, and then he gave an almost imperceptible shake of his head.

I buried my face in his ruff. "The important thing is you're all right. Did you bring the pouch back with you?"

Nick let out a plaintive meow and I set him back on the floor. He waddled into the den and into the farthest corner of the room, scrabbling at something just out of my range of vision with his paw. I walked over and saw him squatted in front of a small bookcase pushed up against the wall. His paw was wedged in a small opening between the two that couldn't have been more than a quarter inch. I bent over, gingerly of course, because my ribs still hurt like hell—and wiggled my hand in as far as it would go. I touched soft leather, and after a few minutes pulled out the pouch.

"I don't even want to know when you got here, or how you managed to hide this so our intruder didn't find it—but I'm glad you did. Now maybe we can start making some sense out of all of this. They've got to mean something for someone to try and run me off the road, but what? The sooner we find out, the sooner we can turn everything over to Daniel and Samms and let them worry about it."

The tea forgotten, I carried the pouch over to the desk and tipped it over. The gem and slip of paper spilled out onto my blotter. I pulled my laptop over and booted it up, then keyed in "synthetic gemstones." About two dozen sites came up. I clicked on one and then clicked on the tab marked "Physical Properties." I scanned the options, paying particular attention to the one titled "Allochromatic." It stated Allochromatic gems were susceptible to color enhancement or change, which might account for the odd black etchings I saw. I found another site that had color photos; however, none of them seemed to have those tiny black flecks in them. Perhaps the gem was defective? I picked up the slip of paper and studied the numbers—318 4181516. Maybe an item number? From where? I picked up my cell, dialed Hank. He answered on the first ring. I could tell from his brusque tone he was in the middle of something, so I asked him if he knew a good gemologist who could check something out. After he assured me he did, I took a photo of the gem and paper with my phone, emailed them to Hank, then replaced the actual items in the pouch. I slipped the pouch into the middle drawer of my desk, locked it, and then picked up a pad and pen. I eased myself gingerly into my recliner. Nick lofted himself up and arranged himself on the chair's arm.

"Ordinarily this would warrant dragging out the murder board, but since I'm not in top fighting shape"—I touched my rib cage lightly—"a pad and pen will have to do."

I balanced the pad on my lap. Across the top of the page I wrote:

Murder Victim: Daisy Martinelli

Possible Suspects:

Henri Reynaud

Magda

"Red Death" (Doris Gleason?)

Then beneath that I wrote:

Motives:

Reynaud got Daisy into Meecham, but she admitted the two of them butted heads. I heard them arguing twice. I saw Reynaud outside the locker room upstairs, with two stones that looked like the ones on the grimoire's cover. Question: Could Reynaud have been involved in the first theft attempt somehow, and did Daisy know about it? Was she blackmailing him? Did he make another attempt tonight, and did Daisy catch him? Was she murdered to shut her up? Were the stones Reynaud had the ones from the grimoire?

I frowned at my last entry. It was possible, I supposed, that Reynaud might have attempted another theft and been caught—it would account for the two stones I'd seen him with. But if Daisy had caught him in the room, why was she strangled in the basement? Of course, he could have moved the body . . . but why? After a minute I added:

Significance of stone I found in Daisy's motel room? Same color as stone in grimoire that Reynaud did not have—is there a reason? And what do those numbers found with the stone mean? Purple stone I found outside kitchen vanished from my pocket—how and why? Was that attack meant for someone else—or was it to retrieve that stone? (Which would mean my attack was premeditated)

I gave a little shudder and continued writing:

Magda and Daisy seemed to argue a lot. Magda is Reynaud's sister—could she be trying to protect him from Daisy? Possible she knows if Reynaud is the thief, or they could be in it together.

I chewed the top of my pen almost off before I wrote down my observations on my last suspect:

"The Red Death" aka "Woman in Red" aka Doris Gleason?

DG was a reporter for a London paper, and also worked briefly at the Meecham Foundation. Lived briefly across the hall from Alexa Martin before moving out and having her flat taken by Daisy Martinelli. Coincidence? Alexa and Doris both dropped out of sight at around the same time? Another coincidence? Daisy said she never met Alexa, yet some neighbors claimed they'd seen them speaking. I found that photograph of them at a Walk for Cancer benefit. Why would Daisy lie? Did she have some sort of evidence that tied Doris and Alexa to the grimoire theft?

Daisy hinted Violet would be best off not knowing the truth about her niece. Could Alexa and Doris have been involved in the grimoire theft together? Could Alexa have been injured . . . or killed?

Is the "Red Death" Doris Gleason? What were she and Daisy conspiring on?

I turned to see Nick watching me, his paws folded, head cocked. I set the pad and pen over to the side and tapped my knee.

"Let's try this on for size. What if Daisy were working with Doris Gleason on a story? What if there were more to that grimoire theft than meets the eye. What if . . ." My eyes strayed to the desk drawer. "What if Alexa did make off with something—not the grimoire, but—a red jewel? Maybe someone really did try to kill her!"

I frowned. Something about that stone was important, all right. Maybe even important enough to kill over. I thought again about the warning hissed in my ear the night of the gala—if the assailant was talking about the red stone, then they might have thought I was . . .

"Alexa Martin?" My eyes snapped wide. "Holy Hell, that would mean she's alive! And Daisy and Doris might be working with her to catch the real thief and protect her. If they know each other, they're all connected from somewhere, but where?"

Out of the corner of my eye I saw Nick hunker down next to an old chair. He stretched out on his side and, the next instant, began to bat cubelike shapes out from underneath the chair. I sighed. One never knew just where Nick hid his favorite plaything—Scrabble tiles—but you could always be certain they'd appear at the oddest times. I got up and moved closer; Nick saw me coming and rolled over so I could plainly see the three tiles he'd lined up:

Z, T, A.

I picked them up, laid them across my palm. "Wow, Nick. You've really hit the jackpot with these. They don't even spell out a decent word."

He shot me what I imagined was the cat version of an indolent stare. *"Merow."*

"It might make sense to you, Bud, but it's Greek to me."

Nick got to his feet, laid a paw on my leg.

"Don't tell me you understand Greek," I said, and suddenly it was as if the proverbial light bulb went on over my head. "Nick! You really are trying to tell me something, aren't you? This isn't meant to be a word, is it?"

"Merow," he purred, then pointed his paw straight at my laptop. I hurried over, booted it up. Once it came on, I called up Google and did a quick search. A few minutes later, I leaned back in my chair.

Zeta Tau Alpha
Zeta Tau Alpha is a nationally recognized sorority. Their motto is *Love, the greatest of all things.*
Zeta is very involved in charitable organizations, and often inducts honorary members into its ranks, usually women active in breast cancer research and awareness, philanthropy . . .

I went over to my tote, pulled out the photo and the small pink ribbon pin I'd snatched from Daisy's purse, and turned them over in my hand.

I fished my cell out of my purse and punched in Hank's number again; this time I got his voice mail. I left a message for him to do some digging to find out if Daisy Martinelli, Alexa Martin, and Doris Gleason might all have been made honorary members of Zeta Tau Alpha. Not leaving anything to chance, I texted him the same message.

Nick crawled onto my lap, and I stroked his glossy black fur. "You and those tiles came through again," I said. "After all, as Hank himself had pointed out, fraternity—and sorority—members stuck together like glue, through thick and thin, no matter what. Even through theft . . . and murder."

"Merow." Nick said.

SEVENTEEN

"**M**er-oow!"

I yawned and winked one eye open. Nick was sprawled on my chest, his golden eyes wide. "*Merow*," he said again.

"Yeah, and good morning to you, too," I grumbled. After texting Hank, I'd immediately gone to bed and crashed, fully intending to get about two hours of shut-eye before going downstairs to open up Hot Bread. I turned my head slightly and glanced at the clock on my bedside table and nearly had a stroke. It was eleven-thirty!

"Gosh Nick," I cried. "Why'd you let me sleep so late?" Usually my feline wants his breakfast first thing, regardless of how late I may have stayed up the night before, and he makes his feelings known by knocking off every article on my dresser. "Why didn't you get me up?"

"Probably because I fed him very early."

I glanced toward my doorway. Chantal stood there, dangling the house key I'd given her in the air. "Both Samms and Daniel called me and told me to watch out for you today. I also straightened up a lot of the mess."

"How nice of them, but I'm fine . . . ow!" I gave Nick a gentle push off my tummy and threw off the comforter. My whole body felt as if I'd been run over by a steamroller. "Ooh, dammit. The doctor said the soreness should have worn off by now."

Chantal eyed me. "You didn't get much sleep, did you?"

I rubbed at my back. "I got more than I intended." I cast my friend a sideways glance. "Say, if you're up here—who's minding the store? Mollie had the day off."

Chantal came over and perched herself on the edge of the bed. "Do not get mad, *chérie*. I made an executive decision. I closed Hot Bread for the day."

I struggled to sit up. "You what?"

"You heard me." Both of Chantal's hands flew up in the air. "Ach, *chérie*, sometimes you can be so stubborn! How do you expect to get back into shape if you do not get proper rest?"

My lips twisted in a rueful grin. "As we both know, I stink at resting. I'm better off when I'm active."

"This is true, but you've been through a lot. Your customers will understand."

"Yeah, the Java Nut will be happy," I grumbled. "They'll get all the fallout business."

"And after going there, your customers will appreciate your good cooking all the more." Chantal gave me a little push into a chair. "Sit back, relax, and I will make you a nice breakfast. Or a lunch. Whichever you prefer."

Both my eyebrows wafted skyward. "You who hate to cook will make me breakfast? Did I hear right?"

"For you I would make the ultimate sacrifice." She put a finger to her chin, tapped it lightly. "How about some scrambled eggs?"

I stared at her. "When did you learn to make scrambled eggs?"

"I haven't," she responded cheerfully. "But I have seen you and Remy make them. How hard can it be?"

I couldn't help but be touched by her offer. For Chantal, standing over a hot stove was tantamount to having one's nails ripped out. "I appreciate the gesture, but I can do it." I held up my hand as my friend started to protest. "After all, I'd planned on opening up today anyway. It doesn't take much to whip up omelets, and I promise I'll just sit and relax with you after I make breakfast."

"Deal." She tossed me a wink over her shoulder as she started for the door. "Besides, you owe me details of all that happened last night. I am anxious to hear about your near brush with death."

"It wasn't a near brush; it was just a little accident."

"Oh, I'd hardly call it that," came a voice from the hallway.

I looked sharply at my friend. "Oh no. Is that who I think it is?"

"Samms. Yes. Daniel is here, too," Chantal said with a sheepish grin. "I told them to wait in the living room and I would see if you were up to visitors."

I sighed. Knowing Samms and Daniel, I was positive that both of them would camp out in my apartment until I was able to talk to them. I sucked in my breath and swung my feet to the floor.

"Fine. Show 'em into the kitchen. Guess it's Spanish omelets for four."

Twenty minutes later Samms and Daniel were settled at my kitchen table, both pairs of eyes trained on me as I cracked eggs into a large mixing bowl and added a splash of milk. I whisked them thoroughly, then walked over to the stove where I'd put the skillet on low. "To what do I owe the pleasure of this early morning visit, might I ask?"

Daniel's sharp gaze raked me head to toe. "You still look bushed. Did you get any rest at all, or were those brain cells firing up all night long?" he asked.

"I got some sleep," I admitted. "You two really didn't have to come over here to check up on me."

"That's not the only reason for our visit," said Daniel. "We have things to discuss."

I had put peppers, onions, scallions, and ham into the skillet while we were talking and now added the beaten eggs. "Okay. Like what?"

"Like if you've got any idea who might have been behind that attempt on your life last night," Samms said.

My head jerked up. "We don't know for sure that it was an attempt on my life."

"True," Daniel said slowly, "but it appears logical, considering you were attacked twice in one night."

"The first time was a mistake," I said. "I'm positive my attacker thought I was someone else. For that matter, how do we know that wasn't the case with the car as well?"

Samms arched a brow. "We don't. But we would like to know just what you were doing at that motel."

I've always found the best defense against a direct question one does not want to answer is to regale one's questioners with direct questions they might not want to answer. "Didn't the police do their own sweep of Daisy's room?" I asked.

"Of course, Broncelli sent a team out there. Unfortunately, too late to catch you doing your little B and E act."

"I don't believe you can call it a B and E when you have the key."

"You can when the key isn't obtained by legal means."

I stared at Samms, my nostrils flaring; he stared back at me with equal fervor. This little contest might have continued had it not been for the spitting and crackling of my omelet. I whisked the pan off the stove and started dividing the fluffy mixture on four plates. Chantal had toasted English muffins and put on a pot of coffee while I was cooking, and we all sat down, breakfast in front of us. Only thing was, I had no appetite, and looking at the others' faces, I doubted they did, either. Nick lofted his portly body up onto the counter, where he stretched out and lay, head lolling over the side, his gaze fixed on my two callers. The silence in the room was so thick you could cut it with a knife, and then Daniel cleared his throat.

"Okay, Nora. Enough's enough. We want to know why you decided to investigate Daisy's motel room instead of going home as you promised you would."

I traced the outline of the floral design on my table-cloth with the edge of my nail, wondering how long I could stall. Judging from the granite-hard expressions on the faces of my callers, not long indeed. "I don't suppose pleading the Fifth will satisfy you two?"

Stony silence. Guess not.

"Okay, well." I tapped the rim of my mug with my spoon. "I was just following my gut. I had a feeling Daisy wasn't being completely honest when I questioned her and she said she didn't know anything about . . . another matter."

"You're talking about your looking into Violet's niece's disappearance," Samms said.

I turned to glare at Daniel. "You told him?"

"Yes, he told me. We're partners, working together. That's what partners do." Samms leaned forward. "You seem to forget, you are not a licensed investigator. You're not even an investigative reporter anymore. You're a sandwich shop owner, Nora. Don't you think you should start acting like one?"

I leaned forward. "Violet asked for my help. I didn't just arbitrarily get involved. I don't feel comfortable talking about it, not just because I promised Violet I'd keep a low profile but also because I really have no proof of anything. Just theories."

Samms muttered something very ungentlemanly and sat back in his chair.

I turned to Daniel. "I didn't say anything to you because there was no ID in the purse where I found the key, and I wasn't even certain it was Daisy's. And that's the truth." I waited a few seconds and when neither of them spoke, I continued. "The room was a mess when I got there. Clothes were strewn everywhere, drawers were pulled out, the mattress was upended . . ."

"We saw the photos," Samms interrupted. "So there was nothing of interest?"

I hesitated only a brief moment before shaking my head. "No."

Samms leaned forward. "As a former crime reporter, I'm certain you're aware of the term *spoliation of evidence*?"

I certainly was. Spoliation of evidence referred to the intentional, reckless, or negligent withholding, hiding, altering, or destruction of evidence relevant to a legal proceeding. I looked Samms straight in the eye. "I am. I'm also aware that the theory of the spoliation inference is that when a party destroys or withholds evidence, it's a reasonable assumption said party has a 'consciousness of guilt' or other motivation to tamper with said evidence."

He steepled his fingers beneath his chin. "So you're basically claiming ignorance?"

"I'm saying that if I found anything, and I'm not saying that I did, but if that were the case, in order to be guilty of spoliation of evidence, I'd have to be positive that it was evidence of a crime."

Samms leaned back. "Well said. When did you get a law degree?"

I opened my mouth, ready to let him have it but good, but Daniel laid a hand on my arm. "Okay you two. Lee's right, Nora. You aren't a trained investigator. You put yourself in danger with that fool stunt, and our investigation at risk."

"And I am sorry. I was just trying to find some confirmation that she knew Alexa Martin a lot better than she claimed—that's it. Believe me, if I thought that I knew anything that definitely pertained to Daisy's murder, I wouldn't hesitate to share it with you." As a swift glance passed between them, I frowned. "Can I say the same for you? Are you keeping something from me?"

"Now how could the FBI keep something from Cruz's own Nancy Drew?" sneered Samms.

I curled the fingers of my left hand around my right wrist, stifling the urge to slap him. Before they could steer the conversation back to what I did or didn't find in Daisy's room, I asked, "What happened with the grimoire last night, and don't tell me nothing did. I saw the two of you and Broncelli and some other policemen huddled in front of that room right before I found Daisy's body."

They exchanged a quick look and then Daniel said, "We're not sure what happened. The alarm went off, but when we went to the room, it didn't seem as if anything was disturbed."

"Everything was intact? Were the jewels in the cover?"

"Yes." Samms picked up his knife, tapped it on the tablecloth. "Why are you so interested in the jewels?"

I shrugged. "Those stones are supposed to have this mystical power, right? They might be what a thief would want, and not the grimoire itself."

"One would need the grimoire, though, for its spells,"

Chantal piped up, and shut her mouth abruptly as I shot her a look over my shoulder.

"Spells would only be good if the thief were a witch, or a warlock," I said. "And there are none of those around Cruz, or at least none we know of."

"It's a moot point," Daniel said, a little too quickly, I thought. "The guard on duty left his post very briefly. He claimed he got a text from Broncelli telling him to meet him down the north corridor. He was gone less than five minutes. And, of course, Broncelli didn't send the text."

"Hm. Interesting." I pushed my chair back, carried my mug to the sink. "And that was right around the time I found Daisy's body, right?"

"More around the time you texted for help. We're not entirely certain the two incidents are related," Daniel said. He leaned forward and touched my arm. "Listen, Nora . . . Several people did say they saw you having some heated discussions with Daisy last night. So Broncelli . . ." He paused, looked at me, then at Samms. Samms gave an almost imperceptible nod, and Daniel finished. "Broncelli has you on a short list."

For a second I just stared at them, and then I burst out laughing. "You're kidding, right? Getting me back for not keeping my promise to stay home last night? Broncelli can't possibly be serious?"

Daniel looked decidedly uncomfortable. "Yes and no."

My legs were a bit wobbly and threatened to go out from under me, so I flopped back into my chair. "And just what does that mean?"

Daniel leaned forward and took both my hands in his.

"It means that Broncelli doesn't know you like we do. He's just going by what he hears, and he's got to go through the normal process. We've got to find people who might have had a motive for eliminating Daisy, and several witnesses said they saw you two arguing."

"Daisy argued with other people, too," I cried. "She argued with Reynaud, and Magda."

"That is true." Chantal nodded. "Even Nellie Blanchard was giving her dagger looks all night." At Samms's questioning look she added, "She's a museum docent. She's been there forever. She wanted that job as Violet's admin, but Violet gave it to Daisy."

Samms snorted, a clear indication he didn't think very much of it. "Anyone else you can think of?"

I hesitated. "She did argue with someone else. That woman in the red costume, the one I called the Red Death. They had a pretty violent one in the kitchen, right before I was attacked."

Daniel fixed me with his FBI stare. "And you have no idea at all who this 'Red Death' woman might be?"

I pursed my lips. "At the moment, no, I don't."

Daniel studied me a long minute, then looked at Samms. "We can go through the guest list with Nan Webb. She's got a pretty good eye and knows most of the people who were there, so maybe she'll be able to shed some light

I relaxed a bit. This would stall them for a while, or at least until they figured out the Red Death wasn't on the guest list, which I was pretty positive she wasn't. No doubt Daisy had snuck her in.

Samms's voice broke into my thoughts. "So, Nora, care to tell us just what you and the victim were arguing about?"

Rats. "We weren't arguing," I said. "It was more like a spirited discussion. I wanted to find out what she knew about Alexa Martin, and she kept saying she didn't know anything."

"But you kept at her," Samms persisted. "Why? Did you have some reason to think otherwise?"

I rubbed at the base of my neck, debating how best to answer, when a sudden thought occurred to me. "Did anyone ever find that other cat? The orange and white one that was in the basement with Nick?"

Daniel shook his head. "No. To be honest, we didn't expect to. It was probably just a stray that wandered in, same as your cat, and it probably took off just as soon as it got a chance."

"I think it might be Daisy's cat—I found cat food in her motel room. Or rather, Nick found it."

"Your cat went with you? I should have known," Samms said with a grunt. "It's a wonder the two of you didn't find another corpse."

"Ha, ha. Very funny."

Daniel rose. "Okay, we're going to let you get some rest. But please, Nora, no more investigating on your own. If you should come into any information that's germane to the case, I want you to come to either me or Lee, understood? If you try to pull any more stunts on your own, I can't promise you that Lee or I will be able to protect you."

I nodded. "I understand."

I walked them both to the door, and was just about to shut it behind them when Samms paused.

"Oh, and Red? This goes without saying but . . . don't leave town. You're on the suspect list, remember."

I couldn't help it. I stuck my tongue out and let the door slam . . . hard.

EIGHTEEN

I spent the rest of Monday in bed, and woke up Tuesday morning feeling a whole lot less sore and more invigorated. Chantal had posted a sign that Hot Bread would open up at eleven, but it was more like quarter of when I opened the door to a long line of people, all of whom expressed concern over Sunday's events.

"Are you doing all right?" asked Ginger Bibavich, a short girl with a Dolly Parton–style hairdo and the chest to match, who ran the nail salon. "We heard about your accident."

I gritted my teeth. "Don't believe everything you hear, Ginger. I'm fine. Don't I look fine?"

She peered at me through about six coats of mascara. "Well, sort of. You do look pale and tired. But I guess that's to be expected after all. I mean, finding a dead body alone . . . Girl, I wouldn't blame you if you closed for a week."

"Oh, heck," mumbled Stan Bivan, who owned Cruz Hardware. His craggy features were twisted in a scowl; no doubt he was still annoyed he'd had to get his customary plain bagel and coffee from Java Nut, where they charged him fifty cents more and gave him smaller portions. "Nora ought to be used to finding dead bodies by now, right?"

More teeth gritting. If this kept up I was going to have to pay Ed Levey the painless dentist a visit. "I'm fine, really. But thank you all for your concern."

Ginger beamed at me. "Man, you must be made out of iron, girl! You are one tough cookie, that's for sure."

Stan snorted. "Yeah, real tough. Now can I get an *Oliver Twist* on rye?"

What can I say? It's nice to be loved.

By one thirty the lunch crowd had dispersed and there were only a few stragglers remaining, regulars who liked to linger over coffee before trudging back to their jobs. I poured coffee into two large mugs for both Chantal and myself and we settled down at the wide counter in the kitchen area. I chose a stool that faced the counter and door, so I could see if any more customers came in. Chantal perched on a stool nearer the refrigerator and tossed a bit of ham down to Nick, who'd been scoffing up samples all afternoon. He took his prize over to his appointed place in front of the refrigerator and settled down for a nosh.

"Do you think they will find this woman, this one you've labeled the Red Death?" Chantal asked.

I took a sip of my coffee. "That's a good question. She's certainly managed to be elusive so far."

"Do you think she is the one who murdered Daisy?"

I shook my head. "No, I don't. If anything I think the real murderer is trying to make it look that way."

She leaned forward and whispered, "What did you find, *chérie*? It had to be something incriminating to make someone try to run you off the road."

I nibbled at my lower lip. "I'd rather not say just yet. I need to get a few things confirmed first. Right now I have no proof that it's connected to Daisy's death, and to be honest, I don't want to put anyone else in danger."

Both Chantal's brows shot up. "You think the killer wants whatever it is you took, don't you?"

I nodded. "Yes, I do. I'm just not quite sure why yet, though." I scrunched up my lips in thought. "It's all connected somehow. Alexa Martin, Daisy, Doris Gleason, and the two attempts to steal the grimoire. There's a common thread that links them all. I just can't see it yet."

Nick hopped up on the counter, swished his tail in my face. "*Er-ewl*," he mewled.

Chantal chucked the cat under his chin. "If Nicky could talk, I bet he'd have some good ideas."

"He has plenty of good ideas without talking," I admitted. "He communicates very well, for a cat."

Nick lifted his head and blinked twice. He inclined his head toward my cell phone. Almost at once it chirped. I had a text message.

"Damn cat's a bit psychic, too. Spooky," I said. I

picked up the phone and looked at the text. I was hoping it might be from Hank, but it was from Ollie.

Lab results back. Bingo! Positive. Card was written by N.

I stared at the message for a few moments. "Well, what do you know?" I held the phone out to Chantal. "The lab says that second card is in Nick Atkins's handwriting."

"Oh my." Chantal glanced at Nick, then back at me. "So that means he's alive?"

"Maybe. Or maybe he'd prearranged to have those cards sent. But somehow I don't think so. I do think he's alive. He's just . . . missing, for some reason."

"A case?"

I rubbed at my mouth. "Not sure. There's something else I've got to do. Bronson Pichard told me that Atkins's ex-girlfriend, Angelique Martone, might have a handle on what happened to him. I've got to track her down, too. I just got sidetracked with Violet and Alexa Martin. But now that I know at least one postcard was definitely written by Nick, finding Angelique gets bumped up the food chain."

Chantal threw up her hands. "I do not envy you, *chérie*. You are trying to solve Daisy's murder and find Violet's niece, and now Nick Atkins's ex-lover, all at the same time. That's a very ambitious schedule."

"Yeah, but we can handle it. Right, Nick?"

The cat opened his mouth, affording me an excellent

view of his red tongue and sharp, white fangs. Then he flicked his tail and proceeded to give it a good washing.

So much for teamwork.

When three o'clock rolled around I closed and locked the door, and Chantal hurried off to her shift at Poppies. I cleaned up and then went upstairs. No sooner had I stepped into my den than my cell chirped. I pulled it out of my pocket and flipped it open.

"Thank God you answered," Hank said. "What I've got for you is definitely for your ears only. It's too much for a text, and I didn't want to have to leave a voice message."

Wow, that sounded promising. I kicked off my shoes and flopped in the recliner. "Great. I hope this news is good."

"I hope so, too." He chuckled. "I still can't believe they'd put you on a short suspect list."

I was tempted to ask Hank how he'd heard, but then thought better of it. Hank had many sources, and not even the threat of Chinese water torture would make him reveal them. In my reporting days, Hank had been one of my CIs and had come through for me more than once. Honestly, I didn't much care how he found out his information, just that it was accurate. He hadn't failed me yet.

"Okay. Cheer me up. What have you got?"

"You may have stirred up something with that gem."

I gripped the phone a bit more tightly. "Yeah? How so?"

"Well, it definitely is a synthetic gem, according to my

source, but what's really interesting to him are those odd markings. He said he can't be sure without actually seeing the stone but he said it looked like some sort of encryption."

I hadn't been expecting that. "You mean a code?"

"He couldn't say. Once again, he'd have to actually see the stone, but he did sound a bit concerned. It was all I could do to talk him into staying quiet about it. Nora, what have you gotten yourself into?"

Now there was a million-dollar question. "What about the numbers?"

"Well, he checked and said it definitely wasn't a number for the gem. Most registrations start with a letter, and they have less numbers. He thought it might be some sort of numeric code." He was quiet a minute, then said, "Okay, on to to the rest of it. Apparently Ms. Gleason had a talent for undercover work. She broke one honey of a story months before, involving someone you're familiar with. I refer to Bronson A. Pichard's involvement in art smuggling. That story was one of the main reasons he decided to come back to the US of A. In addition, my source got it on a very confidential basis that Ms. Gleason was now working on another undercover story, one dealing with state secrets and international espionage. She was working with the full cooperation of Sir Rodney Meecham, who, it turns out, has ties to Scotland Yard."

I let out a low whistle. "That would certainly lend itself to a disappearing act, all right."

"There's more, though. The timeline on our friend Daisy Martinelli indicates that she showed up to move into Doris's apartment exactly one week after Doris went missing. Now, I checked into your sorority angle. You were right. Doris Gleason and Alexa Martin are registered honorary members of Zeta Tau Alpha."

Disappointment arrowed through me. "Just Doris and Alexa? Not Daisy?"

"I didn't say that." He cleared his throat. "Some of the girls called Doris *Dee* or *Deedee*, because she used her full name when she registered. Doris Daisy Gleason."

I let out a low whistle. "I never thought of that angle," I confessed. "That Doris and Daisy might be the same person, but it does explain some things."

"If you liked that, you're gonna love this." Hank's voice held that little note of glee he got when he stumbled upon something really, really unique. "I sent the photo of Angelique you sent me to my guy in New Orleans. He called in a few favors, and finally managed to locate someone who could positively identify her."

"Great," I cried. Finally, a break with something! "So where is she now? Did that person know?"

Hank clucked his tongue. "Let me finish, little grasshopper. I said she was identified all right but not as Angelique Martone.

"She was ID'd as . . . Alexa Martin."

NINETEEN

"So, Angelique, the woman of mystery my partner Nick was head over heels over, and Alexa Martin, the mousy niece of your museum director Violet Crenshaw, are the same person? I always knew that girl was hiding something!"

Ollie sat in my den, a cup of Newman's Own Nell's Breakfast Blend in one hand, and drummed the fingers of the other on the arm of my recliner. He'd popped in right after I'd hung up from Hank, and I, still being a bit shell-shocked by the news, had commandeered him at once. I'd put on a pot of coffee and filled him in on all the latest events, from finding Daisy's body right up to my and Nick's motel-breaking, saving the revelation about Angelique/Alexa—the best, if you will—for last. When I'd delivered the news he'd clutched at his chest, and for a minute I feared he might have a heart attack. Fortunately, it turned out to be gas. Ollie's had one too many Italian hot dogs for lunch.

Ollie glanced over at the photographs of Angelique and Alexa, which I'd laid out on my desk. "That's quite a transformation," he observed. "Alexa is far from ugly, of course, but she's very plain. Angelique, on the other hand, is glamour personified. This is indeed a transformation worthy of Professor Henry Higgins."

I eased myself into the loveseat opposite Ollie, both hands wrapped around my own steaming mug of coffee. "It might not be as amazing as we think. Hank told me Alexa was a Theatre Arts minor and worked in the makeup department of her college's regional theatre group. They won first place in a regional competition for makeup for a performance of *The Wiz*, and Alexa chaired that committee."

I leaned across the table to peer at the photos. I could see the similarities now. The shape of the face, the eyes, the way they tilted their head. The same girl, and yet not the same, thanks to the wonder of Mally and Laura Geller cosmetics, a box of Clairol, and a skilled hand. A *very* skilled hand. She would also have been very adept at making subtle changes in Doris's/Daisy's appearance, too, if necessary for their charade.

Ollie took a sip of his coffee. "When did she change her name? Do we know?"

"I'm betting it was right after that first grimoire incident. Alexa Martin dropped out of sight after that and we know she went by Angelique Martone when she was here in

Cruz." I snapped my fingers. "No wonder Daniel had such a reaction when I showed him that photo. He probably knows her as Alexa Martin, too."

Ollie arched an eyebrow. "If Daniel knows her as Alexa, that can't be good. It must mean Alexa is involved in something the FBI is working on. If Daniel's investigating her, it's got to be something big. And I mean real big."

"I'm convinced Alexa was involved with that theft in London, and that she was either shot for real or it was a story designed to make certain people think she might have been killed." I tapped my finger against my chin. "I think Alexa didn't just randomly go to London. I think she went there because Doris was working on a story that involved international espionage, and she needed help only Alexa could provide."

Ollie frowned. "I don't follow."

"Long story short, Doris needed Alexa to steal something."

"Ah." His expression cleared. "The grimoire?"

"More likely something from the grimoire." I leaned closer to Ollie. "I keep thinking about Nick Atkins and his reaction to the letter he received, about not being able to trust beautiful women. His reaction seemed rather extreme." I rubbed at my forehead with the tips of my fingers. "I think that letter revealed that Angelique was really Alexa."

"Hm." Ollie's eyes slitted. "Maybe."

"You don't agree?"

"It's just that his reaction seemed a bit extreme for a mere name change. There's got to be more to it."

"I agree." I narrowed my own eyes. "I don't think Nick was upset over the fact that Alexa had changed her identity to Angelique. I think he was upset over *why* she changed it. Why do people change their names, Ollie?"

He laced his hands behind his neck and closed his eyes for a few seconds. When he opened them he said, "Well, sometimes it's just because they don't like their birth name; other times, it's for professional reasons, you know, like Archibald Leach becoming Cary Grant or Lucille LeSueur becoming Joan Crawford. Then again . . ."

"It could be because they've got something to hide, or they want to hide," I finished. "Let's take it one step at a time. What could Alexa Martin want to hide?"

"Her father was a convicted thief, right? Plus, you said Daisy intimated Violet might be less than thrilled with her niece. A criminal record, perhaps?"

"Hank checked. She had a few minor skirmishes when she was a kid, but I wouldn't call lifting a pack of Twizzlers a criminal record. That's not to say, though, that's all she ever stole; it just means she was good enough to not get caught. Still, I'm leaning toward option number two. I think she changed her name to hide from someone."

"Who? Her aunt?"

"No. Someone who wants what she took from the Foundation that night. The red stone from the grimoire's cover."

Ollie's eyes widened just a tad. "And that figures into international espionage . . . how?"

I sighed. "I know it sounds whacked. That's why I didn't want to mention any of this to Daniel or Samms, at least not yet. It's just a theory and not a very good one. But take a look at this."

I went over to my desk, unlocked the middle drawer, and pulled out the pouch. I shook out the gem and held it up.

"Wow," Ollie said. "That's some big garnet, or is it a ruby? I can never tell."

"Neither. It's synthetic," I said.

Ollie's brows drew together. "The stones in the grimoire are synthetic?"

"I think the original stones were substituted with synthetic stones. I found this in Daisy's hotel room. I think this was stolen by Alexa during the attempt in London, and another stone put in its place."

Ollie shook his head. "But why?"

I walked over and dropped the gem into Ollie's hand. "Take a good look at the stone. See anything strange about it?"

Ollie held the gem at arm's length, and then brought it almost right up to his face. He squinted at it this way and that, and finally handed it back to me. "It looks almost like there are little black squiggles on the surface, but I couldn't tell you what in heck those lines represent."

"I know. It's very odd."

We heard a slight noise from the wall unit behind us and glanced upward to see Nick, squatting his portly body across the top shelf that held my DVD collection. He swiveled his head to look at us. *"Meower."*

"No movies, Nick," I said. A few seconds later, Ollie and I jumped back as half a dozen DVDs rained down on the desk. "Geez, Nick," I grumbled as I started to pick them up. "What part of 'no movies' did you not understand?"

A plaintive *merow* from the shelf above answered me. "Spoiled kitty," I muttered. "No movies for a week, Nick." I started to sweep the DVDs into a pile, stopped as the one on top caught my eye. Ollie saw the title and chuckled.

"*Diamonds Are Forever*. So, little Nick is a James Bond fan, eh?" He reached out and took the DVD, turned it over in his hand. "This was one of Nick Atkins's favorites, too. If I remember correctly, Bond impersonated a diamond smuggler to infiltrate a smuggling ring, and went toe to toe with Blofeld to use the diamonds to build a giant laser. It had great scenery in it, too." He smacked his lips. "Lana Wood and Jill St. John . . ."

"Whoa." I held up my hand. "Back it up a bit. They wanted to build a giant what?"

"Laser."

I turned the disk over in my hand. "I remember a friend of mine did a story once about a laser that could write on plastic and other synthetic material."

Ollie stared at me for a few moments, and then as the import of what I was saying dawned on him, his lips formed a perfect O. "You think there's laser writing on that stone. But what?"

"I'm not sure. But whatever it is, it's something people might kill over."

Nick chose that moment to loft himself down from the shelf, land on the desk, sit back on his haunches, and warble a loud "*Merow*."

"I think he's trying to tell us something," Ollie said.

I set the DVD down. "I think he just did." I grinned at the cat. "Okay, buddy. Movie night's back on." To Ollie I said, "I think there's only one way to get to the bottom of this. It's time I consulted with the only person I can think of who might be able to give us some of the answers we need to untangle this mess."

Ollie goggled at me. "And who might that be?"

"The person who steered me toward Angelique in the first place. Wish me luck, Ollie. I'm going to prison."

TWENTY

"**T**hanks for coming through with that paperwork, Louis. I really appreciate this."

It was two days later, and I was in the passenger seat of Louis Blondell's Ford Ranger, on our way to the prison where Bronson A. Pichard was incarcerated. I'd wasted no time once Ollie had left in calling Louis and explaining to him that I needed to visit the cad in prison as part of this great story I was working on for *Noir* (a little white lie, but hey—if it got the job done, why not?). As I expected, he couldn't pass up the opportunity for a circulation-boosting story, so he used some of his "pull" (even I was astounded by the amount of pull he seemed to have) to get the normal application for visiting privileges waived.

"It helps to not have a criminal record," he joked as

we made the turn off the interstate highway onto the exit for the prison. "And, of course, your sister's was expunged by virtue of the fact Pichard committed the murder she was arrested for. That might have been a bit of a sticky point, you know. Victims of the inmate's crime are generally disallowed visiting privileges."

"Yeah, well, I wasn't the victim. Lacey was."

"Still, you were instrumental in his arrest. Anyway, there's one big thing in your favor. Pichard approved your visit."

I sat back against the leather seat. That in itself spoke volumes. That and the fact Pichard was the one who'd sent me after Angelique in the first place.

How much did he know? I was convinced he knew a lot more than he'd previously let on, and by God, before this visit was over I was going to pry every last bit out of him.

"Nora Charles. My dear, this is indeed a pleasure."

I'm no stranger to visiting people in prison. I'd conducted many interviews at the Metropolitan Correctional Center in Chicago, and I'd recently visited my own sister in jail. I can't say, however, it prepared me in any way for this sojourn to San Quentin to visit Pichard. For one thing, San Quentin doesn't mess around. This facility is the oldest prison in the state of California, but also one of the toughest. It was formerly the home to California's only gas chamber and death row, until that was ruled a "cruel and unusual punishment" in 1995 and switched to lethal injection. It has an estimated worth of over $100 million, thanks to its prime location on Bay Area real estate. With its own ZIP code and large population of hard criminals, San Quentin has become one of the most feared incarceration facilities on the West Coast.

I had the feeling Bronson A. Pichard would have been insulted had he been incarcerated anywhere else. He probably got some kind of perverse thrill at being housed in the same institution that had been home to such notables as Charles Manson, Randy Kraft, better known as the Scorecard Killer, and Richard Chase, the "Vampire of Sacramento," just to name a few.

I was positive a man as conceited as Pichard undoubtedly felt right at home, which might only aid my mission. If he felt relaxed, he might be more inclined to part with some information—information I was convinced he had, in spades.

The visiting procedure was just like they show in all those prison movies, or at least fairly accurate. I went through a search, and then was escorted to a room where I sat on one side of a glass wall. The prisoner was escorted in. He didn't look much different from the last time I'd seen him—of course then, I'd thought his name was Armand Foxworthy and I'd been on the wrong end of his gun. He sat down in the chair, picked up the telephone, and motioned for me to do the same. The tinny reception didn't disguise the ebullience in Pichard's voice as he sat across from me, a big smile lighting up his craggy features. His bicolored eyes, a feature that totally creeped me out, crinkled up a bit at the corners, the blue one a bit more than the brown.

"I'm flattered indeed that you traveled all the way out here just to visit little old me," he said, the smile never wavering. Actually it was more of a self-satisfied smirk. Like he'd known all along I'd come calling, sooner or later. "I trust you received my letter?"

I gripped the phone receiver tightly. "Yes, Daniel made sure I got it. I'm attempting to track down Angelique Martone. It's not an easy task. Of course, it might have been made a helluva lot simpler had you also mentioned the fact that her real name is Alexa Martin."

"Tut-tut. What would the challenge have been if I'd done that?" He leaned back a bit in his chair, still with that amused cat-ate-the-canary expression on his face. "I never said that it would be easy. But if you want answers, it's a necessary evil." He paused and fairly beamed at me. "How is your little lifesaving cat? Nick, right? He is still with you, I assume?"

"He's fine, thanks. I'm sure he'd be very flattered by your interest in his welfare."

"You bought him a steak on me, I hope." He let out a short laugh. "I've been bested by many people in my life, but to think that it was a cat who was primarily responsible for my downfall—and Atkins's cat, to boot. Whenever I think of it, I can't help but chuckle. I mean the irony of it all."

When I'd come into the room I'd been admonished not to touch the glass. I glanced over my shoulder to make sure the guard near the door wasn't looking my way and I tapped my nail against it. "Why did you say Angelique was the one person who could tell me what happened to Nick Atkins?"

He looked at me as if I'd just escaped from the loony bin, the eyebrow over his brown eye raising just a tad. "Why, because she is, of course."

"Why? How is that possible?" I leaned closer to the glass. "Is it because of what was in that letter Nick Atkins got the night he had that fight with her?"

His eyes narrowed down to slits. "I imagine Nick got lots of letters. Are you asking if I know details about one in particular?"

"Even you must admit you seem to know lots of things you shouldn't."

He chuckled. "True. I've always been one to keep my ear to the ground. In my type of business, forewarned is forearmed. But to answer your question, no. I know nothing about a letter."

I had the impression he was lying, but I didn't have any evidence to call him on it. I bit down hard on my lower lip. "I think that letter told Nick who Angelique really was, and I think you had something to do with it. How did you find out she was really Alexa Martin?"

"As I've said, forewarned and all that. I was always very careful to have excellent and loyal contacts. As it turned out, Angelique—or Alexa Martin—was a friend of someone who didn't have my best interests at heart."

"Doris Gleason."

His eyes widened a bit, but his expression didn't change one iota. "Yes. You see, Doris is a very enterprising young lady. She's a reporter, same as you were, only she'd never give that up to take over the family business, such as you did. She's a girl with her eye on a star, that one. She wants to get a Pulitzer Prize. She thought exposing my art fraud schemes might do it, but when that failed she set her sights a bit higher." He tapped his receiver with one long finger. "There's much to be said for the world of international espionage, my dear Ms. Charles."

"You're involved in espionage?"

His lips twitched, just a bit. "I've been involved in a great many enterprises, over the years."

Ah, now I was getting somewhere. I hoped. With Pichard I could never be sure. "And Doris and Alexa were both involved in that?"

"Yes—to a point. Doris was more so. She only involved Alexa because . . ."

"She needed her to steal the grimoire," I finished as he hesitated. "Or, rather, something from the grimoire."

His eyes gleamed. "You're partially right. The grimoire itself was never an object of desire, at least not to the people we're talking about."

"So it was the jewels, then?" I gave another quick glance over my shoulder but the guard wasn't even looking in our direction. "She needed Alexa's expertise to steal them, and they were partially successful. She got one, didn't she?"

He shrugged. "I don't know. Did she?"

"Let's not play games. You know she did. You also know she played dead and changed her name to avoid someone tracking her down." I pushed a stray curl out of my eye. "What I want to know is, how do they figure in international espionage, and what's Nick Atkins's connection? You know, don't you?"

Pichard tucked the phone under his chin and held out his hands to inspect his nails. "They get so ragged in here." He sighed. "Anyway, to answer you: Many people desire the jewels because of the mystical power they are purported to have. What they don't realize is there is nothing the least mystical about them. They possess a different sort of power." He inclined his head a bit closer toward the glass. "You wonder about Nick Atkins figuring into all this? Well, that is why you need to speak to Angelique, or Alexa, or whatever she's calling herself these days. She knows the extent of Nick's involvement better than anyone. Whether or not she'll share that with you, though, is anyone's guess."

I pressed the heel of my hand to my forehead. A humdinger of a headache was starting to throb, right between my eyes. "Was Alexa really shot that night, or was that just a cover story?"

"What do you think?"

"She was shot," I said at last. "And she changed her name and appearance to hide, but from who?"

He shook his head. "You'll have to ask her that, or Doris."

"Doris Gleason is dead."

He met my gaze without so much as the flicker of an eyelash and leaned into the glass as close as he dared. "Then Alexa is in greater danger than ever now. She has no champion to protect her, as you do. You'd be wise to find her, and quickly."

"She's in danger because of that jewel, isn't she?"

"She is in danger because she took . . . something very desirable."

I frowned. "Has it got something to do with what's inscribed inside the jewel?"

Pichard's eyebrows shot up. "You know about that? The only way you could know is if . . ."

His complexion paled almost to a pure white, and he pressed himself against the glass as close as he dared. "Get rid of it," he muttered.

"It *is* why they're after her," I cried. "Whoever 'they' may be. What's so special about it?"

He cast a furtive look around and then hissed. "Look," he said, "I told you that in spite of you and that cat being responsible for my being here, I like you. You want to know what Angelique—excuse me, Alexa—knows about Nick Atkins. Stick to that. Don't get involved any further with the grimoire and for pity's sake . . . get rid of that stone."

"I'm afraid I'm already involved." I didn't feel the need to mention the fact I'd been run off the road and my apartment had been ransacked on account of finding that stone—he probably knew that, too. The guy had so many connections, even from behind prison walls, it was scary. "If you know what's so valuable about that stone, please tell me," I implored.

"I'll give you some advice. Look past the obvious. Think outside the box."

Wow, and I'd come all this way for such great advice. I really had to kick myself later. I attempted one last question. "Fine. If you can't, or won't, help me any further with the stone, then have you any idea why Nick might have gone to New Orleans?"

He looked blank. "New Orleans?"

"Oh, come now. Someone with your connections has got to know about those mysterious postcards Ollie's been getting."

There was a moment of silence on both our ends, and then Pichard asked, "What did the postcards say?"

"Not much. A lot of nothing, if you ask me. The messages were very short. Ollie thought there might be some hidden meaning, but—"

Pichard was nodding his head up and down. "I remember Ollie, Nick's partner. He's right you know. Nick loved his puzzles and his codes. He used to spend hours on the Internet, looking up different ways to send messages and scribbling in those infernal notebooks he always toted around with him. No doubt some of the answers you seek about Nick are in those postcards. It wouldn't surprise me a bit."

What would surprise me would be getting an answer that made a modicum of sense. I leaned back and signaled to the guard. "Well, this has been swell. I'm sorry I won't be able to do it again anytime soon."

"You're disappointed. You shouldn't be. You have the tools to find out what you need to know. Alexa is out there. Find her and ask her about Nick. I guarantee she'll be able to tell you something, but you must do it quickly. And for goodness' sakes, get rid of that stone."

I hesitated, then asked, "Do you think it's possible Alexa might be the one who murdered Doris?"

He shifted the phone from his right ear to his left. "Alexa wouldn't kill Doris any more than Doris would kill Alexa. No, it's someone else."

"And you know who, don't you?"

Out of the corner of my eye I saw the guard approaching. Pichard hissed into the receiver, "I appreciate your visit, Ms. Charles. Sorry I can't be of more help. I do hope you'll come again and let me know how it all turns out."

"Yeah, you'll be first on my list." I started to lower the phone back to its cradle, but he signaled me to pick it back up. "What?"

"One last piece of advice. When it comes to figuring what Nick's trying to tell you in those cards, all you need do is one simple thing."

"Which is?"

Those eerie bicolored eyes seemed brighter than ever as he whispered, "Listen to your cat. He and Atkins have more in common than you think."

TWENTY-ONE

"Well, that interview with Pichard was definitely an experience. Very *Silence of the Lambs*-ish. I could have used an interpreter."

I was seated across from Chantal in a cozy back booth at the Poker Face. The bottle of merlot on the table between us was down to its last dregs, and both our glasses were sorely in need of a refill. I picked up an onion ring—Jose made great ones, even better than mine, and that's saying something—and twirled it around a few times before popping it in my mouth.

"It does sound as if he enjoys mind games." Chantal took a bite of onion ring, set it down on her napkin, and eyed her empty glass. "But I also get the sense he was sincerely trying to tell you something."

"I'd sure love to know who his sources are," I said as

I popped another onion ring into my mouth. "He knew about Nick's postcards; he knew Angelique is Alexa. The only time he really seemed fazed was when he deduced I had the red stone Alexa stole from the grimoire. That really upset him." I chewed at my bottom lip. "I mean it *really* upset him. He kept telling me to get rid of it."

"Well, if Alexa went into hiding over it, and Daisy was killed over it, I would take it seriously. The smart thing to do would be to turn it over to the FBI."

"Yes, I realize that. I want to follow up on a few more leads first, get all my ducks in a row. I don't want to approach Daniel with a half-baked theory; I want to present him undeniable facts."

Chantal raised an eyebrow. "Only Daniel?"

"Okay, okay. I don't want to approach either Daniel or Samms with a half-baked theory. Happy?"

Chantal leaned forward, her hand clasping her chin. "Both of them will be upset with you for taking that stone from the room and not telling them right away."

I twined an auburn ringlet around my finger. "Oh, ya think? And it's not only them. I'm sure Broncelli won't be happy, either."

"They could accuse you of tampering with evidence."

"Possibly, if one can prove the stone is evidence. Right now, I'm not quite sure just what it is. At least, that's my story and I'm sticking to it." I reached out and patted my friend's hand. "Don't worry. I've got it hidden in a safe place."

"I sincerely hope so, for your sake, *chérie*. Regardless of how you think your theories will sound, I do not think you should delay in telling Daniel and Samms."

I could see my friend was really worried about me. I reached out and covered her hand with my own. "Okay, how about a compromise. If nothing turns up within forty-eight hours, I'll call Daniel and Samms and drop the whole thing in their lap. Happy?"

A huge sigh escaped her lips. "I guess it will have to do."

We polished off the dish of onion rings and then Chantal asked, "What did Pichard have to say about Atkins and the postcards?"

"In a nutshell . . . he told me I should listen to the cat, that he and Nick Atkins have a lot in common."

Her eyes popped. "Why would he say something like that?"

I threw up both hands. "I have no idea."

"Maybe he was being sarcastic."

"Nope, I don't think so. He seemed very serious."

Chantal drained the last drop of wine from her glass. "Well, he is probably right, *chérie*. Besides Ollie, Nicky is probably the only one with whom Atkins spent a great deal of time. He was teaching the cat to play Scrabble, for goodness' sakes. Nicky probably does know how he thinks."

I dropped my chin into my palm. "It's times like this I wish he could just talk and tell me. It would certainly save a lot of time."

"Well, since Nicky cannot talk and tell you what is what, maybe the cards can." She reached into the voluminous tote at her side and pulled out a purple velvet pouch. She shook it, and a deck of tarot cards spilled out across the tablecloth. She picked the cards up, shuffled them three times, and then passed them to me. "You know the drill," she said. "Three piles, and cut them with your left hand."

I did as she directed. She turned over the top card on the pile nearest me. "Hm." She frowned, and then turned over the other two. She leaned forward, cupped her chin in her hands. "Hm," she said again.

"Enough with the hms, already," I said. "What do they mean?"

"Well . . ." She tapped at the first card with one long nail. "The Two of Wands, a very good card for you. It means success is imminent, that you are moving in the right direction, and that your efforts are about to pay off. Then this one." She tapped at the second one. "The Queen of Cups. Card of the nurturer. Ordinarily I'd say this card refers to me, because she is representative of a psychic or a tarot reader, but that is not the sense I get." She closed her eyes. "This is a secretive person who might be sincere in her offer of help but beware! If you should cross her, there is a price to be paid. And then . . ."

"Out with it," I said, as she lapsed into silence. "What's wrong with the last card?"

"Nothing is wrong with it." She pushed her hand through the flipped-up ends of her hair. "The Moon is one of the more mysterious cards of the tarot. It often signifies illusion and mystery. When this card appears, logic and reason take a backseat. This card encourages you to look to your intuition for the answers you seek."

I let out a breath. "That doesn't seem too bad to me. That's what I usually rely on. Frankly, I'm more curious about that second card, and who this secretive woman might be."

Chantal swept the cards back into one pile. "I think you will find out soon enough, *chérie*."

A shadow fell across the table just then, and I jumped. Lance stood over us, a fresh bottle of merlot clutched in his hands. "Someone call for a refill?"

I held my glass out. "About time you came over. I'll forgive you for scaring the beejesus out of me. We're dying of thirst here."

"Well now we can't have that, can we?" He smiled, opened the bottle, and deftly refilled our glasses, replacing our almost empty bottle with the new one. "Big pow-wow this afternoon, eh? I can smell the rubber burning from across the room."

I stuck my tongue out. "Very funny. Ha ha. No, Chantal was just giving me a tarot reading."

He gestured toward the deck. "So I see. What's the matter? No good?"

"It is hard to say," Chantal said. "It all depends on interpretation."

"Most things do." He gestured toward the empty plate of onion rings. "Right now I'm interpreting you need something a bit more substantial to eat, or is this mainly a liquid repast? If so, Bruce is off tonight, so you'll have to wait here until closing time for chauffeur service."

I smiled up at him. "Aw, thanks for the concern, but it isn't really necessary. We couldn't look each other in the eye if we couldn't down a bottle of wine without getting tipsy. Besides, we both live within walking distance."

He looked us up and down and gave his head an emphatic shake. "Uh-huh. Sorry, but I wouldn't be doing my duty as a responsible bartender and owner to let you two loose on an unsuspecting town with too much to drink and nothing to eat. So unless you both want to spend the next seven hours here, what will it be?"

"We could have coffee," Chantal began but I silenced her with a look.

"Trust me, you don't want Jose's coffee," Lance said.

I made a face at him. "This is a ploy. You just want us to sample some of Jose's cooking since he's been taking lessons, right?"

Lance grinned. "Am I that obvious?"

"Only to we who know you well." I looked at Chantal, then at Lance, and heaved a giant sigh. "Fine. What's the special tonight?"

"Ah, I'm glad you asked. Jose just learned how to make it this week, and he doesn't do a half-bad job, if I say so myself. Smothered enchiladas."

I made a gesture of sticking two fingers down my throat.

"Now, now," Lance chided. "Is that nice? I don't come into your establishment and make fun of your specials."

"That's because my specials are palatable."

"Hey, no one ever said they come here for the food." Lance grinned. "Usually my customers are too sloshed to care what they're eating. In this case, I've actually sampled some of his recent culinary efforts, and they're not bad."

I wrinkled my nose. "You never could lie."

"What, it grew?" He tapped at the tip of his nose with his finger. "Okay, I might be stretching the truth a bit—but I have every confidence he'll improve with practice. At least, he'd better improve for the money it's costing me to give him these cooking lessons."

"Heck, you should have asked me. I'd teach him, probably for less than you're paying now."

"No, you would boss and badger him and he'd throw down the towel and never pick up a skillet again. I've seen how you get in the kitchen. Besides, you're a crummy teacher." He shot me a maddening grin. "But if you're not in an adventurous mood, there is some decent chicken salad in the kitchen."

I frowned. "Chicken salad? When did that get on your menu—oh, oh." I wagged my finger in his face. "Your mother made it, right?"

"Guilty. I brought a bowl of it in. I was going to make it for my lunch." He made a sweeping gesture with his arm. "Might I offer you ladies chicken salad on white toast?"

I looked over at Chantal. "His mother does make good chicken salad. I remember every time he'd tell me she made that, I found some excuse to sneak into his locker and switch it with mine."

He wagged his finger at me. "So that's where my lunches used to disappear to! And here I always blamed Morgan Hyland because his locker was right next to mine. Next you'll say that's the main reason you dated me."

I winked at him. "Yeah, and we all know why you dated me. To get close to Lacey."

His cheeks turned flame red, and he brandished pad and pen. "Enough of memory lane. Now, that's two chix sal on white toast, right?"

"Make it three."

Daniel's head bobbed up behind Lance's shoulder. I spun my neck around, saw he was alone, and breathed an inward sigh of relief. I definitely wasn't in the proper frame of mind for more of Samms's wisecracks.

Daniel slid onto the bench next to me and gave Lance a brief nod. Lance hesitated, then mumbled, "Three Chix Sal on white toast. Got it," and shuffled over to the kitchen door. Once he'd disappeared, Daniel leaned back and casually drummed his fingers on the table. "I understand you went visiting today, Nora."

I gulped. I'd expected Daniel to find out—he was FBI, after all—only not quite this fast. Chantal slid out of the booth so fast she seemed like a blur. "Excuse me," she squeaked. "I have to check in with Remy. I'll be back."

"Traitor," I muttered.

Once she'd moved over to the bar area, I glared at Daniel. "Okay, you've chased both of 'em away. You're pissed because I went to see Pichard, is that it?"

"I'm pissed because you didn't tell me that was what you had in mind, yes."

Heat seared my cheeks. "Oh, forgive me. I didn't realize I had to check with you on every little thing I did."

"Visiting someone who almost killed you in the place where they're incarcerated is hardly what I'd consider a little thing."

"Pichard doesn't hold a grudge, so why should we?"

Daniel's lips scrunched up into a peculiar expression, as if he were counting to ten inwardly. He let out a slow breath. "Were you always this exasperating?"

Before I thought, I blurted out, "Yes. Just ask Samms." I flinched a bit under Daniel's pointed stare. "We didn't exactly see eye to eye on things when we worked on the college paper."

"Oh." He leaned back, laced his hands behind his neck. "So was your expedition fruitful? Did you learn anything?"

"I learned Pichard loves to talk in riddles. But if you mean did I learn anything helpful? No. Not really."

He stared deeply into my eyes. "Why do I have this feeling you're keeping something from me?"

I widened my own eyes and placed one hand across my heart. "Moi? Keep secrets from the FBI? How could I?"

"If anyone could, it's you."

I swallowed. I did feel a tad guilty about keeping secrets from Daniel, but I pushed my guilt to the side and batted my eyelashes. "Why, is that a compliment? If so, thanks. Now it's my turn to ask you, is there anything new with the investigation into Daisy's murder?"

"Well, we've definitely identified the red scarf as the murder weapon. And we've found a few witnesses who remember seeing that woman you mentioned, the one in red. Not only was she engaged in an argument with the deceased but they've identified the murder weapon as being worn by her."

I frowned. "Do you feel these witnesses are reliable?"

"As reliable as any. Broncelli seems to like 'em, and he's the one in charge."

Good old Broncelli. "Okay. So what's the next step?"

"Well, we'd like to question her, of course, but finding her is going to be another matter entirely. For one, no one saw her without her mask, so there's really not much of a description to go on, other than general build. They said her hair color was red, but of course she could have been wearing a wig. We've got Nan Webb, Violet Crenshaw, and Nellie Blanchard going over the invite list to see if they could possibly pick out any unfamiliar names, and we'll start there."

"The workers were allowed to bring guests, too," I said. "I had to give Nan Chantal's name."

"We checked that list," Daniel said. "Everyone was accounted for."

Everyone, no doubt, but Daisy's guest. I was betting dollars to doughnuts she'd never signed anyone in, especially if Alexa were the guest.

Both Chantal and Lance came up to the booth just then. Chantal slid onto the bench and Lance set three chicken salads on white toast before us. He looked from Daniel to me, back to Daniel again.

"Did I interrupt something?"

"Yes."

"No."

Daniel and I both answered at once. I muttered, "Saved by the sandwich" under my breath and took a bite. I looked up at Lance.

"Tell your mother anytime she wants to make chicken salad for Hot Bread, she's more than welcome."

He beamed. "I'll pass the compliment along."

Daniel's phone buzzed. He pulled it from his pocket and glanced at the text message, holding it so I couldn't see (the rat!), then slid the phone back into his pocket and stood up.

"Lance, I'm afraid I'm going to have to take this to go. Chantal, always a pleasure. Nora, I'll talk with you later."

"Oh, I'm sure you will," I sang out, wiping some mayonnaise from the corner of my lip with my napkin. The men shuffled off to the bar and Chantal leaned forward.

"Was he very mad about your little sojourn to prison?"

"Not as mad as I expected."

I leaned back, lost in thought. Chantal regarded me intently and then said, "You've got something else on your mind."

"Yep. I think something else happened after Daisy's body was found, something that concerns the grimoire that they're trying to keep quiet."

"Well, apparently it's intact. I know several people went today and saw it. One girl even showed me a photo of it that was taken the night of the gala—that nice young girl who works at Flo's Boutique, Hilary Anderson. Seems her current boyfriend is Wally Behrens—the roving photographer at the gala, remember?"

I knew Hilary; she was a frequent customer at Hot Bread. "I think I just might have to pay Hilary a visit."

"Tonight is Flo's late night. The boutique's open till

nine, and I think Hilary's working. You should be able to catch her."

I started to pull out my wallet, but Chantal waved me away. "I've got this one," she said.

"Thanks. I'll call you later." I gestured toward the bar where Lance and Daniel stood, talking. "Tell them I had to run, that there was an emergency or . . . or something."

Chantal sighed. "No matter what I say, *chérie*, they will not believe it."

Well, I couldn't argue with that.

I blew my friend an air kiss and exited the Poker Face, and as I did so, I happened to glance across the street. Parked there was a long, black sedan—very similar to the one that had run me off the road. The windows were tinted so I couldn't see inside. Someone was in the car, though, because a moment later it glided away from the curb and turned the corner, vanishing from view.

A chill ran along my spine. Then I squared my shoulders, put all thoughts of the black sedan from my mind, and turned in the direction of Flo's Boutique.

TWENTY-TWO

Flo's Boutique was Florence Hammer's baby, and it had been a staple of the Cruz economy for as long as I could remember. When I was in grammar school, my mother had brought me to Flo's to pick out my Easter outfit from her well-stocked children's wear department in the basement; when I was in high school I'd gotten my spring formal and junior prom dresses from her evening wear section, which took up a good part of the second floor; the main floor was for accessories, jewelry, regular day-to-day clothing for the "modern woman," as Flo herself put it. Even though she was now on the sunny side of sixty, she still came in daily to oversee things.

The sign in the window read OPEN, the hands of the clock pointing to nine p.m. as closing time. I stepped inside and looked around. There was a young girl behind the cosmetics counter assisting two women who looked sorely in need of some face cream, and over to the side, behind the scarf counter, stood Hilary Anderson. The curvy blonde was knotting a gay green, purple, and fuchsia print scarf around her neck, and as I approached, she looked up and flashed me a toothy smile.

"Nora Charles! Hey, how have you been? Sorry I haven't gotten over to your shop this week, but it's been crazy here, plus I've had two papers to do for night school." She spread her hands. "Next week, I promise. I miss my *Emma Stone Capri Sandwich*. It's so fab."

"That's okay, Hilary. No apology necessary. It's been a crazy week for me, too."

"Oh, yeah, the gala." Her eyes widened. "I heard your food was to die for—oops!" She clapped her hand across her mouth. "I guess that was a poor choice of words, considering what happened." She looked quickly around the store, and then leaned toward me. "Did they catch the killer yet?"

"Not yet."

"Ooh," she moaned. "It's so horrible, to think someone capable of strangling such a sweet girl like Daisy is out there."

"Did you know Daisy?"

"Not real well. I'm taking art history this semester, so I had to go to the museum a few times. She was very helpful to me." Hilary combed her fingers through her short crop of hair. "I know she was very excited about that medieval exhibit. I heard her on the phone one day. Man, I don't know who she was talking to but she sounded really psyched. She said that this exhibit would be the culmination of all their work."

"Their work? Not hers?"

Hilary shrugged. "I assumed she meant that other guy, you know? That tall one who looks like Vincent Price. They worked together, but you'd never know it. The two of them always tossed dagger looks at each other." She gave me a small smile. "I'm sorry I couldn't go, though. I understand it was a huge success, in spite of everything. Everyone I've talked to that went raves about your food."

"Yes, it was very nice. I guess you got a sense of that, you know, from the photos. I understand your boyfriend is the photographer."

Hilary blushed. "We've only been going out a few weeks, but Wallace is such a gentleman. He's a real good photographer, too. He was taking the pictures for free to get publicity for his business, but when Violet saw his work she insisted on paying him a nice sum for the photos. She even signed a release so he could sell the ones she didn't want to a newspaper or magazine. The *Cruz Sun* already made him an offer."

"Wow, that's great. I bet he got some great shots of the exhibit, too."

"Not as many as he wanted. Right around the time they let everyone in is when you found, you know, the body. But he did get a few. Nearly a dozen, I think."

"Too bad he didn't get any shots of the grimoire. That's the jewel of the collection."

"Oh, but he did!" Hilary bobbed her head up and down. "He managed to get one right before the murder, and then he went back with me today and took some more. I've got one, see?"

She ducked underneath the counter, reappearing a moment later with a photograph clutched in her hand. She passed it over to me. "Wally printed this out for me today."

I looked at the photo of the grimoire, jewels glistening, on its pedestal. The date stamp on the bottom had the date of the gala, and the time: ten p.m. Right around the time I'd sounded the alarm.

"It looks great. He took a few photos, you said?"

"Yep." She cut me an eyeroll. "Wally's a perfectionist. He hates to miss any small detail, so he always likes to take two shots of everything."

"I'm doing an article on the exhibit for *Noir*," I gushed. "I'd love to get copies of both these photos, if you think Wally would sell them to me. As a matter of fact, I plan on working the gala into the article, so a copy of the entire set would be great."

"I'll ask, sure." Hilary took the photo back and slipped it into her purse. "If you're willing to pay, I don't see there'll be any problem. I can let you know tomorrow, if that's okay."

"That's perfect."

Her nose wrinkled. "Just between you and me, that grimoire sure didn't look like much, did it? I mean, I know it's old and all, but for magic gems, I've got to tell you, none of 'em had much luster. I've got cubic zirconia with more zip than those."

An elderly lady approached the counter and tapped

her knuckles imperiously on the glass. "Young lady. Might I see some of those scarves in the case?"

Hilary tossed me an apologetic look as she hurried off to wait on her customer. "I'll call you tomorrow or better yet, if I can get some photos from him, I'll stop by Hot Bread. Would that be all right?"

"Excellent. And there's a complimentary *Emma Stone Capri Sandwich* with your name on it."

She was beaming as I strode out the door. At least someone was happy today. I myself wasn't quite sure just exactly what it was I was hoping to find in those photos. Maybe inspiration would hit when I saw them. God knew I needed to catch a break soon.

Ollie was waiting for me when I arrived back home. He uncurled himself from his position on my stoop as I approached.

"Hey," I greeted him. "What are you doing here?"

He reached inside his jacket pocket and pulled out a postcard. "Got this in today's mail."

I glanced at it. The picture was of a fountain in Audubon Park in New Orleans, surrounded by trees. I flipped the card over and saw the familiar, cramped handwriting. I passed the card back to Ollie.

"Let's go inside."

We went into the shop and Ollie settled himself at one of the back tables. Almost immediately Nick crawled out from under a nearby one and proceeded to wind himself around Ollie's ankles. While he reached down to scratch the cat behind his ears, I put on a pot of coffee, then took some cookies out of the display case, put them on a plate, and walked over to the table. I sat down and pushed the plate of cookies in front of Ollie; he in turn, pushed the postcard in front of me. I turned it over and read:

I love it here! Maybe you can come down. One never knows. No accounting for taste, eh? A bit chilly today. Can't complain. As usual, things are popping. Same old stuff. Every day I miss you.

"N"

I pushed the card back. "This makes about as much sense as the others. Maybe he suffered a concussion or something."

Ollie shook his head. "Nick knows what he's doing. Trust me, there's some message in every single one of these cards. We just have to crack his code."

"Well, Bronson A. Pichard agrees with you on that point. What I'd like to know is—why is Nick writing in code at all?"

"I've been thinking about that myself," Ollie admitted. "I guess he doesn't want anyone who might see those cards to know what he's really up to."

"Then why the hell doesn't he just call, or write you a detailed letter," I said irritably. "Why must there be all this subterfuge and mystery? If he's sending coded messages there must be a reason, and, also according to Pichard, the only one who might be able to shed some light on that is Angelique slash Alexa Martin."

Ollie let out a low whistle. "It's some sweet mess, isn't it?"

"To say the least."

Nick hopped up on the table and pranced over to the postcard. He leaned over, sniffed at it.

"Merow."

"Well, look at that," Ollie exclaimed. "I think he knows Nick sent that."

"Either that or he just likes postcards."

Nick sniffed at the card again, and then his tail thumped down. *Thump! Thump!* The tip of his tail brushed the lettering on the postcard each time. After the ninth thump I stood up.

"Really, Nick, enough's enough."

The cat waved his tail in the air, blinked at me, then turned to Ollie and blinked at him. Then he jumped down and wiggled underneath the table.

Ollie let out a chuckle. "I do believe you insulted him."

"Yes, he is sensitive." I picked up the card and read it again. Then I looked at Ollie. "Nick thumped his tail nine times."

"Did he? I lost count."

"He did." I set the card in front of Ollie and tapped at it. "There are nine sentences on this card."

"Hm, so there are. Maybe he's trying to tell us Nick's code. Maybe it's every ninth word."

I grabbed a pad and pen and pored over the card, counting and writing, then sat back and looked at the words.

"One can't every," I said. "That definitely isn't it."

Ollie scrunched his lips up. "Every ninth letter?"

I repeated the procedure. "EOONTSIOUAAVI." I read the letters out loud. "Makes no sense at all, except maybe he's got a vowel fetish."

"Maybe it's a code within a code."

Nick poked his head out from underneath the table. "*Merow*," he warbled, and then jumped back up. He turned around twice, blinked at me, and then thumped his tail—hard—nine more times before leaping off and disappearing back underneath the table.

Ollie looked at me. "Nine seems to be the operative number, but for the life of me I don't know what he could be trying to tell us."

"Neither do I, but it's got to be something." I bent down, raised the edge of the tablecloth, and peered at Nick, huddled in a ball there. "You know what it means, don't you?"

Nick blinked twice, then laid his head on top of his front paws.

I straightened and nodded at Ollie. "Next time you come over, bring the other postcards. I'm going to do some research on code-cracking, and then you and I are going to figure out just what it is he's trying to tell us."

"Maybe he's not trying to tell us anything?"

I shook my head. "Bronson A. Pichard told me when it came to figuring out those messages, we should listen to the cat. And no matter how crazy that sounds . . . it's just what I intend to do."

TWENTY-THREE

The next morning was busier than usual. Word had gotten out, via the various news articles courtesy of the gala, about Hot Bread's tremendous food, which netted me about two dozen brand-new customers. Chantal, Mollie, and myself were kept hopping straight through breakfast and lunch, with barely a moment for ourselves. Things finally quieted down a bit a little after two, and we all settled ourselves in the kitchen for a light snack—none of us had had time for even a coffee break all day.

"Wow, if this keeps up you might need to advertise for more help." Chantal chuckled, pouring herself a mug of steaming coffee. "Those reviews must have been extremely flattering."

"I read the one in the *Clarion*," offered Mollie, biting

into a toasted cheese sandwich. "They said Hot Bread was definitely a place to watch."

I flopped down in the chair next to Chantal and took a bite of my own tuna sandwich. I poured some iced tea for Mollie and myself and then said, "Do either of you know anything about codes?"

They both stopped, sandwiches halfway to their mouths, to stare at me. "What, do you mean like Morse code?" asked Mollie.

"Probably like a secret code," Chantal said with a knowing wink.

"Ooh, like in Nancy Drew? Or James Bond?" Like Chantal and myself, Mollie was a big mystery buff. "Let's see—do you mean a code or a cipher?"

"What's the difference?" I asked.

"Well, most of the time when people talk about breaking a code, what they're really talking about is a cipher. A code is usually a system where every word or phrase is replaced by another word, a number, or a series of symbols. A cipher is a system where every letter of your message is replaced by another letter or symbol."

I arched a brow. "I don't even want to know how it is you know all this."

Mollie grinned. "It's just something I got interested in. I took an online course in cryptology. There are two types of ciphers commonly used. Transposition and substitution. Substitution ciphers are easier to break, but transposition ciphers aren't as easy to use. A substitution cipher entails substituting one letter and replacing it with another letter or symbol. A transposition cipher is where one transposes or rearranges the position of the letters."

"Sounds fascinating," I said as Chantal stifled a yawn. "Could you give me an example?"

"Of what type? There is the Caesar cipher, the keyboard cipher, the date shift cipher . . ."

Even though I'd originally asked with Nick's postcards in mind, the slip of paper with the numbers on it that had been in the pouch in Daisy's room floated through my mind. "How about a date shift cipher?"

"Okay," Mollie said, a bit too eagerly. She got up, grabbed a pen and a pad from behind the counter, and sat back down. "Pick a date."

"Nora's birthday," Chantal said promptly. "November 3, 1977."

"Great." Mollie wrote down 110377. "This is the code you use to encipher your message," she said. "Suppose you want to say, 'I enjoy the movies of Hugh Jackman.' So under the message, you write the six-digit number until you come to the end, like this: 1 10377 110 377110 37 7110 3771103."

"Oh my God, that's the code?" Chantal looked at it askance.

Mollie shook her head. "No, silly, we're not done yet. Next thing you do is write out the whole alphabet, from left to right. Then you shift each letter of the plain text forward in the alphabet indicated by the number below it. For example, the letter I corresponds to the number 1, so move forward one position in the alphabet, making it J; E shifts two positions, making it G—and so on."

Chantal leaned back in her chair and ran her hand through her curly bob. "That sounds waaay complicated."

"It's not, really. I mean, once you've written out your message, if you want to decipher it, you simply reverse the process: write out the numerical code, and then go back that many spaces in the alphabet. One big advantage to using this cipher is that it's fairly random. You could also combine ciphers, creating what's known as a stacked cipher—and then there's concealment. That's got hidden messages. It usually works much better with a string of words that makes sense with one another, a legitimate sentence."

Chantal eyed her. "I'm impressed, Mollie. You sound like a graduate of spy school. I think Nora should recommend you to Daniel as a consultant."

Mollie blushed. "It's just something I enjoy. I've thought about studying it, maybe angling for an FBI career after I graduate college."

"Really? That's wonderful, Mollie," I said. "If you like, I can ask Daniel which schools are the best for that."

Mollie's face lit up. "Would you? I'd appreciate that."

The bell above Hot Bread's door tinkled just then, signaling the arrival of another customer.

"Oh, man! And I haven't even tried out this *Hugh Jackman Sub* yet," Chantal moaned, casting a longing eye at the sandwich on the plate in front of her.

I rose and smoothed down my apron. "I'm very impressed, Mollie, and I definitely want to pick your brain about codes some more. Right now, though, you gals just sit there and enjoy your very belated lunch. I've got this.

After all, after waiting on half a dozen customers at once, one person will be a breeze."

"Great," Mollie said. "But I'll take my sandwich to go. I've got finals coming up this week."

While Mollie wrapped her sandwich, I headed toward the counter. Hilary Anderson stood there, her blond hair windblown, studying the list of specials. As soon as she caught sight of me, her face split into a wide smile. She reached into the tote bag slung across her shoulder and pulled out a packet, which she waved in the air.

"I've got your pictures, Ms. Charles." She set the packet down on the counter. "The whole set, like you wanted."

"Great." I picked up the packet and looked at Hilary. "Tell Wally I really appreciate this. What do I owe him?"

"He'd made a set for one of the out-of-town papers, but they decided they didn't want 'em. He told me to tell you he'll just take a *Ryan Gosling* on rye to go, since he didn't have to give back the advance."

"Is he sure? I'm perfectly willing to pay the going rate."

Hilary laughed. "Hey, don't look a gift horse in the mouth. All he wants is a *Ryan Gosling* to go. It's his favorite sandwich."

I liked the mortadella, salami, and provolone on a tomato wrap with Dijon mustard myself. As I reached into the case for the cold cuts I said, "Well, tell Wally thanks. And if it should happen the photos lead to a solution of the murder, I'll front his lunch for a week."

"Can't beat that deal. But it might turn out to be pretty

expensive for you." Hilary wrinkled her nose. "Golly, but that boy can eat!"

Chantal and Mollie left while I was making Hilary's sandwiches, and when I was done I walked her to the door, closed it, and then sat down at a table with the packet of photos. There had to be several dozen—Wally must have snapped a photo every five seconds. I started to sift through them, and Nick came out from underneath one of the back tables, hopped up, and sat on the far end, watching.

There were lots of group shots, several shots of just the food tables before anyone had gotten at them—those were really good. I'd have to talk to Wally about possibly making some enlargements and hanging them on the walls of the store. There were some good shots of the bar, and Lance posing in his pirate regalia, a bottle of whiskey clutched in one hand, lots of group shots (mostly of young girls in skimpy costumes LOL). There was an excellent shot of Nan and Violet, both of whom looked regal—and one of Nan, Violet, and Daisy all together and smiling. There were a few more shots of Daisy, all clustered together: Daisy standing by the punch bowl, by the bar, near a crowd of laughing girls—and then the last two photos in particular caught my eye. One showed her in a corner, talking to Magda. Both women looked decidedly uncomfortable, but that wasn't what arrested my attention. Off to one side, partially hidden by the French doors, was a red cape and a red-booted leg—the Red Death, perhaps?

And far off to the other side, it looked as if Reynaud were approaching the women, cape swirling around his shoulders. I glanced at the time stamp and saw it was a few minutes after eight.

The last photo featuring Daisy showed her talking to one of the Harry Potters, her head thrown back in a laugh. Standing off in one corner, throwing her dagger looks, was Magda again—and off in the other corner, looking decidedly unhappy, stood Nellie Blanchard.

Nick walked across the table and butted my wrist with his head.

"Yeah, I know. If I knew just exactly what it was I was hoping to find, this would all be a lot easier."

I flipped through more of the costumed revelers, and then came to the ones Wally'd taken of the exhibit itself. I had to admit: Everything did look impressive. I flipped through them until I came to the ones he'd taken of the grimoire. I looked at the first one. There it sat, on its pedestal, its jeweled cover winking in the overhead light. The timestamp on the photo read 9:35 p.m. I flipped through a few more and then another grimoire photo popped up, slightly out of focus, but depicting the same scene: grimoire on pedestal, jeweled cover winking. This timestamp read 10:15 p.m. Well after the discovery of Daisy's body. I laid the two photos side by side on the table and pored over them. I couldn't see any discernible difference, but the graininess of the second photo made an accurate comparison a near impossibility. I shuffled through the rest until I came to the one of the grimoire he'd taken the next day, laid that one beside the other two, and peered at them all intently. Of course I was no gem expert, but it did seem to me that the stones in the last photo weren't half as bright as the ones in the prior photos. I held them up to the light, squinted. Was it just wishful thinking on my part, or did the blue and green stones seem just a bit smaller in the second photo?

"Yowl!"

Nick's paw slashed out at the second photo. I drew it back before he could put a claw mark on it.

"I'm not imagining it, am I? They aren't the same stones. Someone got in there and substituted them." A mental picture of Reynaud holding those two stones reared itself in my memory. I might have a handle on who—but how? And why?

I set the grimoire photos on the side and thumbed quickly through the others again. I saw one of Daniel, Samms, and Broncelli, taken early in the evening—the men were all smiles. There was another more candid shot outside the grimoire room, taken after Daisy's body had been found. No smiles there. Broncelli all but sneered into the lens.

Nick's paw shot out again, knocking those photos out of my hand and onto the floor.

"Er-ewl."

"Yes, I don't particularly care for him, either," I grumbled as I bent to retrieve the photos. "But Daniel looks nice in these, so we'll keep them. We can always cut out Broncelli—and Samms."

I paused, studying Samms standing there in his black pants and shirt. His tight, body-hugging pants and shirt. The guy had muscles; pretty ripping ones, too. He'd kept in good shape over the years; probably had a gym membership . . .

And I cared just why, exactly? "The past is in the past, Nora," I muttered to myself. "Follow your own advice."

Nick's paw lashed out again, the tip of his claw poking a tiny hole right above Broncelli's tie. "Hey," I said, holding the pictures out of his reach, "calm down, will you? These pictures might be evidence . . . what the hell?"

One second Nick was sitting on top of the table, the next he was a black blur, jumping off and racing from one end of the kitchen to the other. He stopped by the stairway that went up to my apartment, let out a loud yowl, and resumed his imitation of a feline Flash.

"Nick!" I yelled. "Stop it."

"*Er-OWWWWWL.*"

I'd never seen him act like this. I'd heard that sometimes cats took fits but I'd never actually seen one—was this what was happening now?

Or was there more to his strange actions?

The third time he squatted in front of the stair door and yowled, I threw down the pictures and stood up.

"Okay, Nick. Enough's enough. What will it take to get you to act like a normal cat again?"

He reared up on his hind legs, started clawing at the door. I reached over and opened it, and he shot right up the stairs—no, flew might be a more accurate description.

He flew right up those stairs as if someone had doused his tail with benzene and set it aflame.

"Fine, Nick," I called up the stairs. "I'm coming up and you'd better be nice and calm by the time I get there—or no supper for you tonight, young man. And I had some nice turkey skin I was going to give you, too."

I heard a plaintive meow and then . . . nothing.

I ran up the rest of the stairs and pushed open the door that led into my apartment. "Nick? Where are you?"

I walked into the den and as soon as I'd crossed the threshold I stopped, the hairs on the back of my neck pricking at attention. I was suddenly overcome by the feeling that I wasn't alone in my apartment.

I lowered my voice to a half whisper. "Nick? Are you all right?"

No answer. I moved back into the hall and looked around. Everything was quiet, but the feeling I wasn't alone still gnawed at me.

Nick flew out from nowhere, raced down the hall, and skidded to a stop in front of the closet. He uttered a low growl and then hit the folding door with his paw. The door creaked back, opening a fraction of an inch, just enough for a little orange and white face to peep out.

I stared, stupefied. "That—that's the cat from the gala. The one who found the body. The cat who belongs—"

"To me," said a soft voice from just behind me. "The cat belongs to me. I need your help, Nora."

TWENTY-FOUR

For a minute all I could do was stare at the dark-haired woman before me. She looked almost exactly as she did in Ollie's photograph, only better, darn her. Even with pale skin and dark circles beneath worried eyes, she still looked as if she'd stepped right out of the pages of *Vogue* magazine in the tight black jeans and simple purple turtleneck she wore.

Finally I found my voice. "You're Angelique Martone," I said. "Or I guess I should call you Alexa Martin, right? How did you get in here?"

Her lips curved in a wistful expression. "Angelique, Alexa . . . there are days when I am not sure just who I am anymore. As for how I got in here . . . I'm pretty good with locks."

"A man named Bronson Pichard tells me you're the

person who can shed some light on Nick Atkins's disappearance."

Her eyes widened slightly. "Nick is still missing?"

"I think you know he is."

Nick, who'd been busy sniffing the other cat, turned suddenly to face Alexa. His back arched, his lips peeled back, and he let out the mother of all hisses.

Alexa nodded toward the cats. "He is Nick's cat, right? Sherlock?"

I nodded. "His name is Nick now." At her startled look I added, "I named him that before I knew who his owner was."

She let out a low laugh. "The cat never really warmed up to me, which is a shame, since I'm an animal lover. I think he knew I was lying to his owner, but I had my reasons."

"He is a very perceptive cat. You lied about your identity, right? Because you knew Nick had been hired by Violet to find you?"

"I lied about my identity, but not because I was trying to hide from my aunt. Had I known she was the least bit interested in finding me . . . who am I kidding? It wouldn't have changed anything. I had to be thought missing, or better yet, dead, not only for my safety but for anyone connected with me." She took a step closer to me, Nick hissed again, and she stepped back. "You took the stone from the hotel room, didn't you?"

I nodded. "That's what they ran me off the road for, and ransacked my apartment hoping to find, isn't it? There's something about this stone that's very special.

Would it have anything to do with the laser writing etched in it?"

Her eyes held a gleam of admiration. "Doris was right about you. You are smart. We can help each other, Nora."

I folded my arms across my chest. "I'd say right now you need my help more than I need yours."

Her lips slashed into a thin line. "I did not kill Doris. She was my friend, probably the only true one I've ever had."

I nodded. "I believe you. However, the police will be a different matter. Several people, myself included, heard you arguing with her the night of the gala."

She let out an exasperated sigh and pushed the back of her hand through her thick, luxuriant black tresses. "That is because she was so stubborn. She insisted she could handle things on her own. She didn't want me to help her."

"Because you were supposed to be missing or dead, right?"

"If it was revealed that I was indeed alive, then it would have put us both in a very precarious position."

"Because you stole that red stone."

She nodded. "Yes."

We stood for a moment or two in silence, which I broke with a light cough. "We're talking in circles here, and not really getting anywhere."

"This is true." Her gaze softened as she looked at me. "You wish to learn the truth about Nick Atkins and the reason why he disappeared. Pichard was correct. It is possible I might be able to help."

I leaned toward her. "You know where he is?"

She shook her head. "I didn't say that. I can tell you what I know about Nick, and why I think he might have wanted to drop out of sight, but that's about all I can do." She paused. "I will need something from you first."

I should have seen that coming. "What is it you want?"

"I need your detective skills to help me clear my name in Daisy's murder, and bring a dangerous criminal to justice."

"Is that all? Would you like me to whip you up a sandwich, too?"

"It's a very serious matter, Nora. You can ask your friend Daniel. He appreciates the gravity of the situation."

Even though I'd suspected Daniel was acquainted with Alexa, hearing it confirmed still surprised me. "So the FBI's involved in all this?" When she didn't answer I added, "I know Doris was a reporter, working on some sort of story that concerned international espionage."

Alexa nodded. "That is true. These people are very dangerous, make no mistake."

"It wouldn't be the first time I was up against someone dangerous."

Her lips slashed a thin line. "Not like this. I have nothing to offer you, Nora, except the little I can tell you about Nick. I would ask much more of you in return."

I managed a small smile. "Let me be the judge of that."

I made a strong pot of coffee and then Alexa and I sat down at my kitchen table. I put out two big bowls of Friskies for the cats; Alexa's cat hunched over her bowl and gobbled hungrily. Nick pecked at his and then he moved off to squat in front of my stove, his sharp golden gaze trained on us. For Nick to abandon his food bowl, he must sense something big in the wind.

Alexa took a sip of coffee and nodded at him. "Your protector."

I looked at the cat fondly. "You can say that again. He's saved my life more than once."

"You are lucky." Alexa cast a glance at her own cat. "Valentina is a good companion, but at the first hint of danger . . . well, let's just say she gives new meaning to the phrase *scaredy cat*."

I laughed. "Nick's just the opposite. He runs toward guns, not away from them." I sobered and cupped my mug in my palms. "Okay, enough small talk. It's time you had the floor. Why is that stone so valuable that people want to kill over it?"

Alexa set her mug down and leaned back in her chair. "I'm not sure how much you know about my past."

"I know your father was estranged from his sister, Violet, and he raised you after your mother died."

She nodded. "My father never married my mother, but it wasn't because he never asked. She just could never bring herself to marry . . . a thief. That was what my father did best, you know, and it's true what they say . . . genes will out. I discovered at a very young age that I'd inherited his talent—I have very nimble fingers." She held out her hand and flexed the digits in front of me. "My mother would have had a stroke if she knew just how much like my father I was. It started out with small things—a pack of gum here, a candy bar there—but as I grew older, I discovered a way to get the pretty things we couldn't afford. Nice underwear, angora sweaters, pretty dresses . . . it came easily to me. Too easily.

"The worst was when I stole a diamond bracelet from a local jeweler. Just my luck, they'd installed new video cameras that day I wasn't aware of. They had me on tape, and the only thing that saved my indiscretion from going public was the fact I was still under eighteen. I was living with my father by then, and he was appalled—although I can't help but feel there was a little part of him that was actually proud I'd inherited some talent of his. Anyway, the records were sealed by the court, I did some community service, and then—my father got sick. In the meantime, I'd decided to turn over a new leaf, and I went to college. I studied Art History, because I also had a talent for drawing and I'd always loved to look at the paintings and sculptures by the masters. I thought I could get my degree, maybe get a museum job as a docent, eventually work my way up, and someday, maybe, my own paintings or sculptures might be on display somewhere. I was a year away from graduation when Dad died—and then Doris called me.

"I'd met Doris two years ago at a Zeta Tau Alpha fundraiser. We had a mutual love of art and hit it off right away. Doris was more interested in journalism, though, and she'd received an offer to study abroad and attend school in London while working at the Meecham Foundation. Anyway, two days after my father passed away I got a call from her. She wanted to know if I could come to London. She'd see to it that I got a job at Meecham—if I helped her out with a story she was writing. I asked for details, but she was adamant: I had to go to London first, and she'd fill me in later. Needless to say, I jumped at the chance. I was being given an opportunity for a fresh start, in an entirely new country where no one knew of me or my past. I cleaned out my accounts and was on the next flight out of the USA.

"I took the job with Meecham, and I have to say, at first I was disappointed. It consisted of writing articles and categorizing exhibits—really boring stuff. Doris worked from home on other projects—I later found out she wanted it that way because she was holding down two jobs at the same time. Anyway, I'd just about decided to give up the job and go back to the States and finish college when Sir Rodney brought in the grimoire.

"At first glance, you'd wonder just what was so special about it. I know I did. It looked like any other old book. The silver scrolling on the cover was pretty nice, but the jewels weren't anything to write home about—and I know a thing or two about jewels. As a matter of fact, it didn't take me long to realize the jewels on its cover weren't real. I thought about bringing it to someone's attention, but that would entail my explaining just how I was so expert in the field of jewelry—so I confided it to Doris. She got so excited, I thought she was going to have a heart attack right on the spot. Then, a few days later, she started asking me for details—how I knew they weren't real, what looked different about them, yada yada. She made such a fuss I told her that maybe I should mention something to Sir Meecham, and that's when she took me into her confidence. She admitted that the reason she'd called me to England and gotten me a job with Meecham was the grimoire. She'd wanted my opinion on the jewels, because it bore out what a source of hers had told her weeks before. The grimoire was being used as a tool to smuggle a valuable formula to a foreign power. Or rather, the jewels in its cover were."

I set down my cup and leaned forward. "So it wasn't just the red stone? They all have writing in them?"

Alexa nodded. "The jewels are really all a formula for a highly sophisticated nerve gas. According to Doris's source, there was a contact within the Meecham Foundation who secretly worked for an undercover organization, and they intended to switch the stones and transport them to a lab in the United States. So Doris hit upon an idea. She wanted me to steal the stones first."

My eyes flew open. "Good Lord. Talk about a nutty, dangerous idea!"

Alexa chuckled. "Yes, in hindsight it did have a lot of flaws. Doris, however, saw an opportunity to impress her contact and get a Pulitzer Prize–winning front-page story. She talked me into breaking into the foundation and taking the stones." She paused. "What we didn't count on was someone else breaking in on the same night, with the same idea."

My eyebrows rose. "So someone else was there to steal the stones?"

"Apparently there was someone else involved, besides the mole in Meecham, who also wanted the stones to sell to a different foreign power. Lord only knows what might have happened if the guard had not come in when he did. I managed to get away with the red stone, but I was shot in the side, and I ended up taking a header out the window. Fortunately Doris was there and she came to my aid. I woke up in a hospital two days later. Turns out the bullet had only grazed my side, but I'd suffered a mild concussion, two broken ribs, and a broken wrist from the fall." Her lips twisted into a rueful grin. "When I was in college a friend of mine was drunk and fell off the roof of the sorority house. She suffered similar injuries. The doctor said it was because her whole body had gone limp when she fell. Thank God that was what happened to me." She let out a breath. "After that we both decided that it was best for Alexa Martin to disappear. She feared whoever was involved at Meecham could easily uncover my past and put two and two together. I vanished, changed my appearance and my name, and took a flight back to America a week later. I settled in Carmel, got a part-time job in a bar. That's how I met Nick."

"And the other stones?"

"They remained untouched in the grimoire until the night of the gala. Someone switched them."

I nodded, remembering I'd thought the stones had looked different in the photograph. "And of course they realized they were missing one."

"I believe they knew that going in, and suspected Doris of having it. I think that's why she was killed."

"Do you have any theories on who the inside person might be."

"Doris was fairly certain Reynaud was involved. Even though the man's past looks excellent on paper, Doris recently was able to uncover the fact he contributed a good amount of funds to an underground group suspected of terrorism."

"What were you two arguing about the night of the gala? I was outside the kitchen and heard you. I remember she said something about you being in danger."

"She was pretty sure that Reynaud overheard Violet tell Nan about asking you to find out what happened to her niece. She felt Reynaud knew I was alive, and that I had the stone. She feared for my safety, as I feared for hers."

"What did she want you to do that night?"

"She wanted me to steal the remaining stones. She'd worked out a plan to lure the guard away from his post so that I could slip in and switch them."

"Sending him a text from his superior?" I nibbled at my lower lip. If that were the case, she must have been killed immediately afterward.

"I am not sure how she intended to distract the guard, but at the last minute, she told me to abort the plan. She'd discovered something—she wouldn't tell me what—that led her to believe someone else was involved, and it might not be Reynaud after all. She said she didn't want to move forward until she was certain."

"And you have no idea what she might have found out that changed her mind?"

"No. She said it was too dangerous and the less I knew, the better." She gave a short laugh. "I got mad and pushed her and threw my cape at her. I was horrified when I found out there was a red cape wrapped around her body."

"Doris was strangled with a red scarf—were you wearing one? I couldn't remember."

Alexa shook her head. "No. Anyway, I did not kill her, no matter what the police will think."

"I believe you. Did you happen to drop anything in the corridor behind the kitchen that night? A small purple stone?" When Alexa shook her head, I added, "I found one lying there when I was looking for you and Doris. Then I got conked on the head myself. Right before I blacked out, someone whispered, 'Watch your step, Red. You shouldn't take what doesn't belong to you.' Shortly after, I realized the stone was missing. I wasn't sure if I'd just lost it or if whoever knocked me out took it."

"As far as I know, the only stones of any value are the red, green, and blue ones. I know nothing about a purple stone. It would make more sense that in your red cape, you were mistaken for me."

I got up, went into the den, and returned with the pouch. I pulled out the stone and slip of paper and laid them in front of Alexa. "This was in the pouch with the red stone. Do you recognize the numbers on that paper?"

She picked it up and studied it. "It could be a numeric code," she said at last. "I am not very good at cracking them, however."

"I've recently gotten a crash course in just that subject." I scraped my chair back, got a pad and pen from one of the drawers, and sat back down. I wrote out each letter of the alphabet, and then at the top of the page wrote down the numbers:

318 4181516.

Following Mollie's method, the numeric message now became:

CAH DROP.

Alexa wrinkled her nose. "That makes no sense, does it? What is a cah drop?"

I sighed. "I have no idea." I stared at the paper for another minute or two, and then something clicked in my head. I looked up at Alexa excitedly. "Maybe we're looking at this all wrong. Maybe it's not a code at all. Maybe it's something much simpler—like a phone number. Geez, I should have thought of that right away! Dummy!" I gave my forehead a resounding slap.

"Oh, I don't know," Alexa said. "Sometimes the most obvious answer is the most overlooked one."

"True." I pointed to the first group of numbers. "318 could be an area code."

"There are enough numbers in the sequence it could be a phone number," Alexa agreed. "318-418-1516. I wonder if it is."

"One way to find out."

I went into the den, returning a few seconds later with my cell phone. I punched in the number and hit the speaker button. A few seconds later we heard, "Monroe Homicide."

"Sorry, I dialed wrong," I murmured and disconnected. "Why would Doris have put the Monroe Homicide's number in with the stone?"

"To hide it? She must have had a reason."

Something clawed at the edge of my consciousness, some memory that wouldn't break free. I looked at Alexa. "Let's go downstairs. I have the gala photos in the shop. I want to go over them again. I have a feeling the answer to all this is somewhere in those pictures."

I locked the stone back in my desk, slid my phone into my pocket, and then Alexa and I went back down the stairs and into Hot Bread, Nick following close behind. The gala pictures were still where I'd thrown them when Nick went wild, on the back table. I motioned for Alexa to sit down and then I handed her a stack of photos. "Look these over."

"Sure. What am I looking for, exactly?"

I bit down on my lower lip. "That's the devil of it. I'm not sure exactly. I'm hoping something will just hit me when I see it."

I thumbed through the pictures in front of me, and suddenly there it was, staring me right in the face. I picked the photo up, peered at it closely, and then suddenly it made sense. Crazy sense, maybe, but . . . sense. I held the photo out toward Nick.

Nick glanced at it, then let out a loud yowl.

"I'm glad you agree," I said.

Alexa looked at me sharply. "You've found something?"

I nodded slowly. "I think I've figured out who the person is who wants the stone, and who killed Doris . . . Now I just need to find a way to prove it."

A muffled *thunk* from the front of the shop made me pause.

"What was that?"

"It sounds as if something fell," said Alexa, but I put a finger to my lips. We sat in silence for a few more minutes, but all remained quiet.

"I guess it was nothing," I began, and then paused again as the bell over the front door gave a quick jingle and then stopped, almost as if a hand had clamped it to prevent making any more noise. A second later we both heard an unmistakable creak, and our eyes locked.

Someone else was in the shop.

TWENTY-FIVE

I rose from my chair, my heart beating a rapid tattoo in my chest as I considered my options. I put a finger to my lips and eased my cell phone out of my pocket. I punched the 1—Daniel's number—and bit back a cry as it went to voicemail. I was just about to shoot off a text when a message popped up on my screen: BATTERY LOW. "Swell," I muttered. "I've got to remember to charge this thing." Praying there was enough juice in it for one quick text, I dashed one off to Daniel . . . SOS. Then I slid the phone into my pocket and leaned closer to Alexa.

"I shot Daniel a text, but just in case he doesn't get it, I think we should make a run for it."

Alexa nodded agreement and we tiptoed toward the back door, Nick padding along silently at our heels. I was just about to turn the knob on the back door when it hit me.

"The stone," I hissed. "I don't want to leave it here, especially since I'm pretty sure that's what they're after." I pressed my car keys into Alexa's hand. "The Lake's Bakery truck was blocking my driveway when I came back. I've got a rental right now. It's the silver SUV parked down the block. Go find Daniel and Samms. They're most likely at the police station, and bring them back here—fast." I gave her a little push. "No one else. Got it?"

She looked at me, her face pale. "Yes, but I don't like leaving you alone."

"I'm not alone. I've got Nick. Now go . . . fast."

She hesitated, then nodded. Alexa vanished out the back way and I turned around toward the stairway that led to my apartment. Out of the corner of my eye, I caught a glimpse of a dark shadow moving silently and swiftly through the store. I frowned. If I crossed over to my apartment entrance, I'd be in plain view of the intruder. The door to the basement was over to my left. If I could get downstairs, there was another exit that led around the back and I could enter my apartment from the outside entrance. Making up my mind swiftly, I veered to the left and slowly eased open the basement door. I groped for the light switch, groaning softly as I remembered the bulb had blown and I hadn't replaced it yet. Gritting my teeth, I plunged down the steps in the pitch black, staying to the right to avoid the creaky spots on the steps, feeling my way with my sweaty palm pressed against the cold cement wall.

Upstairs, I could hear light footsteps padding around. Then I heard several loud clangs and realized whoever it was must be pulling my pots and pans off the wall.

Of course. They'd already searched my apartment for the stone and come up empty—now they were searching my store. I shuffled forward a little faster. If I didn't hurry up, Hot Bread might be declared a disaster area.

It seemed like an eternity had passed until I reached the doorway. I started to open the door, and the ensuing creak sounded like a thunderclap in the stillness. I paused, then slowly began to inch the door open again. It still creaked, but not as loudly. I finally got the door all the way open and I hurried up the short flight of stone steps into the alleyway behind the store. I paused for a minute, sucking the fresh air into my lungs, my heart still in my throat—and then a heavy arm snaked around my throat and a heavy hand clamped over my mouth and nose.

"You think you are so clever," a raspy voice whispered in my ear.

I knew that raspy voice. Magda!

I struggled to pull her hand away, but the old woman held on like a magnet. She was, apparently, much stronger than she looked. She swung me around and gave me a push back toward the way I had come.

"We wouldn't want anyone to see us, now, would we?" She leered as she jabbed a hard object into the small of my back, something that felt painfully like the cold barrel of a gun.

We went back through the basement and up the stairs. When we reached the store, Magda shoved me down on the floor and then towered over me, brandishing the gun as if it were a lasso. I crab-walked backward, right into a pile of my good pots on the floor.

"What the hell do you want?" I blazed, hoping I sounded indignant instead of how I really felt.

She crouched over me, her horsey face shadowed in darkness, and laughed evilly in my ear. "I think you know what I want. You have the stone. You have to have it. It wasn't in Daisy's room, and you were there. You took it. Give it back."

"If I had it," I answered, "I surely wouldn't give it to you. That stone, and the others, belong in the possession of the US government."

Magda gave a loud snort, as if she found my comment highly amusing. I plunged on. "Daisy, or should I say Doris, knew someone from the Meecham Foundation was involved. She'd originally suspected your brother."

Another snort. "Reynaud has rather . . . unique political associations, but he is not a traitor. Me, on the other hand . . . well someone had to bring money into the family." She gave a dry chuckle. "Reynaud has always tried to look out for me. He never liked the people I hang out with, but I make much money from being associated with them, more than my stupid brother ever will at that museum. He almost ruined everything. He found the stones I planned to switch in my locker."

That explained what I'd seen the night of the murder. It had been Reynaud trying to protect his sister, not commit a crime. "You got them back from him, though, and you did switch them."

She gave me a peculiar look and shook her head. "No, I didn't. I never touched them."

I frowned. "Are you telling me the truth? Doris had

an inkling of what you intended to do. Isn't that why you killed her?"

Her frown deepened into a scowl. She shook her long, greasy hair so it cascaded over one shoulder. "I did not kill that girl," she rasped. "I did not kill anyone. I am a smuggler, not a murderer."

"Then if it wasn't you, it had to be the person you partnered with. The other thief. Someone very clever, someone no one would ever suspect in a million years, because of his position and reputation."

"Very good, Ms. Charles. You are quite the sleuth."

He'd melded out of the shadows so silently, I wondered how long he'd been there. Curtis Broncelli glared down at me, then he leaned down, grabbed me by my upper arms, and hoisted me to my feet as if I were nothing more than a rag doll. "How long have you known I was involved?"

"Not long. Tonight, actually. Something bothered me when I figured out those numbers weren't a code, but a phone number for Monroe Homicide. I remembered hearing you'd worked at Monroe Homicide at one point. Then, when I was looking over the photos of the gala, it suddenly hit me. In one shot that was taken early in the evening, you were wearing a tie tack with a purple stone. Later on, in another photo, the tie tack was gone. I'd found a purple stone outside the rear entrance to the kitchen, right where Alexa and Daisy had been arguing." I touched the back of my head gingerly. "You knocked me out," I accused. "That flash of black I saw was the black suit you wore that night. You must have seen me pick up the stone and you knocked me out to get it back, and whispered that warning in my ear."

"It's a distinctive tie tack. I received it for twenty years of meritorious service with the Secret Service. When I saw the stone was missing, I knew I had to get it back because someone, no doubt, would put two and two together, as you did. You can imagine my chagrin when I saw you pick it up. You, of all people. The girl Daniel'd been bragging about."

Daniel? Bragging about me? I felt a sudden surge of pride.

He shrugged. "A trifle over the top, perhaps, but desperate times . . ." He let the rest of the sentence hang.

I decided to go for broke. "One or both of you searched my apartment, and ran me off the road the night of the gala."

Magda bared all her teeth in a semblance of a smile. "Guilty on both counts. And, as you well know, I did not find what I was looking for."

I remembered Nick sprinting out the car window with the pouch, but said nothing. I frowned and looked quickly around.

Where was Nick?

Broncelli kept on talking. "You've got that stone here somewhere. I know you do. We've kept pretty close tabs on you. It's doubtful you've hidden it anywhere else. Although you might have given it to that pretty friend of yours, the one who owns the flower shop, for safekeeping. We just might have to try her next."

"Leave Chantal out of this," I growled. "She doesn't have it."

"Then tell us where it is."

I clamped my lips together and glared. Broncelli leaned closer so that his nose almost touched mine. "I've got a very angry Chinese national who very much wants the complete formula, for which I need the original stone. I'm sure you can imagine what he'll do to me if he doesn't get it, so I'd advise you to stop stalling and tell me where it is."

"Chinese national?" Magda plucked at Broncelli's sleeve. "I thought it was the Germans we were getting the formula for."

Broncelli ignored her outburst, focusing fully on me. "I've learned quite a few inventive ways to torture people during my years with the Secret Service and FBI. You'd be amazed at some of them, really. And you'll get first-hand knowledge very soon if you don't open up and tell me what I want to know."

"From what I understand, you have a very long and respected career in law enforcement," I said. "Why be a traitor to your country?"

"Why indeed. I can give you four million very good reasons." He laughed lightly.

"Two million," amended Magda. "We are still partners, Curtis."

In spite of my precarious position, I couldn't resist playing devil's advocate. "Yes, tell her if you're still partners, Curtis."

"Shut up," Magda spit at me. She glared at Broncelli. "You talked me into joining forces with you, double-crossing the buyer I had for yours. You'd damn well better come across with my portion."

He whirled on her, lips drawn back in a snarl. "Your buyer was a small renegade group—they would have paid a pittance for this. After the way you bungled everything I should cut you out entirely. You had strict orders that night. If my bullet missed Alexa, you were to finish what I started. Instead you let her get away."

Magda's face paled. "She was bleeding so much and it all happened so fast. I thought, no, *we* thought she'd died, remember?"

"Until we found out otherwise. She was the girl dressed as the Red Death that night. We haven't managed to track her down yet, but we will. We need to get rid of that loose end."

I breathed a silent sigh of relief that apparently they weren't aware Alexa had been here tonight. I lifted a brow at Broncelli. "So then Doris discovered you were the traitor and you killed her?"

He shook his bald head. "Make no mistake, I surely would have killed her had I thought she suspected the truth, but I did not. I had no idea she suspected me. We were both quite confident Reynaud was high on her list."

I frowned, looking from one to the other. "That's impossible. One of you had to have killed her."

"I didn't," sniffed Magda. "As for her suspecting my brother, well, I knew she would never be able to prove anything. Besides, if he were going to be fool enough to take that rap for me, who was I to stand in his way?"

Wow, what sisterly love. Made me want to puke. But it still didn't make sense.

Broncelli glared at me. "I know what your game is.

You are trying to distract us, but these flimsy tactics will not work . . . Are you ready to tell me where the stone is yet?"

"I—I don't have it."

"Liar." He jerked a gun from the waistband of his pants and aimed the muzzle at my chest. "You have ten seconds. Ten—nine—eight . . ."

I stared into the big black barrel and prayed for either a miracle or divine intervention and then . . .

"EEROWL!"

"MEEEEOW."

Two blurs descended upon Broncelli and Magda—one black and white, the other orange and white. The black blur shot out a claw and knocked the gun into a far corner, leaving behind a trail of blood. The orange and white blur entangled its claws in Magda's hair and pulled her head back, hard. I took advantage of the distraction to scramble to my feet.

"Oh no you don't."

Even with his hand dripping blood, Broncelli still reached for me. I knew I had to act, and fast. I doubled up my leg and kicked my foot straight into his groin with as much force as I could muster. He dropped to his knees with a pitiful cry. I spun around. Nick squatted in the corner, near a pile of pots. He shoved the heaviest one toward me with his claws. I snatched it up and brought it down hard on the back of Broncelli's head. He moaned, and then lay still.

Magda, meanwhile, had managed to disentangle Valentina from her hair. She tossed the cat into a corner and reached for her own gun, tucked in the waistband of the gauze skirt she wore. Nick spun into action again. Rearing himself up on his hind legs, he sprang, spitting and clawing, into the air, hitting her full in the chest just as she leveled the gun at me. His fangs buried themselves in her wrist. She let out a sharp yowl and the weapon clattered to the floor. Valentina leapt gracefully forward, kicked it with her front paws right over to my feet. I reached down and snatched it up.

I brandished the gun at Magda. "Sit down and shut up."

Eyes glittering, she eased herself into a chair, clutching her bleeding wrist and moaning. "He bit me," she growled. "I'm going to need a rabies shot."

"Nick doesn't have rabies. And as far as a shot goes, don't tempt me."

On the floor, Broncelli moaned. I debated hitting him with another pot or maybe just giving him a shot in the arm; nothing serious, maybe a flesh wound. He started to rise on one elbow, moaned again, then his eyes rolled up and he keeled over on his side. I was still considering giving him another whack on the head for good measure when he let out a deep sigh and then lay motionless. I prodded him with my foot.

Out cold. Finally.

I'd just straightened when the back door suddenly burst open. Daniel and Samms entered, guns drawn, and then stopped as they took in the scene before them.

I dropped the gun and planted both hands on my hips.

"Geez, about damn time you got here."

Samms and Daniel each pointed at the other. "Blame him," they chorused, and I laughed and bent down to pick up Nick, whose pink tongue darted out to lick my cheek.

"It's okay, guys. I've got all the calvary I need right here."

TWENTY-SIX

The following evening found a cozy group gathered at a back booth in the Poker Face: myself, Chantal, Daniel, Samms, Rick, and Alexa. Lance, who'd spent a great deal of the evening fawning over Alexa, approached our table, coffeepot in hand. "Refills?" he asked.

I shot him a look. "Of Jose's coffee? Really?"

Lance clucked his tongue at me, but I noticed his gaze was riveted on Alexa. "Now, now, be nice. How about if I bring over some nice Kahlúa to add to it?"

"Great." Chantal clapped her hands. "I'm a sucker for Kahlúa."

Lance hovered over Alexa's shoulder. "How about you, Alexa?"

She wrinkled her nose. "It's all right. Myself, I prefer amaretto."

"Funny you should mention that. I've got some amaretto-flavored coffee in the back. I can have Jose put another pot on."

I had to smother a grin. "You do? Since when?"

He shrugged. "Oh, I'm not sure. A week ago, maybe? Jose mentioned flavored coffees were big so I thought maybe we'd give it a shot."

I held up my mug. "I think the Kahlúa will do for now."

He hurried off to the bar and returned about five minutes later, a bottle of Kahlúa in one hand and a bottle of amaretto in the other. He set the Kahlúa in front of me and the amaretto in front of Alexa.

"Knock yourselves out. On the house." He gave Alexa another wide smile. Alexa smiled back. For a split second I felt the slightest twinge of irritation. Did he or didn't he have a king-sized crush on my sister? The irritation dissipated as I told myself Lacey had always been totally oblivious to Lance's interest, and if he wanted to shower some attention on Alexa, and Alexa showered some back, so what? They both deserved a break.

I picked up the bottle of Kahlúa, poured a generous helping into my mug, passed it over to Chantal, and looked at Daniel. "So, where's the stone now?"

"Safely in the hands of the US government." He leveled me with a stern look. "You do realize hanging onto it was a really insane and dangerous thing to do, right?"

I took a long sip from my mug, which now tasted more like Kahlúa laced with a little coffee. "All's well that ends well?" I turned back to Daniel. "How long was Broncelli under suspicion?"

"Actually, quite some time," Daniel admitted. "It all started back in Monroe. Broncelli's excellent record in Homicide brought him to the attention of the FBI field office captain, who recruited him. Not long after, he got involved with an underground group who paid him quite handsomely for coming across with some classified documents. It escalated from there, particularly more so when Broncelli was promoted to the International Task Force. Several important formulas and plans found their way into enemy hands, things Broncelli had access to, but no one could prove he had a definite involvement. IA had him on their person of interest list hoping to catch a break."

"His excellent service record kept him pretty much above reproach for a long time," Samms added. "That same quality was what made him so valued as a double agent. He'd been around long enough and had enough contacts, knew the ins and outs, so he was very adept at covering his trail."

"Why would a man who held such a respected position throw it all away and commit treason?" Chantal mused.

"Simple." Rick smiled at her. "He has two ex-wives with expensive tastes and he himself loves to play the ponies. It all made him an easy target. The terrorists were willing to pay top dollar for the information Broncelli was able to provide."

"These stones were his biggest score. And he might have gotten away with it, except for two things: He got greedy, and Doris Gleason got involved."

"That is true." Alexa nodded. "Doris had been using

her various newspaper contacts to track down that underground group for months, for an exposé. Her source revealed to her that the formula was going to be smuggled to an undisclosed location in Germany—through the gems—and their contact was an inside source at Meecham. She suspected Reynaud right off because of his political affiliations. Doris wanted to catch the traitors red-handed; she thought the story would earn her a Pulitzer, and it probably would have. What she wanted to do was get the jewels herself to smoke out the persons involved, and that's when she called me."

"Meanwhile, our boy Curtis got an attack of the greeds," Samms said, picking up the gauntlet. "He'd gotten an offer from a different foreign power for the formula at double the original price. So he planned to steal the stones himself, make it look like a robbery to throw off his original bidder, and sell them to his second source. He needed someone on the inside, and Magda, who'd been involved in underground and smuggling activities for years, was ripe for the picking. She'd already acquired a buyer on her own, one she was only too happy to dis when Curtis dangled a larger fee in front of her."

"The night Curtis planned to steal the stones, two things went wrong," Daniel said. "First off, Alexa picked the same night. Secondly, the alarm that Magda supposedly disconnected malfunctioned somehow and the guard rushed in. Alexa got away with the red stone, which contained the largest part of the formula, but Broncelli saw her when she went out the window."

Alexa nodded. "Doris looked up and caught a glimpse

of him in the window and realized he'd seen me. That's when she decided we should adopt new identities. She contacted her source, who in turn contacted the British secret service, who contacted the American FBI, and they determined I should go back to the USA where it was safe. Then they started concocting a plan to smoke out the traitor. And guess who they put in charge of the case?"

"Broncelli," Chantal and I said together.

"Right. Of course, he had no idea it was a setup. He saw it as his opportunity to smuggle the gems in the grimoire over to the US, where the second bidder resided, and use Doris to smoke Alexa and the other jewel out. He arranged with Meecham to bring the exhibit to California, where he knew Alexa was hiding."

"Why go through all that? He was in charge. He could have just tracked Alexa down and gotten the jewel," Chantal said.

"He could have but Alexa's exact location was known to only a handful of people and on a need-to-know basis. Broncelli wasn't on that list, and he didn't want to call attention to himself by making too many inquiries. When the arrangements were made for him to take Mac Davies's place in Homicide, he figured it was a golden opportunity dropped in his lap: He could smoke Alexa out, switch the jewels, make off with all the money, and leave Magda holding the bag."

"Broncelli had no idea Doris had seen him that night," Alexa put in. She tapped the checked tablecloth with one long, bloodred nail. "Their paths must have crossed at some point during the gala, and I'll bet the fact he was dressed all in black jogged her memory. That's why she was so insistent we had to be certain before going ahead with our plan and accusing Reynaud."

I turned to Daniel. "That's why she seemed so nervous. They must have confronted each other at some point during the evening, and Broncelli killed her to avoid exposure—or he had Magda do it."

Daniel shook his head. "They were telling the truth. Broncelli didn't kill Doris. Neither did Magda. They both have alibis for the TOD."

He reached into his jacket pocket and passed me two photos. One showed Broncelli, Daniel, Samms, and two other policemen grouped together. The other showed Magda chatting with, of all people, Nan Webb.

"See?" He tapped the edge of the pictures. "Both photos were date- and time-stamped right at the time the coroner estimated Daisy was murdered—so neither one of them could possibly have done it. As far as the murder goes, we're back to square one."

"Great." I stared at the pictures and frowned. "Looks like I can't finish up my article for *Noir* yet, can I?" I still had a gut feeling the key to solving Doris's murder was staring me right in the face, only I was too blind to see it.

"*Er-ewl.*"

I'd forgotten that Nick was in the bar, too, because he'd been so quiet—uncharacteristically so, I might add—underneath the table. I glanced down. He was on his back, forelegs in the air, a piece of what looked like red string curled between his paws. I reached down to take it away, and he rolled over onto his paws, eyes wide, ears perked.

"How did you get that, you little devil?"

Alexa peeped underneath the table and laughed. "He might have stolen it from Valentina. I noticed her playing with similar strands."

Chantal laughed. "It is amazing the things they find to amuse themselves with, no?"

Alexa nodded. "Yes, never mind buying them expensive toys. Just leave a frayed piece of clothing lying around and presto. A new toy."

Frayed clothing? Something clicked in my memory. I peered underneath the table again.

Nick curled his paw around the red strand and held it out. "*Meower*," he said.

And then, in a sudden burst of God knew what—Inspiration? Enlightenment? An epiphany?—it just all became crystal clear.

Thanks to my cat's eclectic taste in toys, I was 99.9 percent sure I knew who murdered Doris. Now all I had to do was prove it.

TWENTY-SEVEN

Daniel brought me home around eight thirty. We stood on my stoop, and he pulled his hand through his thick crop of dirty blond hair. "Once all this is over," he said, "and we find out who really killed Doris, I think we should celebrate."

"I'm all for that. What did you have in mind?"

"Something both of us will enjoy. A date where no dead bodies pop up to spoil it. Different, no?"

"Me-owww!"

Daniel chuckled. "Sounds like Nick thinks that wouldn't be much fun."

We both laughed, and then Daniel took me in his arms and planted one on me. His mouth was warm, his lips soft, and for a few moments I just lost myself in the sheer bliss of the moment. When we finally broke apart, he trailed one hand down my arm. "Well, I'd better get back down to the station. Lee gets cranky when he has to fill out paperwork."

"He never was fond of paper pushing," I mused. "Seriously, how did he get involved in all this?"

"It was part of the plan," Daniel admitted. "Lee knew Broncelli from their days together in Monroe, and he always felt something was off about him. When we approached him to help us out, he was only too willing."

"So all that stuff about his leaving St. Leo was just a cover story." At Daniel's nod I added, "I guess he'll be going back to his old job, then?"

"No." Daniel rubbed the back of his neck. "My superior at the FBI has offered him a job on our Special Task Force, and he's accepted. He'll be working with me and Rick, out of our Carmel office."

I arranged my features into what I hoped looked like a bright smile. "Yeah? That's terrific." *Not.*

At my feet, Nick let out a low growl. He wasn't too thrilled, either.

Daniel gave me another kiss—this one a bit shorter—and then he headed back to his Range Rover and, with a brisk wave, sped off. I watched him go, then hurried up the stairs to my apartment, Nick cantering along behind me. I walked into the den, pulled the packet containing my set of gala photos out of the drawer, and shook them all out on the table. I thumbed through them, and, on the next to last one, found what I was looking for. I slid the photo into my jacket pocket and reached for my purse and car keys—and then stopped.

Nick stood by the door, waiting expectantly. I nudged him with the toe of my shoe.

"Sorry, bud. You can't come with me."

His eyes widened. *"Merow?"*

"This won't take long. I have to get proof positive for Daniel of the identity of Doris's killer. Once that's done, I can finish that article for *Noir* and then . . ." I waggled an eyebrow at the cat. "We can celebrate."

Nick cocked his head at the word *celebrate* but then he meowed more decisively and planted his cobby-shaped body along the length of the door, paws folded beneath him, head lifted defiantly.

I sighed. I knew that stance. It meant he wasn't inclined to budge till he got his way. Apparently my promise of a celebration wasn't good enough to dissuade him from wanting to accompany me. "Listen, bud, I know you want to protect me but it won't take long. And I don't want to have to worry about you."

The eyes narrowed and he grumbled deep in his throat, almost as if to say, *Who worries about who?*

"Fine," I muttered. "I know how to deal with your mood, mister."

I hurried into the kitchen to open a can of Fancy Feast yellowfin tuna, his very favorite. He came running the minute I popped the tab on the can. I filled his food bowl and he wasted no time in hunkering down in front of it. As he slurped up the tuna, I slung my purse over one shoulder and paused, my hand on the doorknob. "Works every time." I chuckled. "Oh, and just in case I'm not back in a half hour, you have my permission to do whatever it is you do to go get Daniel and bring him to the museum."

I heard a soft meow as I pulled the door shut.

The museum was shrouded in darkness when I pulled into the parking lot, and I breathed a sigh of relief. I knew there would be no more guards since the grimoire mystery had been solved, and none of the office staff seemed to be working late tonight. I parked far back, under a spreading elm, and made my way toward the rear service entrance, thanking God I hadn't had a chance to return the kitchen key. I let myself inside and moved silently and swiftly down the corridor into the main lobby, up the stairs and past the offices into the employee's locker room. Just as before, only a few of the lockers had shiny locks dangling from their handles; I hoped the one I sought wouldn't. I started pulling open doors, and midway through the first line I gave a short intake of breath and stepped back.

Bingo. I reached inside and pulled out the long black dress. I hung it on the front of the locker and held it out by the sides, inspecting it carefully. I turned the edge of one sleeve up, and my breath caught in my throat.

Several small red strands clung there.

I remembered something a fellow reporter had said to me once: *It's always the ones you least suspect you've got to keep your eye on.* Well, that was certainly true in this case.

I eased my phone out of my jacket pocket, fired off a

couple of shots, and emailed a set to Daniel and one to myself. I'd just replaced the dress in the locker when I heard the unmistakable creak of a floorboard behind me. I whipped my head around.

Nothing.

I felt goose bumps start to break out on my arms and the back of my neck, so I closed the locker door and tiptoed back out into the hall. Everything was dark, silent. As still as death.

And then, out of nowhere, Nellie came charging at me.

She held a bronze paperweight I'd seen on Nan's desk in one hand; there was no time for me to move out of her way, so I braced for the onslaught. I saw her mouth drop open and heard her cry out like a wounded animal, then her face contorted as she brought the paperweight down. I sidestepped just in time, watching as the force of her swing propelled her to the floor.

"You had to stick your nose in where it didn't belong. Who gave you permission to come here and go through my locker?"

My breath was coming in short bursts. "Nellie. I—I didn't think you'd be here."

She snorted. "Obviously. What are you snooping around here for?"

"I think you know." I took a quick glance over my shoulder at her locker. "You came to get rid of the evidence, I suppose?"

She charged at me again, swinging the heavy paperweight like a baseball bat. I ducked out of the way once more, backing into the first open doorway, which proved to be Nan's office. I ducked behind her desk, flattening myself against the floor, and cringed as the paperweight connected with the desktop and wood splintered above me.

"How did you find out?" she spat. "I was so careful. I made sure no one saw me."

My hand closed over the photo in my pocket. "You can thank Wally Behrens and his camera. I remembered seeing a photo of you, and there were several red strands clinging to the edge of your sleeve. The scarf you used to strangle Daisy had frayed ends. It hit me tonight, when I saw my cat playing with some red strands."

"You and that damn cat." Her voice was a low growl. "You just don't know what it's like. You're in business for yourself, and before that you had a job where they respected you. You have no idea what it's like to be stuck in a menial position, to know you can do better, and to have some upstart come in and jerk it all out from under you."

I was trembling so hard now it was hard to keep my teeth from chattering. "Nellie, stop acting crazy. Can't we talk this over sensibly?"

She towered over me, chest heaving, eyes glittering. "What's to talk about? You're going to have me arrested for murder."

I licked at my dry lips with the tip of my tongue. "Nellie—listen. I wasn't always respected in the journalism field. It took years before most of the guys treated me as an equal. I understand how frustrated you must have been when Violet gave that job to Daisy."

"She didn't have half the knowledge I did. And she

wasn't even going to stay! I heard her talking with her friend, the one dressed all in red. She said as soon as she got what she needed, the two of them could leave Cruz forever! Imagine that! She didn't even appreciate the chance Violet gave her!"

Nellie started to pace back and forth, turning the paperweight over in her hands. I eased myself up, mentally gauging the distance from where I now stood to the door and how fast I might get there, if only Nellie would move to the other end of the room.

I started edging toward the doorway. "What happened the night of the gala?"

Her upper lip curled back. "I followed her down to the basement. She had a cat down there. She was bringing it some scraps. I confronted her, told her that I'd overheard her, and she wasn't going to get away with it. I told her young folks nowadays just have no respect for much of anything. That's when she shoved me out of the way. Told me if I knew what was good for me, I wouldn't say a word about anything I'd overheard. Then she laughed and said that even if I did, Violet and Nan both thought I was a bit touched, so maybe it wouldn't matter. That's when I really lost it. There were some old costumes down there in that trunk. I saw that red scarf and I grabbed it. She had her back to me so I just looped it around her neck, pulled hard, and held on fast." She clucked her tongue reminiscently. "It didn't take long for her to die, with that stupid, puzzled expression on her face. I dumped out all the clothes in the trunk and shoved them into another box, and put her inside. Then I found a red cape that looked like the one her friend was wearing and looped that around her shoulders." Nellie sniffed. "She wasn't here that long, but she acted like she owned the place. Sucking up to Violet and Nan, flaunting her fancy education. She talked down to me like I was some addle-brained twit who didn't have a clue about a museum. She felt she was entitled to that job—can you imagine that? She was entitled—and I was the one who did all the heavy lifting! I was the one who was at Violet's beck and call, who did whatever Nan wanted! Daisy deserved to die."

I decided to try to appeal to her sensible side, if there was one. "Nellie, it was a crime done in the heat of passion. No one who knows you would blame you."

Her face took on a crafty expression. "Sure they would. They all think I'm crazy, right? Well, they've gotta find me first."

With that, she heaved the paperweight right at my head and took off through the doorway. I ducked, narrowly avoiding being hit squarely in the forehead, and took off after her. I grabbed her around the waist just as she reached the top of the staircase. I pushed her flat on her stomach and used my weight to hold her down, pressing my knee into her spine between her shoulder blades and twisting one of her arms behind her back.

"Ow," she cried. "You're hurting me." Then suddenly she went limp and began to sniffle. "I didn't mean to kill her, honest. It, I mean she, she just got to me, that's all. I'm not a killer."

I felt a wave of pity for her and let go of her arm. "It will go easier on you if you turn yourself in Nellie."

No answer. She just lay on the floor, her breathing ragged. I got up, and moved away. I pulled out my cell phone, but before I could hit number 1 I heard a noise behind me.

Nellie stood right behind me, her face wet with tears. She had Nan's letter opener in her hand. She must have slipped it off the desk in the confusion. She waved the long, sharp blade under my nose.

"I can't go to prison," she rasped.

As the sharp point rushed toward my face, I dropped my phone and reached out and grabbed her wrist with both hands. I pulled down hard, throwing us both off balance. She tumbled to the floor, me on top of her, a jumble of arms and legs as we both struggled for the letter opener.

Nellie was mad as a hornet now, and her suppressed fury made her stronger—and more determined. She sprang to her feet first and gave me a sharp kick right in the ribs. I doubled over, but this time she was too quick for me. Her fingers closed over the letter opener and with a loud cry she started for me again. All I could do was lay there, pain shooting up my side, and cross my arms over my head in a feeble effort to protect myself.

"Drop that!"

Nellie paused, the blade only inches from my face. I lowered my arms enough to see Daniel standing at the top of the stairs, his gun leveled at Nellie. Behind him was Samms, gun also drawn, and behind him, a tiny black blob. Nick.

Samms moved forward while Daniel held his gun on Nellie and he pinned her arms down and planted a pair of steel cuffs on her wrists. Then he heaved her to her feet. Daniel, meanwhile, had reached me and gathered me into his arms.

"Hey, slugger. Where does it hurt?"

I touched my side gingerly. "She got me good in my ribs, but I guess I'll live."

Nick padded up to me and gave my cheek a thorough washing with his rough, pink tongue. I reached out and pulled him closer to me. "How did you know I was here?"

"Thank your cat," said Samms. He jerked his thumb at Nick. "He showed up at the station, spitting and hissing and running around in circles. We figured he was trying to tell us something, and he led us here."

I chuckled and whispered into Nick's ruff, "So you understood what I told you about going for help? You rascal."

He licked my chin. I pulled him closer and gave him a big kiss right on the top of his head.

Daniel helped me stand up and gave my arm a squeeze. "Well, thanks to you it looks like all the loose ends of this case are finally tied up."

I shook my head. "Not all of them," I said.

I'd just finished sweeping up after the lunch crowd the next day when the shop bell tinkled and Alexa and Violet walked in. I almost didn't recognize Alexa. She'd dyed her hair back to its natural dirty blond color and discarded her heavier, theatrical makeup in favor of a fresh-scrubbed look, which I decided suited her much better. I set the broom down and hurried over to them. I gave each a hug in turn and then motioned them to sit down.

"Special Agent Corleone brought her to me this morning," Violet said. Her face was creased in a smile, and her hand closed over mine in a hard squeeze. "We've spent the morning getting to know each other, and we owe it all to you, Nora. I knew you were the right woman for the job."

I laughed. "I really didn't do anything outstanding, Violet. Things just worked out."

"Fiddlesticks. You were smart enough to take advantage of opportunities, and to put two and two together. Isn't that what being a good detective is all about?"

She had me there.

She leaned back in her chair and blew out a sigh. "At least it's all finally over. I knew Alexa was innocent but my gosh! Whoever would have thought Nellie capable of murder?"

"She was an unlikely suspect," I agreed. "It just shows what can happen when someone gets pushed over the edge. She truly believed she should have had the admin job, and she resented the hell out of Daisy for it. I honestly don't believe it was premeditated. I think when Daisy dismissed her so curtly that night, something inside her just snapped."

"That poor woman," Alexa murmured. "It's sad, really. She had nothing else in her life except that job and it became a grand obsession."

"Well it's all over now," Violet said crisply. She took

her hand from mine and placed it over her niece's. "The murder's solved, the gala was a huge success, and all's right with the world. My niece and I need to take some time to get reacquainted. We've a lot to catch up on, you know. So we're leaving for a month's stay in London tomorrow. I've rented a lovely town house just off the Thames."

"That's wonderful." I grinned impishly. "And will Nan be running the museum in your absence?"

Violet rolled her eyes. "Yes, and hyperventilating every second, no doubt." She cast a fond look in her niece's direction. "Alexa will be living with me when we return—and getting her degree in Art History, so she can someday take over for me at the museum. In the meantime, she'll be taking over Daisy—er, Doris's old job as admin."

I smiled at them both. "That's great." To Alexa I said, "You'll do a fabulous job."

Violet glanced at her watch. "We really must get going. There's a lot we have to do yet before our plane leaves tomorrow."

I nodded. "Violet, would you mind if I spoke privately with Alexa for a minute? We have . . . a little unfinished business."

"No problem." Violet rose, her hand dipping in her purse for her cell phone. "I should check in with Nan anyway. I'll be outside in the car." She pointed her finger straight at me and winked. "Don't think I forgot you, young lady. I fully intend to compensate you for all this."

I waved my hand. "I couldn't accept any money."

"Oh, it's not money." She smiled mysteriously. "I've got something special set aside for you, for bringing Alexa back into my life."

I waved my hand. "It's really not necessary, Violet. I was happy to help."

"I know you were but that's not the point. Good work deserves to be rewarded. I'll see you receive it within the next few days. And you're going to love it, trust me."

I saw Violet wouldn't be persuaded otherwise, and besides, now she had my curiosity piqued. What could it possibly be? I smiled and said, "Okay, Violet. Thank you."

She swept out of the shop and I went over, locked the door behind her, and then turned to Alexa. "I kept my end of the bargain. Now it's your turn."

"So it is." Alexa eased herself into a chair and rested both elbows on the table. "I believe I mentioned already I'd gotten a job as a barmaid when I first returned to Cruz, and that was how I met Nick Atkins. He fell for me pretty hard, and I cared for him, too—it was really hard not to care about him." Her voice took on a wistful note. "He was a real charmer where women were concerned. He had a way of making you believe that you were the only one in the world who mattered to him."

I'd heard stories about Nick's prowess with the fairer sex from Ollie, and nodded. "So I've heard. But I get the feeling he genuinely cared about you, Alexa."

"Nick never discussed his work when he was with me. He never liked to talk shop. Then one night he came to my apartment with a letter. The letter revealed my true identity as Alexa Martin, the girl he'd been hired to find.

It also revealed, in detail, what had gone down at Meecham and my part in it." She exhaled a long breath. "He asked me why I'd lied to him. He said if I'd been straight with him he might have been able to do something."

I eased myself into the chair next to her. "Really? He said that? But what could he have possibly done?"

She shrugged. "I have no idea. He stormed out, and I didn't see him for weeks. Then one night he showed up at my apartment. He said he understood why I did what I did. I'd just put him in an awkward position, but none of that mattered anymore. He asked me if I'd do a favor for him."

"What sort of favor?"

She raised her gaze to meet mine. "He wanted me to shoot him."

"What?"

"He said something had happened and he had to leave town, but he was caught in the middle of a situation and faking his death was the only way he could get out of it. He told me to wait underneath the pier, and when he approached, he'd drop a handkerchief as a signal and I was to shoot him. He even messengered me the gun, loaded with blanks."

I felt as if someone had just jerked a rug out from under me.

"So his shooting was a setup? Engineered by him?"

Alexa nodded. "He said there would be a witness who could testify he'd been shot, even though no one would find a body." Her hand shot out to cover mine. "I believe Nick was—and may still be—involved in something really, really big and very dangerous."

I drummed my fingers idly on the table. It seemed as if my original theory might indeed be correct: that Nick was on the run from the mob. I almost fell off the chair, however, at Alexa's next words.

"That night he came to me with the letter—he tried to hide it, but I caught a quick glimpse of the letterhead. It was from MI5. British Intelligence."

My mouth fell open. "MI5? Why would Nick be getting correspondence from them?"

"Can't you guess?" Alexa lowered her voice to a whisper. "Because he either works with them or for them.

"Nick Atkins is a spy."

TWENTY-EIGHT

It was the following Monday, and I'd just locked up for the day and settled down at the rear counter to go over some bills when a *tap-tap-tap* sounded at my back door. Nick rose from his comfy position in front of the refrigerator and ran around in a circle as I let Ollie into the shop.

"Nick certainly seems glad to see you today," I said.

"And well he should be. Nice article in *Noir*, by the way."

"Thanks." My lips drooped a bit. "Too bad it couldn't have had a happier ending."

"You reunited Violet with her long-lost niece, helped shut down some terrorists, and brought a murderer—albeit a misguided one—to justice. It's not a bad ending." Ollie reached into his pocket and pulled out the postcards. He touched the top one. "There's a brand new one—just came today."

Nick reached up and clawed at Ollie's pants with his forepaws.

Ollie chuckled. "Look at him, the rascal. He's all primed to solve the mystery." He dangled the postcards in front of my face. "You did say to bring these by, right?"

I motioned toward a rear table. "Yes. Sit down. I've got some news for you, too. I had a little chat with Alexa you should know about."

He settled his burly frame into a chair. "Got some good, strong coffee? Judging by the expression on your face, I've got a feeling I'm gonna need it."

I poured us two steaming mugs and then related my morning conversation with Alexa. When I finished, Ollie took a long swig and sat for a few minutes before replying.

"I guess deep down I always knew he was alive, but a spy?" He scratched at the stubble on his chin. "That's a bit over the top."

"I've leafed through his journals. Nick himself was over the top, wouldn't you say?"

He laughed. "True. But Nick as a James Bond type? I don't know. It's kind of hard to swallow."

"Alexa wasn't positive about the letterhead," I said. "The spy thing is her own theory. But you must admit, Nick's request to her is rather . . . odd. Why disappear in such a dramatic fashion?"

"Someone has to be after him." Ollie nodded. "The mob, maybe? After all, he did figure out the truth about Adrienne, and Lord knows what else he never saw fit to share."

"I'm hoping the answer is here." I tapped the stack of postcards. "Let's have a look at the latest one."

He plucked the top one from the pile and flipped it toward me. "Here you go. And if you thought the other messages didn't make sense, wait till you get a load of this one."

I picked up the postcard. The photo was a long shot of the Hilton New Orleans Riverside Hotel. I turned the card over, surprised to see every inch of space covered in Nick's cramped handwriting. I read the message out loud:

> Ollie. No Doubt. Sky's beautiful. Every day! Can't complain. River's perfect. Every day! Time's wastin'. Must go. I miss you. Sherlock, too. 'Specially him. I gotta leave. Ollie, take care. No worries.

> "N"

Nick lofted himself onto the table while I was reading and sat, his head cocked, his eyes wide. When I finished, I set the card down on the table. Nick turned around in a circle, planted himself atop the card, and then his tail came down . . . hard! *Thump! Thump! Thump!* A total of fifteen hearty thumps in all before he rose, stretched, and leapt gracefully back to the floor where he meandered back to his spot in front of the fridge and lay down, head on paws.

Ollie scratched at his head. "Well . . . that was odd." He said at last.

"Not really. He's trying to tell us something." I got up and crossed over to the rear cabinet. I opened the bottom drawer, pulled out a slim book, and rejoined Ollie at the table. "When I visited Pichard in prison, he told me if I wanted to figure out Nick's secret messages, I should listen to what the cat had to say."

"Yeah? Well ain't that somethin'." Ollie slapped his knee. "What did he expect Nick would tell us?"

"How to figure out Nick's code."

Ollie blinked. "Oh, Nora. How could Pichard possibly know that?"

I shrugged. "Who knows? Pichard's one spooky character, and even though I think most of his mannerisms are just for shock effect, in this instance he's right on the money. Nick has been trying to tell us how to crack the code all along." I took the pile of cards and laid them out, one by one. "Here's the first card. The first time I read this message for Nick, he thumped that tail of his four times. And the second—he thumped his tail nine times. The third postcard got a grand total of seven thumps, and now this last one got fifteen."

Ollie looked at me, perplexed. "And you think this tells us something?"

"Absolutely. He's telling us how to decipher Nick's message." I held out the book. "I borrowed this from my cashier, Mollie, who's studying cryptology, believe it or not. There's a chapter in here on ciphers. See for yourself."

I held the book out to him and pointed to a highlighted portion. "Read the part on acrostic codes."

Ollie skimmed the printed words, and then looked up at me. "I still don't get it."

"Nick loved puzzles, right? He loved the game of Scrabble so much he wanted to teach it to his cat. He also loved crosswords, and there's a type of crossword puzzle called an acrostic. In a crossword acrostic cypher, the answer is spelled out by the initial letters of words in the cryptic portion of the clue. This"—I tapped the highlighted text—"is a type of code referred to as first sentence acrostic. Now this first postcard has four sentences, the second nine. The third has seven, and this last one has fifteen. Plus, the first few times, Nick pointed with the tip of his tail to the first letter in the sentence, like he's doing now."

We glanced over at the cat, who indeed lay sprawled across the table, the tip of his tail pointing to the first letter of the first sentence of the postcard lying near his rump.

"So he's telling us . . . there's a code here?"

I nodded. "An acrostic first sentence code. The first letter of each sentence should spell out a message."

Ollie whipped a pen out of his pocket. "Let's see if little Nick is right."

I got a pad from the counter, ripped off two sheets of paper, and we each took two cards and sat in silence, scribbling for several minutes. At last we were finished, and laid the papers side-by-side.

Ollie had the first two postcards. His read:

IM OK.

HAD TO GO.

291

And mine:

IM ON A CASE

ON SECRET MISSION.

Ollie let out a low whistle. "Well I'll be a monkey's uncle. Old Nick was trying to tell me something after all." He glanced up sharply. "This last message—ON SECRET MISSION. You don't really think . . . I mean, is it possible he is involved in some sort of espionage?"

I fingered the card and then abruptly stood up. "Honest? I'm not quite sure what to think. This postcard's dated two days ago, so we know he's alive . . . for the moment, anyway. As for the espionage aspect, well, maybe we'll find out the truth someday."

Ollie swiped at his forehead. "Or maybe we won't. Nick always enjoyed projecting an air of mystery."

I walked around the table to stand behind feline Nick, who'd raised himself to a sitting position. "You know, I've often wondered just how Nick found his way to my doorstep that night. I know he's pretty adept at getting himself around but I've got to wonder if it was merely chance or by design."

Ollie's eyes widened. He stared first at me, and then at the cat. "You think Nick Atkins left him there? You think he purposely left him on your doorstep? But why would he do that? He didn't even know you."

I shrugged. "I don't know. Maybe Atkins will turn up one day and be able to explain. Maybe we'll never hear from him again. Right now we know he's alive and as far as Nick's ownership goes, well . . . I'll cross that bridge when or if I ever come to it." I flopped back into my chair and pointed my finger at Ollie. "I'll tell you this, though. I'm not giving him up without a fight."

"I still don't think you have to worry about that," Ollie said. "I think the two of you were always destined to be together."

Nick ambled over to me, butted my elbow. I grasped his middle and pulled him onto my lap. "I think so, too," I whispered into his ruff. "Nick and I are a team, and that's the way it's gonna stay, right, pal?"

Nick twisted his head, looked at me, blinked twice, and then gave a loud meow of approval.

I leaned my head against his and didn't even try to stop the wet moisture gathering at the corners of my eyes.

I couldn't have agreed more.

FROM NORA'S RECIPE BOOK

HUGH JACKMAN SUB

Long Italian roll
Horseradish dressing
Roast beef, cut very thin
American cheese, sliced thin
Monterey jack cheese, sliced thin
Hot and sweet peppers
Shaved lettuce
Tomato slices
Oregano

Toast roll. Slather both sides with horseradish dressing. Layer on roast beef, American and Monterey jack cheeses, hot and sweet peppers, shaved lettuce. Top with tomato slices. Garnish with oregano.

EMMA STONE CAPRI SANDWICH

Breaded chicken cutlets, sliced thin
Italian bread
Fresh mozzarella
Fresh tomato slices
Arugula
1 tablespoon olive oil
A pinch of fresh ground black pepper

Place chicken cutlets on Italian bread, top with fresh mozzarella. Place in toaster oven for approximately 2 minutes. Remove. Top with tomato slices and fresh arugula. Drizzle olive oil over the top of the arugula. Sprinkle with freshly ground black pepper.